A VIRTUOSO
IN AMERICA

A VIRTUOSO IN AMERICA
Book II, Adrian

A Novel

Fred Raymond Goldman

HISTORIUM PRESS
MACON GA / NEW YORK NY
www.historiumpress.com

A VIRTUOSO IN AMERICA: BOOK TWO, ADRIAN

Copyright @ 2025 by Fred Raymond Goldman

All rights reserved.

Library of Congress and Copyright Registration on File.

Second Edition
First Edition under the title "Concerto: Adrian, Book Two"

Hardcover ISBN: 978-1-964700-22-9
Paperback ISBN: 978-1-964700-23-6
eBook ISBN: 978-1-964700-24-3

In loving memory of my parents,
Helen and Louis Goldman

PART ONE
New York City

1
A SPECIAL EVENING

On Monday Evening, September 4, 1939, Adrian Mazurek, concertmaster of The Eleventh State Symphony Orchestra in New York City, stood in front of his bathroom mirror and finished tying the bow tie to his tuxedo. He lingered a while staring at himself and thought about how far he'd come since arriving in the United States fourteen years ago. Back then, he was a shattered young man who sought refuge in his education at The Walter J.S. Sanfried School of Music to overcome his tragic past. He'd focused on his studies to become a proficient violinist and avoided close relationships, lest people think poorly of him once discovering the reason for his retreat from Poland. Since then, he'd developed into a confident and respected artist who associated with the most prominent musicians of the time. Despite that, he'd kept his prior life a secret. Now he was in love with Suzanne and wanted to make a life with her. He was prepared to tell her about his earlier years in Poland before proposing marriage after the fundraiser tonight. He was sure of her love, and that she'd accept his proposal readily.

The limousine arrived half an hour later. Adrian was waiting outside his building. He slid into the back seat. Suzanne was sitting in the middle. Her father, Marcus Reitman, the Director of Development for the orchestra, sat on the opposite window side. Mr. Reitman greeted him with a friendly nod. Suzanne moved over to give Adrian more room to balance his violin case on his lap. They were on their way to the home of Count and Contessa Uberti, who were hosting the fundraiser. The contessa was on the Symphony's Board of Directors. Adrian was their guest of honor.

Adrian had been attracted to Suzanne immediately at a welcoming party for Alistair McGowan in November 1937. The occasion was Mc Gowan's selection as music director and conductor of the symphony. Suzanne was with her fiancé, Bill Henderson. A hunting accident resulted in his death three months later, a month before their scheduled wedding. Adrian waited for what he considered to be a respectable time to ask her out to dinner. They dated intermittently until this past April when they became exclusive.

Adrian studied Suzanne. Her dark brown hair fell softly to her shoulders, accentuating her skin, clear and creamy. The bright red of her lipstick defined the fullness of her lips. He looked into those deep brown eyes of hers and thought of Chana. *She, too, had been beautiful like Suzanne, with the same smooth skin and full lips. Had she had survived, would she have felt comfortable being driven in a limousine to the home of a count and contessa, where he'd perform to a hand- picked array of New York's elites. Would she have been able to bask in this moment with him, like Suzanne?*

He'd come to realize Chana and Suzanne were different people. Suzanne was mature, a person in her own right, well established in her career and secure in herself. Unlike Chana, she could manage whatever came her way, including the demands of his profession. What's more, he and Suzanne shared many of the same interests and values, which, to him, made them compatible. There was no reason not to propose to her. He wouldn't hurt her like he had Chana and leave behind a mess as he had in Poland.

Suzanne interrupted his reverie. "What are you thinking?"

He turned his attention back to her. "Nothing. What's that perfume you're wearing? You smell delicious."

She gave him a playful punch on his arm. "It's Joy. You should know my favorite perfume by now."

"Be careful. My arms are my fortune. I've got to play well for the contessa and her dinner guests if we're going to raise enough money to meet the orchestra's contractual demands."

Mr. Reitman patted his daughter's knee. "Amen," he said smiling. "Perhaps you'd better keep your hands off Adrian tonight, my dear."

Adrian leaned over and gave Suzanne a light kiss on the cheek. He knew she'd be fussy about getting her lipstick smeared. She immediately pulled out her gold compact to check her lipstick and hair.

Adrian felt good about tonight. Playing the violin was his love. It was something he did with his life, a gift with which he'd been blessed and to share with others. He was pleased the contessa had personally invited him to help the orchestra raise money. They had had a connection since his early days in New York as a student at The Sanfried Music School, where she had served on its Board of Directors.

The contessa and Mr. Reitman had gone to great pains to plan a special evening. The Depression had placed a financial strain on the institution. Due to previous contractual obligations with the musicians, lower ticket sales, and annual deficits, the Endowment Fund had taken a hit. Currently there was a significant deficit from the 1938–1939 season and, a new round of negotiations with the musicians was about to begin.

They'd invited an exclusive group of guests, hoping their donations and bequests would place the symphony on sound footing. Adrian's presence would not only provide entertainment but put a familiar face to the symphony. People would find it a privilege to share an evening with him. Reviews of his concerts by *The New York Times* and other large east coast city papers labeled his performances as entrancing, hypnotic, and heart-stopping, and stated he had the ability to create sounds and evoke emotions greater than intended by the composer. Adrian had learned the invitation to tonight's gathering had drawn an immediate response, leaving others the Contessa hadn't invited to feel disappointed.

Adrian was having second thoughts about the first selection he'd chosen to perform this evening, a short piece he'd composed. He'd recently become intrigued by the trend in avant-garde music, which went beyond the expectations one might anticipate hearing from a classical performer like himself. His piece was unconventional, with little melody or form and with erratic, scratching sounds. Now, he wasn't sure this selection was right for this conservative gathering.

Once at the contessa's apartment, he'd look the guests over and determine whether they'd appreciate a composition in this style. He had other pieces to substitute if he felt it more appropriate to this soiree.

Adrian readjusted himself in his seat. He tried not to allow his hesitation about playing his own composition take away from his excitement about what was going to happen after the party when he was alone with Suzanne. He couldn't wait to see the look on her face when he proposed.

To take his mind off his uneasiness, Adrian playfully announced to Suzanne and her father,

"If things go well tonight, I have a little surprise up my sleeve."

"Oh, oh," Suzanne poked her father and said, "You'd better stay close to him. He's in one of his mischievous moods. Why don't you tell us, Adrian, so we're prepared for whatever comes and not sit all evening holding our breath?"

Mr. Reitman patted his daughter's knee and said, "Now, now, Suzanne, we all know how focused Adrian is. He's probably been practicing for this performance for weeks. I'm sure he's out to make an excellent impression by being on his best behavior."

Adrian raised his eyebrows. "You'll just have to wait and see," he said.

Traffic had slowed down. "There's a logjam ahead," the limousine driver said. "I'll try to find a way around it, but it looks blocked. We may be late."

"Do your best," Adrian said, tapping his foot. He worried being late might not give him the time he needed to familiarize himself with the guests to determine whether he should replace his own composition with another and allow him a few minutes of practice before his performance. He kept glancing at his watch. Every minute lost would not only take away from his preparing for his recital but would also delay what he had planned with Suzanne afterward.

2
AN OLD FRIEND

The limousine pulled up in front of one of New York's most celebrated buildings on the east side of Central Park, the home to many New York merchants, financiers, and luminaries in the theater and art world. Paul, the contessa's butler, was outside pacing when the limousine arrived. He hurriedly led them to the private elevator that took them to the twenty-ninth floor, which, including the floor above, contained the largest apartment in the building.

Adrian remembered the first time he'd been to the contessa's apartment. He was with a small group of Sanfried Music School students, who remained at school during its closings for Christmas, Thanksgiving and other holidays. The contessa had invited them to spend Christmas day with her. Adrian's jaw dropped when he had walked off the elevator onto the marble floor that stretched the length and width of the foyer and joined the winding stairs at each end that connected to a balcony on the thirtieth floor. He had never seen such an extravagant entry other than the lobby of a concert hall. On that and other occasions that had brought Adrian here since, he'd never gotten over his sense of astonishment of being surrounded by such luxury.

It was in the beginning of his first year at Sanfried that Adrian began to feel a certain affection for him from the contessa. He wasn't sure whether it was because she sensed his loneliness from being so far away from home or because she was attracted to his musical abilities. Regardless of what contributed to it, her kindhearted behaviors toward him had reminded him of his mother back in Poland, with whom he had had a very close relationship before their falling out when he eloped with Chana, and he later came to the United States.

Because of his disconnection with his family in Poland, Adrian appreciated the contessa's attention, and he came to regard her as a substitute mother figure. As his life and his career progressed and he became surer of himself, his relationship with the contessa had become more an accord of equals. He'd become very fond of her, and he felt it was reciprocal, although he still felt a motherly attachment on both of their parts. Despite this, he had never shared with her what it was about his past that had brought him to America.

Paul took their coats and showed Adrian a secret panel in the foyer where he could store his violin. On the way, Adrian saw the count and contessa approach Mr. Reitman and Suzanne. The contessa, a woman in her eighties, was heavily made up and wore a black sequined gown. A diamond necklace and matching earrings added to the sparkle of her dress. The count, tall and patrician looking, appeared to be a little too young for her. It was widely rumored the contessa was the one possessing the wealth, his family having lost their fortune in the Depression.

The contessa pulled Mr. Reitman aside. Adrian felt bad for him. With all their planning for this event, Mr. Reitman hadn't counted on a traffic jam. Adrian wondered if he was berating himself for not foreseeing this possibility and for not arranging for earlier transportation. After securing his violin, Adrian joined the count and Suzanne. The contessa and Mr. Reitman rejoined them. They looked composed, but Adrian wondered how their being late was affecting her, given the careful and precise scheduling for the evening.

Adrian kissed the contessa on both cheeks. "Dear," she said to the count. "Why don't you take Suzanne and Marcus into the parlor? Adrian and I will join you in a moment." Once they were alone, she touched his arm and said, "I'm afraid because of the delay in Marcus getting you here, I must ask you to keep your performance to no more than twenty minutes. Otherwise, the catering staff informed me dinner may be cold." She said this without a hint of apology, as if keeping to schedule was her obligation as a hostess to her guests.

She patted his cheek. "Perhaps if there's time after dinner, you can play whatever else you may have prepared."

Adrian covered his mouth and suppressed an inclination to laugh. This resolved his ambivalence about whether to perform his own composition.

On the way into the parlor, the contessa told Adrian she'd prepared the guests for his aversion to shaking hands before a performance.

Adrian surveyed the room. He and Suzanne were the youngest ones in attendance. Adrian quickly pulled his shoulders back and put on a smile. He reminded himself that the goal tonight was to relieve the guests of some of their wealth.

The contessa's parlor was decorated with Italian and French furniture in multiple seating arrangements, around which, he estimated, twenty guests were conversing. Others mingled on the terrace to the sounds of laughter and the tinkling of ice cubes.

Servants moved in and out of both areas carrying trays of champagne and hors d'oeuvres. Women dressed in the latest fashions swayed elegantly through the room. Men wore the customary double breasted six button dinner jackets with long, broad pointed lapels and square shoulders. The cuffs of their tailored trousers fell slightly over their highly polished shoes. Hearty laughter resounded from some of the inside groupings as well.

Adrian watched Suzanne glide around the room while the count introduced her to guests. He admired the ease with which she mixed among them. Adrian's thoughts again turned to Chana. *Would she have enjoyed participating in an evening like this and have felt comfortable in this setting, like Suzanne?*

Adrian hadn't been born into privilege, at least not monetarily. What he lacked in a family pedigree of wealth and social class he overcame with a friendly demeanor and good manners. Also, he knew how to use his good looks to his advantage. His six-foot-one height, his blond hair, blue eyes, and slim athletic figure were much admired by women. Men frequently looked at him askance until he gained their appreciation and respect through his talent. As the contessa presented Adrian to the guests, he flashed a wide smile with each introduction and bowed with both hands clasped behind his back.

After their mingling among the guests, the contessa excused herself. Adrian used this as an opportunity to pardon himself from those with whom he was conversing, saying he needed to prepare for his performance. He hoped to be able to catch up with the contessa to discuss the setup for his performance, but she disappeared with the butler.

Adrian wished he could have a glass of champagne, but he never drank before a performance. He walked toward the Steinway in a corner of the parlor where someone was playing soft background music. He expected to find an advanced Sanfried student. The contessa liked to give young people recognition by providing them with the opportunity to play background music at her gatherings. Often she had asked Adrian, in his student days, to play his violin during her dinner parties.

Adrian was surprised to find that the person at the piano was Otto. The two had shared a cabin with other entertainers on the cruise ship that brought Adrian to the United States. He and Otto had earned their passage by playing music during luncheon and dinner meals in the ship's main dining salon and in the cabaret and lounges in the evenings. Adrian was coming to America to make a fresh start after the death of his beloved wife two days after the birth of their son. Otto's family was German, but they lived in a multicultural neighborhood in New York where Otto had picked up some of the Polish language. Adrian had learned enough German during the time he had lived in Krakow with his aunt and uncle. His uncle was of German heritage and often spoke in German at home. Adrian and Otto were thereby able to communicate with one another. In his grief, Adrian had shared with Otto his reasons for leaving Poland. Otto was the only person in whom Adrian had confided.

Right now, Adrian needed to get away from Otto. He was a danger to all he had achieved since those days on the ship when he'd told Otto about his past, and Otto was a danger to his future with Suzanne. *What would she feel if she found out about my past before I had a chance to tell her tonight? What would this evening's guests think of me if they knew?* Adrian had learned back then that Otto wasn't above revealing the confidences of others if it benefited him. He used these as extortion against their confirming rumors being spread about him on the ocean liner, specifically his sexual escapades with women passengers. When Adrian had learned of Otto's means of self-protection, he learned to stay on Otto's good side. There was no use now asking Otto to keep his confessions back then confidential. That might give him more of a reason to expose them.

To be polite, Adrian said to Otto, "How is your career going?"

Otto raised his hand in deference to Adrian. "I haven't reached your level, my friend, but I make a living playing gigs like this, and I play in a band in the Village several nights a week. I've gotten interested in jazz. Sometimes you can catch me at the Three Aces Club." Otto pulled a card from his jacket and handed it to Adrian.

"Come hear me one evening," he said.

Thankfully, the contessa interrupted their conversation by asking guests to move onto the terrace while chairs were set up for Adrian's performance.

Adrian was grateful for an excuse to end his talk with Otto. "I've only a few minutes to make sure my violin is still in tune, but it's been great seeing you again." He held up the card Otto had given him. "I'd love to come hear you play," he lied. "I'll look you up," he lied again.

Suzanne joined Adrian. "Who's your friend?" she said.

"I'll tell you later. It's time for me to get ready." He kissed her cheek and went to retrieve his violin, hoping she'd forget Otto and that he'd be gone by the time he returned.

Chairs were set up in the parlor facing the terrace. Adrian felt comfortable with this arrangement. The contessa asked her guests to be seated. When they appeared ready, she began speaking.

"My dear friends, tonight I am happy to treat you to a rare private performance by Adrian Mazurek. His name, I'm sure, will soon be mentioned along with the likes of other great violinists of our time.

I've invited you, as season ticket holders, members of the symphony's board, and music lovers to make a substantial contribution to our orchestra. Bargaining negotiations will begin soon, and we do want to retain the highest quality of musicians and to restore our Endowment Fund. I've laid out envelopes on the piano inscribed with your names for you to place your checks or pledges." She smiled, exposing all her teeth. "I've gone to great lengths to provide you with the finest dinner you will have this year, and I've plied you with enough champagne and scotch to help loosen you to open wide your wallets and checkbooks." The guests laughed politely. The contessa then gestured to a chair in the first row. "Friends, I am pleased to present Adrian Mazurek."

Adrian came forward. He stood straight and tall before his audience, resting his violin and bow just a few inches from the sides of his legs.

"Ladies and gentlemen. Thank you for coming this evening. I've enjoyed meeting all of you and feel honored our hosts have invited me to perform before such a distinguished group. I'm going to play three Caprices by Niccolò Paganini, numbers one, five and twenty-four, three of my favorite pieces to play. I love playing these because they excite me. They take me from the highest notes to the lowest with such velocity, I find them breathtakingly beautiful. It's been said if you listen carefully, you may hear the violin mimicking the human voice." Adrian lowered his head for a few seconds to gather his concentration. Then he lifted his violin and began playing.

Adrian enveloped himself in his playing. The room, with all its distractions, disappeared as he concentrated on the complexity of the Caprices. His eyes remained closed as his fingers moved rapidly, sometimes in quivering like motions, across the fingerboard. He worked his bow along the strings, sometimes gracefully, and from time to time with such forceful movements his chin rose above the chin rest.

Throughout his performance Adrian's facial expressions alternated between sadness, peacefulness, and pleasure, as if he were feeling deeply what the music was conveying. Only once or twice, for just a second or two, did his eyes open, as if by reflex. With his final movement of the bow, Adrian came to a stop, and suddenly, as though he were coming out of a trance, he gave the signal he was finished.

Adrian bowed to the audience and mouthed the words "Thank you" to what seemed to him to be genuine applause and appreciation for his performance. Quickly, the gathering surrounded him with their congratulations and expressions of admiration. Adrian saw the contessa in the background standing with Suzanne and her father, all looking proud and pleased. When the guests' reactions quieted, Adrian replaced his violin in the secret panel in the foyer and retreated to a bathroom. He needed a few minutes alone to pull himself back into the moment of reality. Chana had entered his thoughts too many times tonight. He wanted to shake her from his mind and get back to Suzanne, to touch and feel her and have her touch him. He wanted to feel alive and appreciated by her.

In the bathroom Adrian removed his jacket, rolled up his sleeves, and washed his hands and face. He looked in the mirror. The intensity of his playing had mussed his hair. He unrolled and buttoned his sleeves and put his jacket back on. Then, he pulled out a small black comb from the inside pocket of his jacket. Otto's card was entwined in the teeth of the comb. He extracted it, tore it into little pieces, and tossed it in a wastebasket. He hoped he'd never run into Otto again, especially with Suzanne on his arm. He combed his hair, admired himself for a moment, took a deep breath, and rejoined the party.

3

SURPRISES

T he contessa was waiting for Adrian. She was ready to call her guests in to dinner.

Because of the largeness of the table, there were multiple competing conversations. During a rare pause, one of the guests asked Adrian about his background.

"Where in Poland are you from, Mr. Mazurek?"

"Call me Adrian, please," he said. "I was born in a small village northwest of Krakow. My father came from generations of violin makers. He ran a small school with the help of my mother. He trained young men in the art of making violins, then and now praised world-wide, I might add, one of which I played tonight."

"I wouldn't have thought of Poland as a place where violins were made," Arthur Bartholomew said in a pompous tone of voice.

Adrian ignored Mr. Bartholomew's ignorance. "Poland, especially its large cities, is among the most civilized and sophisticated countries in the world. You should add Poland to your itinerary for your next European tour."

"I'm afraid it may be a little too late to visit Poland with Germany bombing it to pieces," Mr. Bartholomew said.

Mr. Bartholomew's remark startled Adrian. For a few seconds he felt lost in his surroundings and uncomfortably warm. His thoughts went to his relatives in Poland, people with whom he hadn't had contact since coming to America. He hadn't read the papers in the past few days while preparing for tonight and wasn't up on the news. He wanted to hear more from Arthur, and yet, he didn't.

His reflections were interrupted when the contessa encouraged Adrian to tell her guests more about his Polish background.

"Yes, uh," he tried not to stutter. "As I was saying, my parents ran a school to train young men in the art of violin making. Students enrolled in a three-year apprenticeship. My parents accepted new students each year when older students completed their training and joined a luthier guild."

"Luthier guild?" another guest said.

"Yes," Adrian responded. "During his three years, each student was required to build a violin from scratch, piece by piece, part by part, and present it to an association of violin makers before being accepted into a violin makers' guild."

"Did you learn to make violins, the one you played tonight, perhaps?" Philomena Rice asked.

"I'm afraid not, regrettably. I went to public school and afterward hung around the apprentices who lived with us in our home. My mother played the violin. At an early age, when I showed curiosity, she began teaching me." Although Adrian tried not to show it, he felt a heavy feeling in his stomach from hearing about the bombing of his homeland. He laid his fork on the table so no one would notice his hand trembling.

Adrian looked over at the contessa. She had a smile on her face, seemingly pleased her guests were interested in him and that the conversation was flowing. He felt Suzanne place her hand on his. *Does she sense my worry?*

"How did you become so proficient?" another guest asked.

"When I was fourteen, and my mother felt she had taught me all she could, she arranged for me to have an audition at The Krakow School of Music. The school accepted me for a three-year program, but I had to return home after two and a half years when my father died. My professor in Krakow sent my mother lessons to help me keep up. I returned to Krakow to complete my studies six months later when she remarried a widower from Lodz. He was a guild certified violin maker. Soon after, I came to the United States, and The Sanfried School of Music accepted me into its violin program."

The contessa held up a glass of champagne. "And, lucky for us," she said.

Across the table, Samantha Willoughby said, "Have you heard from your family in Poland? Has Germany's invasion affected them?"

Adrian lowered his gaze. "No. I haven't been able to reach them," he lied for the third time this evening. "I've had no response to a telegram." He felt guilty and ashamed about this, but he had tried his best to block his past from his mind.

"That must be very worrisome. I hope they are well."

Adrian avoided Mrs. Willoughby's eyes. With a thickness in his throat, he said, "That's very kind of you."

Discussion of Hitler's invasion of Poland and of today's announcement of the entry of England and France into war with Germany caused some guests to speculate how long it would take for the United States to become involved.

Adrian was relieved when the conversation turned to a talk of the success of the symphony's program for the 1938–39 season. He wasn't a political person, but more importantly, he didn't want anyone to remind him of what was taking place in Poland and how it might be affecting his family.

After the guests completed the last course, the contessa suggested they adjourn to the parlor, where they'd be served after-dinner drinks. With the chairs from his performance removed, the guests spread out comfortably among the groupings of furniture.

The contessa and Mr. Reitman took the opportunity to gather the envelopes with the guests' checks and pledges. After doing so, the contessa announced the guests had contributed $7,500 to the symphony. There was a round of applause, and the contessa thanked everyone for their contributions. Adrian caught the smile directed at him by the contessa and Mr. Reitman's nod of approval.

Susanne took his hand and squeezed it. "You did good," she said.

Adrian felt pleased with himself. He looked at Suzanne, and with a surge of exhilaration, he kissed her cheek. "Wait right here," he said to her. "Now comes the surprise."

Adrian left the room and returned with his violin. He called for everyone's attention and said, "You've given very generously this evening, not only to the symphony, but to me as well with your kindness. To show my gratitude, I'd like to play one more piece for you, a medley from the latest Broadway musical hit, *Panama.* I thought it might be a pleasant way to wind down the evening after such a magnificent dinner."

Beginning with the rousing opening song, "Happy to Have Met You," Adrian bounced among the groupings looking directly into the eyes of each person as he played. Women smiled and blushed, and men raised their drinks to him. Next, he stopped in front of the contessa and plunked, "What Lies Behind Those Lying Eyes?" The sound of laughter filled the parlor when the contessa hid her face behind her hands.

Adrian swung over to two men and played, "Not a Nickle to My Name." One of them pulled out his empty trouser pockets and exclaimed, "That's true. I just gave all my money to the symphony." As if in defiance, Adrian switched his song to the ballad, "I'm Not Sure I Can Believe You?" He heard more laughter and clapping by amused guests.

Adrian felt the guests turning their heads to follow him while he moved from settee to settee, chair to chair, and sofa to sofa. He ended with the show's rousing ending, "Let's All Meet Again in Panama." Adrian saw the guests had taken his hint that the evening had ended when they stood and gave him gleeful applause. Adrian felt high that the night ended on a good—no, *a superlative*—note. He hoped what he had planned for later with Suzanne would have the same result.

After the last of the guests stood waiting by the elevator for Paul to take them down, Suzanne, her father, and Adrian thanked their hosts for a memorable evening.

Before Adrian could retrieve his violin from the secret panel in the foyer, the contessa pulled him aside to thank him for making the evening a success. She cupped one cheek, kissed the other, and looked him in the eyes like his mother had when she was pleased with him. This act of affection reminded him how much he missed the touch of his mother. He remembered playing for her in the kitchen one evening while she was preparing dinner. When he hit the wrong note, she stopped stirring her soup, came behind him, and gently guided the bow with one arm and helped him finger the proper notes on the fingerboard with the other. She went quietly back to her stirring when she felt he played it correctly. It was moments such as these he felt his mother's love. Adrian returned the contessa's kiss with a kiss on her cheek. As he walked away from the contessa, Adrian heard her tell the count she was exhausted and was going to bed.

Suzanne and Mr. Reitman were waiting for Adrian by the elevator with their coats on. Paul helped Adrian with his coat. Adrian stepped onto the elevator still thinking of the contessa's touch and the memories it stirred. After the door closed, he realized he'd left his violin behind. The elevator started moving. Paul said it was too late to go back. He'd take Adrian to the apartment when they reached the lobby.

Once back in the foyer, Adrian retrieved his violin. The side door beyond the staircase was open. Adrian heard the count talking. He began to walk toward the elevator but stopped short when he heard the count shout, "Heil Hitler," and other voices respond, "Heil Hitler."

Adrian listened as the count spoke about the invasion of Poland and the Reich's need for money for munitions, to build railroads, and to feed the German army. He asked them to give generously to "the cause" by donating their jewelry and American dollars. Adrian stood frozen between two impulses, one to escape before anyone discovered he'd overheard their discussion and the other to stay and listen to what was happening. He'd heard enough. His desire to escape won out. Adrian moved to the elevator quietly where Paul was waiting to return him to ground level. The shock of what Adrian had overheard took away his euphoria. It was replaced by a sudden coldness that hit him at the core. He thoughts became fuzzy. He needed time to pull himself together.

Adrian was quiet in the limousine on the way home.

Suzanne laid her head on his shoulder. "What's on your mind?" she said.

"Nothing, I'm just tired. I was more nervous than I thought I'd be. A lot was placed on my shoulders tonight. I'm a little stressed out. Plus, all that wine at dinner didn't help any."

"The contessa did go all out, but look at the money she raised," Mr. Reitman said. "Don't sell yourself short, Adrian. You were brilliant, and it will help the symphony and your career immensely, and that little surprise of yours, pure inspiration, Adrian, pure inspiration. Get some rest tonight you two." The driver waited until a doorman escorted Mr. Reitman into his apartment building.

When the limousine pulled up to Suzanne's town house, Adrian took Suzanne's hand and said, "Would you mind if I didn't come in this evening?" He asked for her forgiveness. "I'm tired, and I just need to go to bed."

"I thought you might like to come in and celebrate," she whispered in his ear.

"Not tonight," he said, aware of her disappointment.

He walked Suzanne to her door and unlocked it for her. When he leaned to kiss her she turned her head and ran inside, slamming the door in his face.

Adrian felt bad, but the truth was too many memories had surfaced in him tonight that wore on his emotions. Those and the accidental witnessing of the meeting in the side room next to the stairs confused him and raised his concern for the contessa. He was convinced she had no awareness of the count's involvement in such activities. His affection for her led him to worry what effect this would have on her if it were to become public.

These thoughts swirled around in his head as he entered his apartment. He kicked off his shoes, yanked off his tie, and dropped into bed, otherwise fully dressed, and he fell fast asleep.

4

A JINX ON THE EVENING

Adrian woke up early, still wearing most of the clothes he'd left on the night before. He rubbed the sleep from his eyes and ran his fingers through his hair as he remembered how last night had ended. He tried to find excuses for what he'd heard from the room off the contessa's foyer, but he couldn't come up with any.

He threw his legs over the side of the bed, sat for a moment, then thrust himself to his feet.

At the foot of the bed, he kicked his misplaced shoes aside, removed his rumpled jacket, picked his tie up from the floor, and tossed them onto a chair. Then he headed to the bathroom, washed his hands and face, and brushed his teeth. After assessing he didn't look too bad, nothing a shave wouldn't fix, he combed his hair and walked back into the bedroom.

I must not have heard right. It had to have been the champagne. But the words were stuck in his head. He couldn't deny hearing that deep baritone voice shouting "Heil Hitler" and the same words repeated back. He tossed the clothes on the chair onto the bed and sat by the window with his face in his hands. *What's my responsibility here? I need to talk with Suzanne about this.* Then he remembered. He'd turned her down last night when she expected him to stay over, when he'd been prepared to propose. *She'll be angry. I hurt her feelings. I'd better call her.* He looked at his watch. It was 6:30, too early to call.

Adrian decided to take a walk and clear his head before calling Suzanne. Outside, he picked up a copy of the morning paper and walked slowly. He decided he'd make Thursday a special night to make up for the disruption last night to his original plan to confess his past and propose to Suzanne. He'd make it more personal and romantic.

Back at his apartment Adrian read the newspaper to see if there was any mention of the unnerving happenings at the Contessa's the night before. There was none. After shaving and showering, he called Suzanne.

"Suzanne, before you lay into me about last night, I think what I am about to tell you might explain my mood when I dropped you off."

"Go ahead, I'm all ears."

That sounded sarcastic, but I deserved it.

He told her about what happened when he went back to get his violin and its effect on him. He said he wasn't prepared to deal with that last night because it was too much of a shock.

"My goodness. I'm shocked just hearing you tell it. What arc you going to do?"

"That's why I'm calling, at least the first reason, to ask your advice." He went over what he thought were his choices, to either tell the contessa what he'd heard, call the FBI anonymously, or do nothing. "I'm worried about the contessa. She's been good to me. I don't trust the count. I'd hate to see her embarrassed by him."

Suzanne paused for a minute. "Are you sure no one saw you?"

"The only person would have been Paul, and he never left the elevator while he waited for me. I don't think he knew what was going on. He kept looking at his watch like he was in a hurry to get somewhere."

"You should wait and see what happens. It would be embarrassing for the contessa to hear this from you. My advice is to send her two dozen yellow roses with a note thanking her for the lovely evening and leave it at that for now."

Adrian wasn't convinced that was the solution, but, not knowing what else to do, he agreed. "I'll do that. And Suzanne, speaking of lovely evenings, if you're not busy Thursday night, I'd like to take you out on the town."

"To what do I owe that extravagance?"

"Oh, just because I love you, and I've been doing a lot of thinking."

"Thinking?"

"Let's talk about it Thursday." He needed Wednesday to make special plans for the evening.

"What time will you pick me up?"

"How does 7:30 sound?"

"It sounds perfect. How should I dress?"

"I love that green dress. It looks so great on you."

"OK, and if anything happens before then, let me know."

"You bet. See you Thursday."

The next morning, Adrian picked up another morning newspaper. On page two there was an article about the arrest of a leader of the New York German American Nazi Organization, referred to as the New York Bund. A tax investigation determined he had embezzled a substantial amount from the Party, and the government planned to prosecute him.

Adrian wondered if the FBI had any information about the count and the others at the meeting. He hoped this arrest would discourage the count from any further involvement in German activities. As a devoted patron of the symphony and recognized throughout New York for her support of the arts, the contessa didn't deserve to be involved in any scandal. More importantly, he was fond of her and didn't want to see her hurt in any way. He couldn't forget that moment when she kissed his cheek, like his mother had long ago.

Adrian made a dinner reservation at Henri's Brasserie, Suzanne's favorite French restaurant. He didn't tell her where they were going. He wanted this evening to be special. After dinner he planned to surprise her by taking her on a carriage ride through Central Park. He'd tell her about his past, profess his love for her, and propose marriage, hopefully by moonlight. The newspaper's weather page predicted a bright sky that night.

On Thursday, January 7, a day he wanted Suzanne and himself to remember always as the day they became engaged, Adrian took a taxi to Suzanne's. She was wearing the green dress he'd suggested. He took a step back from her and whistled. She twirled and curtsied for him.

Suzanne had the makings of his favorite drink waiting, a White Russian. He prepared a glass and sat and drank it while she took care of last-minute preparations in her bedroom. Adrian looked around the living room. It was on the second floor of the four-story townhouse Suzanne had inherited from her maternal grandmother along with a substantial trust. Suzanne used the ground level, which had its own private entrance, as her office. She rented out the third and fourth floor apartments. Suzanne furnished her apartment in the contemporary style, mixed with Art Nouveau. It was comfortable, unlike his rented two-and-a-half room walk up in an old brownstone. Her apartment was like a swanky hotel suite with daily house cleaning service. In fact, she had a house cleaner only on Fridays.

By contrast, Adrian had furnished his small apartment sparely with sheets of music and books, in what he professed to be orderly arrangements of the projects he was working on with the symphony and his students. He slept in a back room that had two large windows facing the alley. He'd hung posters he had purchased from The Metropolitan Museum of Art. "Organized clutter," he called his style of decorating.

"I don't know how you live in such spare surroundings. Surely you can afford better on your salary," Suzanne responded the first time Adrian took her to his place early in their relationship. They never returned there again. He knew she wasn't bothered by the clutter as much as she was by the small bathroom stuffed into what used to be a closet in the bedroom. Thereafter, her apartment became his second home.

Adrian finished his drink. Suzanne soon appeared. He placed his arms around her and kissed her lightly on the cheek.

"Shall we go?" he said.

"I'm ready when you are." She went to get her wrap.

Outside, Adrian flagged a cab. Suzanne squeezed his hand affectionately when he told the driver their destination.

"I hoped you might take me there."

The maître d' escorted them to a table in the back that Adrian had requested. It was the table where they'd sat on their first visit to Henri's.

"You remembered," she smiled.

Adrian looked at Suzanne across the table. She had piled her hair up on her head, and she was wearing ruby earrings that glistened in the light from the candle on the table, accentuating those tantalizing lips. He'd noticed several male diners had turned to look at her when the maître d' showed them to their table. For a moment, he just stared at her.

She raised an eyebrow. "What?" she said.

He could feel his heart beating in anticipation of what he was going to ask her tonight and of her anticipated response. The glow on her cheeks and her beaming expression caused him to momentarily lose awareness of his surroundings. Once more, he felt sure of Suzanne's love for him and of his readiness to make a commitment to her.

"Did I tell you how nice you look?"

"Well, kind of. You whistled when I twirled, but it wouldn't hurt to hear it in words."

"Then shame on me. You look beautiful—no, gorgeous. I'm the envy of every man in the room tonight."

"Thank you. Then all the effort I made to look nice was worth it."

"One of the things I like about you is how naturally beautiful you are."

"Don't kid yourself. It takes a lot of work to look this natural."

Adrian chuckled and was about to reach across the table to take her hand when their waiter arrived to take their drink orders and to leave menus. Adrian ordered another White Russian, Suzanne a glass of white wine.

"You 're being very mysterious tonight," Suzanne said. She leaned forward, placed her elbows on the table, and clasped her hands. "What is this surprise you have for me?"

"It wouldn't be a surprise if I told you. You'll have to wait and see."

Suzanne gave a frown of disappointment and took a sip of her wine.

Adrian couldn't wait to see her reaction to his after-dinner surprise. He'd suggest they take a short walk to work off their meal. Then he'd hail a cab to take them to Central Park, where a horse and carriage would be waiting. He looked forward to the expression of joy on her face and her playful swat on his shoulder. He could feel his skin tingle. It hadn't occurred to him until that very moment that it was in a horse drawn carriage he and Chana eloped on the night of her cousin's wedding. A shiver went through him. He hoped this wouldn't put a jinx on the evening. The thought distracted him from his reach for his drink. He almost knocked it over.

"What's the matter? You seem nervous."

"No, my foot fell asleep. I just stamped it on the floor to wake it up. It threw my body off." He raised his glass and, a little too loudly, said, "To us."

Heads turned toward them.

"To us," she said, clinking his glass then holding it up to those grinning at them from the other table.

"You're feeling a little playful tonight, I see. I like that," Adrian said.

"Perhaps you're rubbing off on me."

He smiled widely. "I like that even more."

"I think I'm ready to order, how about you?" she said.

"Yes, I'll call the waiter."

They both ordered Caesar salads. For entrées, Suzanne ordered escargot, Adrian boeuf bourguignon.

During dinner Suzanne asked if Adriane had heard any more about the arrest of the Nazi sympathizer reported in the *Times* and about any involvement of the count. He said he hadn't and that he'd taken her suggestion and sent the contessa two dozen yellow roses with a note thanking her for being so gracious to him on Monday. He hadn't received a response.

"I wonder if she knows about the count's involvement with the Bund. If this got out, it would ruin her in New York society," Suzanne said.

"You're right," whispered Adrian, glancing around. "We shouldn't be talking about it here. Let's change the subject."

They talked about Adrian's students and their progress and about the beginning of rehearsals for the first concert of the symphony's new season. Adrian felt more relaxed talking about these things, more grounded in the present after the troubling thoughts he had about his past.

"One of my students is exceptional, Suzanne," Adrian put down his fork and leaned toward her. "It's exciting to think someday, when he's famous, I may be mentioned in his biography as his teacher."

Suzanne raised her chin in an act of one-upmanship. "And I may be mentioned as his agent."

"All right, all right. I'll try not to let my head get too swelled," he said. *That's another thing about Suzanne. She knows how to keep me grounded. I need that sometime, so I don't look pompous around others.*

As usual, Suzanne ate only part of her dinner, leaving the waiter to ask if there was something wrong. She assured him there wasn't, that she was just not that hungry. Adrian forked a snail from her plate before the waiter took it away.

"Mm, fantastique." Adrian brought his thumb and forefinger to his lips and waved them in the air. "Give the chef our compliments."

Suzanne rolled her eyes and lowered her head.

They declined dessert, and after paying the check, they left the restaurant. Outside, they walked arm in arm.

"That was lovely," Suzanne said. "Thank you."

5

THE FEARED MOMENT

Adrian and Suzanne left Henri's at 9:30. The night was clear and warm. Adrian looked at the sky. He was happy to see the moon shining. *Perfect*, he thought.

Adrian suggested they take a little walk before he hailed a cab for his surprise.

"Good idea," Suzanne said. "Let's head in that direction." She pointed south. "I've got a surprise for you."

Adrian was thrown off guard by her suggestion. He'd been thinking about the carriage ride all day. He couldn't wait to see the look on her face and hear her response when he proposed. He'd rehearsed the words all morning and afternoon to perfection, the same way he'd memorized the movements of his bow across the strings of his violin when he played a concerto. He didn't want to lose his rhythm.

"Don't worry. "We won't stay long." Suzanne led him to the flashing neon lights of 52nd Street.

When Adrian saw the sign for the Three Aces Club, he cringed. "What are we doing here?" He tried to control the quiver in his voice.

"When you went to tune your violin to get ready for your presentation at the Contessa's, I was curious about the man you were talking with, so I went over to meet him. He told me you knew each other from years ago when you came to the United States on the ship together. He said you hadn't seen each other since you'd entered The

33

Sanfried School. He told me he'd invited you to listen to his band. I thought I'd surprise, you by bringing you here."

Adrian stopped walking and faced Suzanne. He felt a wave of nausea. "I had a more romantic evening in mind, Suzanne, like soft lights and mood music. I wanted to be alone with you. I didn't want to share it with anyone else."

She kissed him on the cheek. "That sounds wonderful. We'll go in to say hello. Then I'll make up an excuse to leave. I promised the man, Adrian," she pleaded. "I'm sorry. I thought you'd be pleased."

Suzanne dragged Adrian inside. He thought if he could get to Otto first, he could warn him not to share anything about his past in Poland. Otto, however, was on the stage with the band doing a set. A greeter led them to a small table near the front. *How am I going to get out of this? Think, think.* Adrian's chest tightened in near panic.

The five-piece combo on the tight stage was playing. Otto was improvising on the piano. Each of the other musicians took turns highlighting their extemporaneous musical skills.

Suzanne looked at Adrian, took his hand, and smiled. "Remember when we danced to this at Beth and Will's wedding? It was their song, and we all joined in after giving them time to dance alone."

Adrian squeezed her hand pretending to remember and wished time would speed up so they could leave. Adrian's mind was racing through the worst-case scenarios that could result from any slip of the tongue from Otto about his past and spoil his intentions for the special evening he'd planned.

Otto looked in their direction and gave them a wave.

Oh no, he's seen us. "Suzanne, I really need to get out of here. I can hardly breathe through all this smoke," Adrian shouted above the music.

Adrian watched her tilt her head to the side and purse her lips as if she were wondering what was going on. "OK," she said, reaching for her wrap on the back of her chair.

The set ended, and before they could depart, Otto had left the piano and now stood at their table with a wide smile.

Damn. Adrian forced a smile back. "Hi, Otto. We only stopped by to say hello. We can't stay, but we couldn't pass by without saying hello." *I'm repeating myself. I must sound like an idiot.*

"Stay for just one drink, please. I haven't seen you in so long. It was great running into you the other night, and I was happy to meet Suzanne." Otto smiled and said, "She's charming, Adrian. You've got yourself a classy woman."

Adrian thought he saw Suzanne bite her lip to try to hide a smile. *He's hooked her. He hasn't changed a bit. He's still the same old skirt chaser he was on the ship.*

Otto waved over a waiter, and they ordered drinks.

Adrian watched Suzanne look Otto over. He and Otto were different physically. Otto's hair was brown, thick, and wavy, and he was broad shouldered. Both had athletic builds, but Otto was broader in the chest with a tapered waist. Adrian had a slim torso and narrow hips. Otto had a darker complexion with a five o'clock shadow. Adrian was pale skinned with a slow-growing, less noticeable blond beard.

Adrian felt himself becoming annoyed when Suzanne started asking Otto questions about himself. They discovered he was divorced and had two children, a son seven and a daughter five. He lived in Brooklyn to be near his kids, worked in a music store during the day, and taught and worked in clubs and odd gigs at night to pick up extra money and, hopefully, to get noticed. He had an agent, but she hadn't been able to get him into the bigger bands that were gaining popularity with the swing trend in music.

Adrian became more irritated when Suzanne told Otto she was an agent and maybe she could help, although she knew little about jazz. When she took a card from her purse and handed it to Otto, Adrian recognized his jealous feelings and wondered if he was as secure with Suzanne as he thought. Tonight, of all nights, he didn't want to think about Suzanne noticing another man, especially this one who had the ability to destroy their relationship. He tried to tell himself he was being silly, but he couldn't shake his uneasiness.

"We should leave, Otto," Adrian said. "Don't you have another set to get ready for?"

"No, I've got time for another drink."

Adrian cleared his throat to tell Otto he and Suzanne needed to get to their next destination when Otto interrupted his thoughts by asking him about his family back in Poland and how Germany's invasion was affecting them.

"Have you been able to reach your mother?" Otto said.

Adrian squeezed his glass. Otto was getting too close. "No, I haven't. Suzanne, we must leave," he said, starting to rise.

"What about your son in Krakow, what's his name, Simon, right?" Otto said.

This was the moment Adrian had feared. Otto had revealed his secret. Immediately a shock went through him. He was unable to speak. It was too late to roll back the clock even a second. He looked at Suzanne. She looked stunned, as if someone had just smacked her in the face. He saw the evening he'd planned go up in smoke.

"Son?" Suzanne eyebrows lifted. Her neck bent forward. "Yes, how is Simon doing? You haven't mentioned him all evening."

Her reaction took Adrian aback. He expected she'd express her feelings more strongly upon learning he had a son he'd kept from her, throw her drink at him, curse at him. Instead, she looked as if she was in control of her feelings, given what she'd just heard. This concerned him more than if she had acted out. All he could do was stare at her. He found it difficult to speak.

"I haven't been able to reach Krakow," Adrian said, while keeping his eyes on Suzanne. "I'll try again tomorrow."

Suzanne stared openly back at Adrian. She leaned back in her seat and folded her arms over her stomach. "Yes, you should do that. At a time like this a boy needs his father."

"It looks like Germany has every intention of taking over all of Europe," Otto said. "I thought we had them calmed down after World War I. I'm afraid we may be in for another war. What do you think, Adrian?"

Adrian ignored Otto's remark. His face remained fixed on Suzanne. Adrian tried to keep himself under control. *She's ready to split. I've got to get her away right now so I can smooth this over.*

Suzanne picked up her purse. "Excuse me," she said. "I need to visit the restroom."

"Is she OK?" Otto asked when Suzanne was out of earshot.

"I think she may have had a little too much wine at the restaurant," Adrian said.

When she returned, Suzanne said, "It's late. I have an early morning appointment."

She picked up her wrap. Adrian got up to help her. "I'll get us a cab."

"No. You stay with Otto and catch up on old times. We can talk tomorrow." She turned to Otto and said, "It was nice to meet you, Otto. Give me a call if you feel I can help you."

Adrian looked at Otto trying to cover his scorn for Otto letting loose his secret before he had a chance to do so himself. Not wanting Otto to see the rift that had just occurred, he said, "I'd better get her home safely. I'll call you so we can do this again."

Adrian chased after Suzanne. He wanted to catch up with her to try to explain, but was it possible? What could he say to justify holding secrets from a woman he'd planned to spend the rest of his life with? He blamed himself for his stupidity thinking he could get by in life by pretending a part of his life didn't exist.

6

THE CONFESSION

Adrian followed Suzanne from the Three Aces Club. He managed to reach her taxi before she closed the door. He got in. The driver turned to see if everything was all right. Suzanne nodded for the driver to go ahead.

They both sat quietly, not looking at each other.

He wanted to take her hand, to squeeze it, but he was afraid she'd pull away.

Suzanne didn't say anything when she got out of the taxi. Adrian paid the driver and followed her into her apartment. She hung up her coat but didn't offer to do the same for him. He tossed his coat onto the back of a chair in the living room. Suzanne sat on the sofa and crossed her arms. She looked down to the floor. When he moved to sit next to her, Suzanne's eyes rose glaringly to meet his. He took two steps back.

"Say something, anything," Adrian said to a scowling Suzanne. "Please, just don't look at me like that. Tell me what you're thinking."

Suzanne's face reddened. "I don't know what to say. I'm speechless." She played with her hands. After a pause she said, "When were you planning to tell me? Why have you hidden this from me?" Her anger was raw.

"I didn't just hide it from just you, Suzanne. I hid it from everyone. For years I've even tried to block it from my own mind. Aside from Otto, you're the only person who knows."

She glared at him. "How did you think you could get away with it?"

"I didn't. I planned to tell you the night of the fundraiser. I was going to propose when we got back to your apartment, but the news of war in Poland, my worry about how that might affect Simon, and my hearing the conversation by Nazi sympathizers threw me for a loop. So, I planned to tell you tonight instead, after dinner. I rented a horse and carriage to ride us through Central Park. I was going to tell you then. Otto telling you about Simon ruined that."

Suzanne shook her head. Her body twisted deeper into the sofa. "Did you think you could drop that information on me, and I'd fall into your arms and agree to marry you?"

Adrian saw the tension in her neck and shoulders. He had to convince her he was sincere, to help sooth her anger and regain her trust in him. There was a willingness in him to believe he could make things right. The thought of losing Suzanne was too painful.

He leaned forward in his chair and licked his lips before speaking. "I'm in love with you, Suzanne. I acted foolishly. I should have told you about Simon when I saw we were becoming serious. You have every right to be angry."

"Right now, I'm just stunned. I thought we loved each other. I had high hopes for our relationship, especially that we'd always be honest with one another." Her voice was firm and direct. "This has been a jarring surprise. I need to know the truth. Otherwise, there's no possibility of my trusting you again."

Adrian felt a lump in his throat. "You're right, Suzanne. I understand how you must feel. Where would you like me to start?" He was berating himself for being naïve in thinking she'd accept such a shock so readily.

Still glaring at Adrian, she said, "You might start with the truth. Why on earth have you been hiding this from me?"

Adrian took a deep breath. "Do you mind if I have a drink?" he said, already making his way to her liquor cart. "It'll help relax my nerves. I want to tell you what you should know and answer your every question.

Suzanne nodded as she played with her bracelets.

Adrian poured himself half a glass of plain scotch and gulped it down. He put the glass back on the cart and walked over to a chair facing Suzanne. He rubbed his hand across the back of his head and looked down to the floor. He couldn't look her in the eyes. Recalling his past was a suffocating weight on him. Those early years in Poland scrambled through his head. He searched his brain to decide where to begin. He loosened his tie and unbuttoned the top button of his shirt. After clearing his throat, he began trying to keep his voice under control.

"What you heard is true. I have a son. His name is Simon. He's fourteen and lives with my aunt and uncle in Krakow. As far as I know, he isn't aware I exist." His hands clenched. "It pains me to say that. I think about him often, but I made a foolish promise to my aunt and uncle not to disrupt his life, not to upset him by revealing they're not his real parents. So, I never contacted him. I've tried to distract myself from him by concentrating on my studies and my career, and," he hesitated, "on you." He paused to see if she'd respond.

Suzanne's head tilted. "Who is the boy's real mother? Where is she?" Her voice cut right through him.

Adrian hung his head and muttered, "She's dead. She died two days after Simon was born."

Suzanne's eyes narrowed.

He decided to tell her the whole story, hoping to gain her understanding and forgiveness. He told her when he was fifteen, he developed a crush on a Jewish girl name Chana and she on him.

"We first saw each other on Poland Independence Day, a holiday of festive celebration. Villagers assembled on the square behind the public buildings where a stage was set up for speeches and performances. My mother and I played the violin for the crowd. I noticed this brown-haired girl with dark eyes staring up at me. There was a shyness about her I found appealing. She was wearing a necklace with the Star of David. In our village Jews and Christians lived peacefully but separately. I knew our families would never approve of our relationship, but I couldn't help myself. I learned she was the daughter of one of the owners of the local furniture factory. They sold spare pieces of wood and veneers to local craftsmen, including my father for his workshop."

"Soon after, I went to their shop pretending I was browsing. When I thought no one was looking, I handed her a note asking her to meet me at the area on the edge of town, where every Thursday farmers and vendors came to the village to sell their farm grown vegetables, animal meats, and other items. The market was busy. It took us a while to find each other. We didn't talk long, but we planned to meet there weekly whenever we could sneak away." Adrian spread his hands. "That's how it started. It was as simple as that."

A police siren blared, interrupting Adrian's remembrances. A window was open. The filmy curtains fluttered with the incoming breeze. He was grateful for the time to gather his thoughts. Adrian watched Suzanne lean forward, kick off her shoes, pull up her knees, and tuck her legs underneath her dress. When she tossed her head to take off her ruby earrings, her hair loosened and fell to her shoulders. She put the earrings in a tray on a table next to the sofa. Her gracefulness with these ordinary womanly acts enchanted Adrian. He interpreted these as her beginning to loosen up and become involved in his story.

"We continued our secret meetings. When I went to The Krakow School of Music a year later, we corresponded through a friend of mine. I came home two and a half years later to help my mother when my father died."

"I recall your saying that at the contessa's," Suzanne said. "That must have been a difficult time for you."

"Yes, it was, very difficult," he said, encouraged by her sensitivity. "As you know, I stayed with my mother to help her run the school and kept up with my violin studies. I practiced every chance I got and found time to meet Chana."

"When my mother remarried, I told Chana I was going back to Krakow to finish my studies. I foolishly asked her to come with me, not comprehending the possible consequences of such an act. She said she would."

"You've never talked much about your youth before," Suzanne said. "What you told the Contessa's guests was more than you've told me. Every time I've asked you about it, you said you spent your time studying, but it looks like you had plenty of time for other things."

Putting Suzanne's sarcasm aside, Adrian said, "It's hard for me to talk about Chana. I feel ashamed. When she and I eloped, I not only took a young girl away from her family and led her to her destruction, but I also created a hardship for my parents by leaving them to deal with the community's wrath."

Suzanne tilted her head to the side and raised her eyebrows. "Led to her destruction?"

Simon went on to explain. "At first, we were joyful living with my aunt and uncle in Krakow. I attended school and Chana took care of Katrina, their daughter, while they worked in their bakery. Katrina was born with hip dysplasia. Chana helped her with her prescribed exercises to strengthen the joint causing her condition. This was Chana's way of repaying my aunt and uncle. Chana told me Katrina never complained about her exercises and was a joy to look after." Adrian looked thoughtful for a moment. "It must have been hard on my aunt and uncle to watch Katrina struggle to walk, but they never said anything to indicate raising her was difficult."

The room grew silent. Suzanne appeared to be thinking about what he said. He waited a minute or two and asked if she wanted him to go on. She nodded.

"When Chana became pregnant, it was a joyful time for all of us. She reached out to her family by writing to them, but they returned her letters. Later her sister wrote to her saying her father forbade the family from communicating with her. It was awful to see the expression on her face when she learned that." Adrian shook his head. "Now, when I look back, I can appreciate why my mother reacted strongly to my running off with a Jewish girl. At that time, my mother's disappointment didn't affect me as Chana's father's rejection had affected her. I had my music, all my family in Krakow were of the same religion, and we lived in the same city. I suppose I wasn't as understanding as I could have been."

Adrian paused and took a deep breath. Sitting there, facing Suzanne, he thought about his actions to make Chana happy. "Life in Krakow was so different for Chana. She missed her family dearly, and she had no loyal friends. My being at school for long hours distressed her, and we quarreled. Sometimes, at night, I'd hear her crying in the bathroom. I tried to comfort her. I did my best to make her happy by expressing my love for her and my joy over the prospect of our having a child. I spent more time with her. My family did their best also. Nothing seemed to help. She became more withdrawn." He hoped Suzanne could understand the stress he was dealing with at that time, that what he'd just told her had aroused her sympathy for him, and she'd be more understanding of why he had kept his past hidden inside himself. He swallowed hard and continued.

"When Chana died two days after Simon was born, I felt guilty and ashamed. I'd taken this beautiful, spirited young woman from her home and provided her with a life of disappointment and sorrow." Adrian bent forward in his chair. His face fell into his hands. He couldn't look at Suzanne. He felt himself begin to cry. He didn't want her to see this. He stood and walked around the room, keeping his back to her.

"I was distraught. I couldn't take care of my son. I stopped going to my classes. I didn't sleep well. I lost weight. I kept thinking about Chana, and I blamed myself for her death." Adrian pulled out a handkerchief and blew his nose. "My salvation came when, through the effort of my teachers, I received an invitation to apply to the Sanfried School." Adrian looked up into Suzanne's eyes. "My aunt and uncle agreed to raise Simon as a Catholic. That was Chana's wish, so he'd be a full part of their family. Chana's expressed she wanted to be buried in the Jewish tradition."

Adrian breathed a deep sigh of relief. "There you have it," he said, depleted of energy. "The whole story." He waited for her reaction.

"Why have you kept this hidden?"

"What purpose would it have served to make it known? I no longer had a claim to Simon, although I've thought about him all the time. It was difficult to share my feelings about this with others. I felt they'd judge me. But I made a success of myself here. I finished school, found a wonderful job, enveloped myself in my career, and built a life."

He reached for her hand, but she pulled away. He lowered his head and gave a bitter smile. "Before you, there was no one I wanted to share my life with. I knew when that time came I'd have to share this with that person."

Suzanne raised her arm to run her hand through her hair "It's quite a story. Very sweet, very heart-wrenching."

The tone in her voice told Adrian she was still angry. His story hadn't aroused any sympathy for him nor any understanding of why he'd held back his past. He was disappointed. He'd been sincere. He expected a more appreciative response.

"If you'd told me all this when we first met, I might have understood. I might have been upset, but I might have been able to get past it because you were honest with me. It's not only me you didn't trust. What about your friends and colleagues?" She paused. Her voice lowered and seemed more controlled. "I'll keep your secret, but some day it will come out. When it does, they're going to wonder why you never acknowledged you had a son. They'll wonder why you were holding back. Is there something wrong with the boy? Is there something wrong about the circumstances of his birth? Is there something wrong with you that you would deny him?" Her voice rose and appeared strained. "What will they think of me? Did I not want your son? Did I prevent you from acknowledging him? Did you ever think of the position you may have put me in?"

Suzanne walked to the window and closed it.

"I want to forgive you, Adrian, but right now I can't." Tears filled her eyes. "I don't know if I ever will. I can't get past how you deserted your own son. You had family to help you until you found yourself. Instead, you ran away and never looked back. What cold-hearted man does such a thing?" She stopped to stare at him. "Don't you wonder what your son looks like, if he looks like you, if he has your talent, if he's happy? It makes me feel you really don't want a child in your life. You either can't or don't want to commit to a family life with me. You've just wasted my time, and I'm furious with myself for letting you do it."

What she said stunned Adrian. She hadn't understood a thing. He stiffened and clenched his hands "You forgot, Suzanne, I wasn't a grown man then. I thought I made that clear. Chana and I were just young, inexperienced kids in love. I was still finding myself. I thought I clearly expressed my regret over how badly my relationship with Chana had turned out.

Adrian stopped to catch his breath. He turned and took a few steps away before calming himself and turning to face her. He unclenched his hands and said, "Whatever happens between us, Suzanne, I want you to know, I'm sorry. You're right. I never considered those things you said, and I beg your forgiveness. I love you, and I do want to marry you and have children with you. I'm hoping you'll forgive me, accept what happened, and marry me. One day I'll find Simon and hope to let him know how sorry I've been. Please, Suzanne, let me prove it to you."

Adrian waited for a response. When none came, he pleaded for her understanding. "I can appreciate how you feel about my giving up Simon, but please don't presume to read my mind, to think my son is never in my heart nor in my thoughts. I'm conscious of him every day. I wonder all the time about what you said: what he looks like, how he spends his time, if he's happy. I have a box full of birthday cards I've bought for him and notes I've written to him about things in my life I want him to know, and about the thoughts I've had of him. I regret the promise I made to my aunt and uncle not to interfere with his upbringing. I have a note to him now in the breast pocket of my overcoat that I want to show you."

Adrian went to where he'd left his coat when they arrived. He pulled out a piece of folded white paper. "Read it," he said. He handed her the note he'd written earlier in the day. It said, *Dear Simon, I'm going to ask Suzanne to marry me tonight. I'm going to tell her about you. I'll tell you tomorrow what she said. Love, Dad.*

Suzanne read the note and handed it back to him. She looked tired. "I'd like you to leave now."

"Suzanne," his voice begged.

She went to the front door and opened it.

Adrian passed in front of Suzanne and turned for one more glance at her. He could see she was determined that he leave.

He walked out with his chin lowered to his chest. Exhausted, he hailed a cab home.

7

A BEER AND A WHITE RUSSIAN

Adrian was in a state of turmoil over the weekend after he'd left Suzanne's apartment, more than he'd felt since he'd left Krakow. Music for him was easy. You read the notes on the sheet, and you played them. The more you played, the better you became. Following the notes gave you control. You could give them your own interpretation. But life was more complicated. People were harder to read. Their faces didn't always show their deeper feelings, and practice didn't always make for better relationships, unless you understood your behavior and had the ability to make changes. His understanding of himself was coming too late. But he loved Suzanne and couldn't stand the thought of losing her. He'd find a way to win her over, to make their relationship work no matter what it took. But she'd have to show a willingness also.

After a miserable three days of pining alone for Suzanne, Adrian realized his only escape was to force himself to work. He'd wait hopefully for her to make the next move, to decide whether she could accept him and his past.

Monday morning Adrian was walking into Union Hall to prepare for an upcoming concert when the contessa's limousine pulled up. He started to enter, pretending not to see her when she called his name. He wasn't ready to face her or anyone else.

Too late. He turned, put on a smile, and walked up to meet her after Paul helped her out of the limo. Adrian returned her kisses on both cheeks.

"Thank you for the yellow roses, dear. They're beautiful."

She looks frail today, like something is weighing on her. I wonder if she's found out about the count. "What brings you here this morning?" Adrian said.

"I'm here to present a ceremonial check from the dinner contributions to our board president. He, Mr. McGowan, Mr. Reitman, and I are having our picture taken for the *Tribune*. You should be in the picture too, Adrian. Come, join us."

"No, I'm not dressed for it. I don't want to intrude." Adrian hoped his annoyance didn't show. It was through his efforts the money was raised. He felt offended he wasn't invited earlier to be in the photograph. Anyway, his thoughts about what happened between him and Suzanne preoccupied him. He didn't feel like being around other people, especially Mr. Reitman.

"Nonsense," the contessa said. "You should be there. I want you there."

"Thanks, but I've got a lot to do to prepare for the season's first concert. I'll be working here most of the day."

"Come, walk me inside, then," she said, and grabbed his arm. "How is Suzann? She's such a lovely girl. I caught you flirting with one another across the room the other evening. When are you going to make an honest woman of her? I think Mr. Reitman would be pleased to have you as a son-in-law."

Adrian wasn't sure how to respond. He wasn't prepared to share with the contessa nor anyone what had happened when he told Suzanne the truth about his past. He wondered if Suzanne had told her father, and, if so, what his reaction was. That would be another reason not to have his picture taken with Mr. Reitman. It would be awkward.

"Soon, I hope, soon," he answered. His face must have betrayed him. He was too quick to smile. He looked down at his watch to show he was in a hurry.

The contessa's eyebrows furrowed. "Are you all right, dear? From the look on your face, I'd say something is bothering you. Why don't you meet me for lunch after I finish here and tell me what's troubling you?"

"I'm afraid I can't," he said, glancing at his watch again. "I have a busy schedule." Adrian not only wanted to avoid discussing his personal problems with the contessa that might expose his secret, but he also didn't want to be placed in any situation where the count's name might arise.

"Then come to dinner tonight at my apartment. I won't take no for an answer. I'll have Paul get you at 6:45. How's that for you?"

Making one more effort for her to release him from this invitation, he said, "Thank you, but I don't want to put you to all that trouble."

"Nonsense. I'll get my cook to make us something special. I'll see you then."

Before he found an excuse to bow out, the contessa had let go of his arm and waved goodbye.

Adrian spent the day at Union Hall preparing for the opening selection of the symphony's 1939-40 subscription season, Edward Elgar's *'Introduction and Allegro for Strings, Op.47."* He'd chosen three other string members from the orchestra to make up the string quartet with him. He reviewed his notes for the bowing he'd go over with them. Then he went over the other three pieces on the program for that evening. These preparations took his mind off his troubles with Suzanne for a while.

On his way home, Adrian wished he'd been swift enough to come up with an acceptable reason why he couldn't meet the contessa for dinner. He wasn't in the mood to be in anyone's company. He forced himself to shave, shower and change and wait for the contessa's limousine. While shaving, Adrian practiced several responses for when the contessa might bring up his relationship with Suzanne to determine if that was the reason for his looking troubled that morning. He studied his face in the mirror as he said them aloud to see if his expressions gave him away. *"You know how involved I get readying for the new season. I haven't given Suzanne the attention she needs. She feels neglected. I'll make it up to her,"* or *"One of Suzanne's clients is posing a problem. It's preoccupying her. She'll work it out,"* he'd assure the contessa.

When Adrian arrived at the apartment, the contessa took him to a small parlor on the opposite side of the stairway from where he'd overheard the count and his Nazi sympathizers. Adrian noticed the yellow roses on a table nearby. He wondered if the contessa had them purposely placed there for his benefit. Paul took their drink requests. Adrian asked for a White Russian. He was surprised when the contessa asked for a beer.

"I don't drink beer in public, but I do like one when I'm alone," she said.

Adrian chuckled to himself. This was something he wouldn't have expected when he first came to know her. Now that they had become more familiar as adults, he was getting an intimate look at her more approachable side.

They chit-chatted while waiting for Paul to return.

"How did the picture-taking go?" Adrian asked, with a bit of sarcasm.

"Oh, everyone was full of smiles and compliments that I raised so much money. I did make it plain, Adrian, you deserved credit, that you charmed the guests with your playing and by your ebullient personality. I hope I made them feel guilty for not asking you to be in the picture. I did tell the *Times* people to make sure your name was in the picture's caption as the guest of honor."

"That was kind of you, contessa."

"Nonsense," she responded. "I've been an admirer of yours ever since you appeared at the Sanfried School, and please, call me Rose. My devoted friends call me Rose. My father named me Henrietta Roselynne, but I hated Henrietta. It reminded me of a stuffy old maid. I demanded to be called Rose at the age of sixteen, and it stuck."

Hmm, thought Adrien. *I wonder if Suzanne knew this when she suggested I send the contessa roses.*

Their drinks arrived. When they were alone, the contessa said, "Now tell me, Adrian, what's going on in that handsome head of yours. You seemed upset when I asked about Suzanne this morning."

Adrian was taken aback at the abruptness of the question, but he realized he shouldn't have been. She'd implied that was the reason for inviting him to dinner, and he'd planned for it while shaving. If he told her the truth, how would the contessa react?

Adrian's worry over the possibility of losing Suzanne overrode his feeling of the need to hold back his concerns with the contessa. He decided to take a leap of faith and confide in her.

Adrian put his drink down. He stood, walked around the room, picked up a photograph, stared at it for a few seconds, and replaced it. He needed to collect himself, to make sure he was making the right decision. He returned to his seat and told her the story as he'd presented it to Suzanne. He told her Suzanne's reaction and poured his heart out about how he felt he may have destroyed his relationship with her. The contessa listened without a single interruption, only occasionally shifting in her chair or sipping her beer. When he finished, Adrian felt exhausted. He hadn't touched his drink the entire time. He grabbed it, and though it was now watery, he gulped it down.

Adrian sat back with the empty glass in his hand and waited for the contessa's reaction.

The contessa ran a finger around the rim of her glass. "We all have our little secrets, things we don't want people to know."

He wondered if she was referring to the count. He felt a rush of sympathy for her. He looked down and shook his head.

Looking up, she said, "You had immense talent when you arrived at The Sanfried School, but I saw a sadness in you. I wondered if it contributed to your studying and working so hard and leading you to become what you are today." Looking him directly in the eyes, she said, "I see I was right. I understand what you must have been going through keeping such a story to yourself, the guilt you must have felt."

Adrian stared back at her. Relieved by her response, he felt a complete release of all tension. He sat back and let it sink in.

"Perhaps," she continued, "your struggle with Suzanne is a blessing in disguise. It might be a breakthrough in your relationship now that it's out in the open between you. Give Suzanne time. She's a strong woman. She's received a shock. I understand what that means."

Adrian felt little satisfaction from these words. He'd derive more comfort if he knew Suzanne had come to feel the same. He wondered what the contessa meant about understanding what it meant to receive a shock. Was this another reference to the count? He looked at her. That look of worry he'd seen earlier that morning was back. She was picking at the buttons on her blouse.

"No one knows what I'm about to tell you, Adrian. I tell you out of my affection for you and my need to unburden myself, just as you have." Her hands gripped her elbows, and she leaned back in her chair. "I've kicked the count out," she said, with a twist of satisfaction in her voice.

"A representative from the Committee on Immigration and Naturalization paid me a visit the day after the fundraiser. He told me about the count's association with the Nazi movement, right here in New York." She undid her arms and pounded her knee. Her voice rose. "How dare he do this here where my friends are, where he might humiliate me. The government has been following him for several months. The Committee chairman, an old family friend, has agreed to let me handle it privately, but he suggested I move quickly before a scandal breaks."

Leaning back, she kicked her leg up and said, "I've given the count the old-fashioned boot. I've sent him back to Italy. If he wants to mingle with Nazi sympathizers, let him dine with Mussolini." She leaned to one side and swept a speck from her dress. She again lowered her voice. "I know people look upon me as a fool, an old rich woman keeping a younger titled gentleman who's lost his fortune. That they talk about me behind my back hasn't escaped me. But I could not have them think of me as a Nazi sympathizer. I've told people he's gone back to Italy to settle an uncle's estate. I've made it clear. I never want to see him again."

As Adrian listened to the contessa tell her story, all thoughts about his own problems fell to the side. "I'm so sorry, Rose," he said. "Here I am spouting off about my problems when you're hurting. It was rotten of the count to do that to you. You're well respected here. People will be sympathetic. Please let me know if I can do anything for you."

"I didn't mean to burden you with my troubles, Adrian. It was my desire to help with yours. Come, let's have dinner." She got up and pulled a cord. Paul appeared, and soon a servant brought them their meal. They ate at a table set in the room for them.

"If you want, I'd like to help you in any way I can to locate your family. I've got influential friends, many in government. She rattled their names off to Adrian. There may be little chance of contacting your son directly with all that's going on in Poland, but if there is, I'll see if someone can at least try to find out how they are."

Tapping her cheek with her forefinger, the contessa said, "I might even try contacting Eleanor Roosevelt. Our families have a long history, both being from New York. We meet occasionally, and she may be able to give me ideas about how to help you in your search."

Adrian couldn't believe what he was hearing. Names from the upper echelon of American society were being tossed about as possible help to him. It concerned him that such people might find out about the skeletons in his closet. However, if he wanted to find his son, he had to put such feelings aside. People didn't need to know the full story, he realized, only that his family was in trouble, and he was doing his best to help them. Having made a declaration of his secret to both Suzanne and the contessa, he was determined to face his past and try to reunite with his son.

The next morning Adrian went to Union Hall early. He decided to do more preparation for the Symphony's upcoming season's opening concert before heading to The Sanfried School to teach an early afternoon class on the use of the violin during the Romantic Period. He walked onto the stage of Union Hall and set up four chairs for the quartet for the Edward Elgar piece and a music stand for the conductor. He pretended it was the night of the concert, though it was weeks away. He rose from the chair where he'd sit during the performance, the one closest to the conductor. He walked to center stage, where maestro McGowan would stand. He raised his bow for the oboe player to sound the "A" note to start the tuning of the orchestra. McGowan would arrive on stage once the orchestra was tuned, and Adrian would shake his hand. Adrian savored this ritual. He practiced it often when he was alone in the Hall and thought no one was looking. It made him feel a part of a great tradition and a part of a prestigious orchestra. He worked hard to be. It would have been, he hoped, a source of pride to his family in Poland.

He'd written about such experiences in his unsent notes to Simon. He wondered if Simon had found the violin he'd left behind in the bureau in the basement of the bakery of his aunt and uncle. *Did it interest him? Has he inherited my talent for the violin? If so, might this create a bond between* us *if we were to ever meet?*

Adrian heard clapping. He turned toward the seats. Despite the few lights he had turned on for the stage, the auditorium itself was dark. He couldn't see who was there. He bent forward with his hand over his brow and squinted. It was Suzanne.

He laid a hand on his heart. *She's forgiven me.* He felt a floating sensation, as if all his burdens had been removed by her presence. He moved closer to the edge of the stage.

Suzanne walked toward him. "Isn't it a little early to begin preparation?"

He threw up his arms. "You know me. I like to get an early start."

Suzanne rolled her finger in the air. "And that little bit of action when you stood stage front, lifted your bow, and greeted the conductor…is that part of your early preparation?"

Embarrassed, Adrian dropped his chin and scratched his ear. "You saw that, huh?"

Her voice softened. "Adrian, I came to see you. I thought we could have lunch together."

Surely, she was here to try to set things right between them. For a brief second, he felt vulnerable. *Suppose I'm wrong. What if she's here to break off our relationship completely?* From the tone of her voice and her friendly demeanor, he knew he was wrong.

"Sure. Let me make a call. I'll meet you in the lobby."

"Thank you, Adrian."

Adrian made his call, arranged for a substitute for his class at Sanfried, and freshened up before joining Suzanne. The words of the contessa came to him, giving him hope that his sharing the truth with Suzanne was a breakthrough in their relationship.

They walked to a small Italian café nearby. It was crowded, but the hostess found them a small table in the back near the kitchen. The restaurant was noisy from the chatter of the lunch crowd. Waiters coming and going through the swinging doors of the kitchen added to the hubbub.

A waiter took their orders, and after a moment of silence between them, Suzanne placed her hands on the table, closed her eyes, and took a deep breath. "Adrian, I've had a few days to think things over," she said softly. "I can't say I'm sorry for the way I acted. You gave me quite a shock, but I understand how hard that must have been for you. I've come to realize how this has affected your life. I thought about the other night, how you pulled out that folded note to Simon. It convinced me you were sincere. I said some cruel things. I was only thinking of myself, and I ask you to forgive me."

Adrian smiled. He felt a mixture of relief, happiness, desire, and love all rolled into one. His body relaxed. "Thank you," he said. He reached across the table for her hands and kissed them. He set his eyes upon her.

"Suzanne," he said. "I want to marry you and have babies, little girls who will look just like you. Before you answer, there's something you should know."

"What's that?"

"I'm going to search for my son, no matter what or how long it takes. If, and when, I find him, I'll honor my pledge to my aunt and uncle, but with the war in Europe, I must know he's all right and that I made the right decision. If he is in danger, I want to try to bring him here. Can you live with that?"

"I wouldn't have it any other way," she said.00

8

THE BLESSING

Over coffee the next morning, Adrian said to Suzanne, "Before you start calling your friends, would you give me this morning to tell your father about our engagement and to ask his blessing?"

"How sweet," she said, folding her hands at her chin. "Of course. While you're there you can ask him about what we talked about last night." She smiled and said, "Now that I've got you, I want to make it legal as soon as possible.

Adrian placed his napkin on the table, stood, went over to Suzanne, and kissed her goodbye. "I'll phone you right after to tell you what he said. Just let me do one thing, and I'll be out of your hair."

Adrian went to his desk and wrote a brief note to the contessa. *Thank you for your advice. Suzanne and I are engaged to be married. Details to follow. Love, Adrian.* He put the note in an envelope, placed a stamp on it, and headed to Union Hall. He'd mail it on the way.

Family disapproval on both sides had marred his first marriage. Adrian was determined not to let that happen again. He felt he owed his future father-in-law the respect of telling him about his background. He hoped Mr. Reitman, after hearing his story and his profession of love for Suzanne, would offer his blessing. Adrian straightened his posture, took two easy breaths, and headed toward Mr. Reitman's office.

Adrian found Mr. Reitman at his desk with his door open. He tapped on the door.

"Adrian, please, come in," Mr. Reitman said and pointed to a chair.

Adrian closed the door behind him and sat. "Thank you. I'm glad to find you here this early." Despite his show of confidence, Adrian found his stomach churning.

Mr. Reitman leaned forward. "You can't raise money lying in bed. Tell me, what brings you here so early? You look worried."

Adrian smiled broadly. "As a matter of fact, I have good news I hope will please you. I asked Suzanne to marry me, and she accepted. I came to ask your blessing."

Mr. Reitman pulled himself up from his chair and walked around to Adrian. They shook hands.

"Nothing could make me happier," Mr. Reitman said. "To tell the truth, I've been expecting this. Of course, you have my blessing, my boy. May I call you Son?"

"I'd like that," Adrian said. It had been many years since someone called him that. He had a deep regard for his future father-in-law and hoped what he had to tell him would bring them closer together. Adrian licked his lips. "You may not be so happy after what I'm about to tell you."

"Oh?" Mr. Reitman's smile slowly faded. His eyebrows rose.

"Please sit down, sir," Adrian said.

Mr. Reitman moved back behind his desk, sat, and folded his arms across his chest.

Adrian twisted his watch back and forth around his wrist while he told Mr. Reitman about his relationship as a teenager with Chana. He told him about her death following childbirth and the reason for his subsequent move to the United States. While speaking, Adrian watched for any signs of displeasure on the part of Mr. Reitman that might change his mind about giving his blessing.

When Adrian finished, Mr. Reitman uncrossed his arms, leaned forward, and picked up a paperclip from his desk. He rolled it around his fingers then tossed it back on his blotter. He shifted his body to the left and leaned his elbow on the arm of the chair, still not responding.

"I've shocked you, sir."

Mr. Reitman pulled out a handkerchief and blew his nose. "To be honest, yes. You've caught me off guard. I've always known you and thought of you in a certain way. What you've told me is unsettling." He put his handkerchief back in his pocket. "I assume you've told Suzanne about this?"

"Yes, sir. I did. I wanted her to hear it from me before I asked her to marry me."

"How did she respond?"

"At first, she was shocked, like you, but when she understood why I'd kept this a secret from everyone, she accepted my proposal.

Mr. Reitman sat up straight and rubbed his chin. "I have great faith in Suzanne's judgment. If you tell me she knows about this and has accepted it, then I shall too. I can tell by your expressions and demeanor it hasn't been easy for you to tell me this. The fact that you've been honest says a great deal about your character. Still, I'm going to need a little time to adjust to this, Adrian. I hope you understand."

"Yes, sir, I do, but I hope you'll never be unsure of my love for and my devotion to your daughter."

"You're both mature and responsible people. I appreciate your coming to me to share your story. I'm sad for your suffering, but I admire what you've made of your life." Mr. Reitman placed his hands flat on his desk. "You have my blessing, Son. All I ask is that you keep my daughter happy, and you give me grandchildren while I'm still young enough and able to spoil them."

"Thank you, sir. That's our intent." Adrian paused, "Before I leave, I do have two requests. One is you don't share what I've told you."

"You've got my word. And the second?"

Adrian told him what he and Suzanne wanted. "We'd like to keep it a surprise if it works out."

"That's a tough request, but I'll see what I can do."

"Thank you. Suzanne will be happy when I tell her. Thank you for your understanding and for your blessing. I hope I always act in a way to make you proud."

Adrian was about to walk out the door when he turned, and said, "I have a third request.

"What is it, Son?"

"May I call you Dad?"

Mr. Reitman rose and walked to Adrian. "Of course," he said, patting Adrian's shoulder, his eyes moistening.

Back in his office, Adrian called Suzanne and told her that her father would try to honor their request. She said she'd start preparing her part right away on the expectation that her father would come through.

9

DINNER WITH FRIENDS

Adrian had no illusions. At some point in time, the fact he had a son whom he'd kept a secret might become known, particularly among their circle of friends, a close-knit group of six couples. He hoped when that happened it wouldn't affect their relationships. He and Suzanne would need their support. In the meantime, he and Suzanne decided, rightly or wrongly, there was no need for their friends to know. What difference would it make? It might only upset them. There was no purpose in their knowing, nothing they could do. The war had made it impossible for Adrian to reach Poland to find out about Simon. There was the possibility Adrian would never see or hear from his relatives there again. He tried to think positively, however. He'd continue to make it his lifetime goal to reunite with his son and seek his forgiveness.

On Saturday evening, September 23, Adrian and Suzanne were dressing to have dinner with Clair and Larry at their home.

"What time are we due there?" Adrian said, unbuttoning his shirt.

"Around five-thirty."

"Anyone else going to be there?"

"No, just us."

"I like Claire. I'm glad you and she are close. You've known her a long time, haven't you?"

"Ever since we were randomly paired as roommates at Wellesley. We didn't know each other in New York. We took to each other

60

instantly. We've been joined at the hip since. Next to my cousin, Charlotte, Claire is my best friend."

"I used to think she and Larry were an odd fit, but I've grown fond of him," Adrian said while putting on a clean shirt.

"He puts on an act, but he's not what he seems. Despite his gruffness, he's quite sensitive."

Adrian tucked in his shirt. "How did they meet?"

"I told you this story, didn't I?" Suzanne said, brushing her hair. Claire was exhibiting her work at a gallery in Greenwich Village. Larry came in and bought one of her paintings. She went to thank him, and he asked her out to dinner. They found they had a lot in common. They've been together ever since. I was a bridesmaid at their wedding."

"Have I seen the painting?"

"You can't miss it. It's the one over the sofa opposite the living room fireplace." Suzanne walked over to Adrian and straightened his collar. "There, you look nice."

"You too." Adrian planted a kiss on her forehead. "I'll get our coats."

"Grab an umbrella too. I hear the patter of rain on the window, and don't forget the bottle of brandy you got for Larry."

"I won't." He looked at his watch. "It's getting late. I'll hail a cab. You wait here."

Adrian soon returned with an umbrella. "The cab's waiting." He helped her on with her coat and held her arm as they walked to the cab. He held the umbrella over her. "Be careful. It's slippery," he said. Once they were safely in, Adrian gave the driver the address. Adrian asked Suzanne, "Are we the only ones invited tonight?"

"Yes, and if Larry calls me Suzy, I want you to swat his arm."

Adrian smiled. "You're the one who's developed that move to perfection, my dear." Adrian paused. "How come among our friends I'm the only one Larry hasn't assigned a nickname?"

"He respects you and your position too much. He appears to be a simple man, but underneath that gruffness, he's quite sophisticated."

Changing the subject, Adrian asked, "Have you told Claire about our wedding plans?"

"Of course not. We've decided to keep that a secret, remember? If I told her, the others would know as soon as she could get to them and spoil the surprise."

"Just checking," Adrian said. "It will be spectacular if we can pull it off. Is it like Claire not to keep a secret?"

"It's exactly like her. She loves having all the gossip before everyone else and being the first to spread it around."

"I thought you were quite fond of her."

"I am. I love her dearly. That doesn't mean I'm not aware of her faults. She's the typical younger of two sisters. She gets attention by trying to outdo the other. In her case, it's spreading news before others know. Don't get me wrong. She's not a bit malicious. It's, well like I said, her way of getting attention. Surely you've noticed that."

Adrian shook his head. "No, I haven't."

"Men. You can be such fools when it comes to women."

Adrian looked at Suzanne and grinned. "Anything this fool should know about you?"

"If you haven't found out by now, you never will."

Adrian looked at Suzanne's hand. "Are you anxious to show off your ring? If Claire sees it before the others, it may spoil it for you.

"I'll swear her to secrecy."

"I thought that wouldn't work, second sister syndrome and all."

"I'll keep my gloves on."

"Even through dinner?"

"I'll tell her I have a contagious rash," Suzanne said playfully. "She won't want me to touch her silverware."

"Yeah, Adrian said sarcastically. "That ought to work."

The light drizzle turned to a downpour. Adrian held the umbrella over their heads as they got out of the cab and walked toward Clair and Larry's brownstone. Two bicycles sped by them causing

Suzanne to stumble. Adrian caught her but not before she broke the heel on her shoe. When Adrian reached down to pick it up, the umbrella drooped, and they both got soaked.

"Damn," Suzanne said as she limped toward the brownstone on Adrian's arm.

Larry was waiting for them at the door. "Hooligans," he shouted to the bicyclers in his gravelly voice. "Quick! Come in," he said to Suzanne and Adrian. "You're soaking wet. Let me have your things."

After hanging their coats on the Victorian coat rack in the hallway, he turned to Suzanne and said, "Are you okay, Suzy?"

Adrian saw her wince. She hated it when he called her that. Larry had a penchant for calling all of their friends by nicknames, or street names, as Suzanne called them. Larry owned a construction company. His employees knew each other by their nicknames. After so many times being called "Suzy", she gave up correcting him. He was too likeable to hold it against him very long.

"I'll be alright," she said shaking off the chill and removing her wet shoe. "I broke a heel."

Don't worry. Claire will get you some slippers. Clair's finishing setting the dining room table. Let's meet her there. She'll get you some dry clothes. He led them down the hallway.

"Oh Larry," Adrian said. "With the rain and all, I left a bottle of Delford Amagne in the cab."

"Good choice. Too bad," Larry said and led them to the dark dining room.

Shouts of surprise greeted them when they entered the room and Larry switched on the chandelier above the dining room table. Suzanne and Adrian became the center of a circle surrounded by five other couples offering their congratulations. Suzanne held her hands to her face repeating, "Is this for real?" Adrian shook the men's hands heartily and kissed all the women on both cheeks.

When the circle broke, Claire said, "I know I told you it was only going to be the four of us. That was just a ruse to give you both a surprise engagement party."

"You stinkers," Suzanne said to Claire and Larry. "All of you," she said turning to the others. "But we love you for it, don't we Adrian?"

"I'm very touched, my friends. I'm at a loss for words. Thanks for this. It means a great deal to us. He put an arm around Suzanne's shoulder and kissed her cheek.

Claire lit the candles on the dining room table. "I've got to run into the kitchen and check the rack of lamb," she said. "It's ready sooner than I planned. Larry, come help me and Nelly." Nelly was the housekeeper Claire and her mother shared for occasions like this. "Everyone, refresh your drinks. Someone take care of Suzanne and Adrian. We'll be right back."

Adrian admired the room. It was large and comfortably furnished with an extended dining table set with Claire's special dinner plates and bowls, crystal wine glasses, and silverware. A Victorian sideboard with the fixings of a bar sat along the wall behind which was the kitchen. Adrian watched the dangling prisms from the chandelier play tricks with the flickering lights from the candlesticks as they cast moving shadows around the room creating a soft, romantic atmosphere.

Adrian looked in the mirror over the sideboard. He saw himself and the room it reflected. *This is what I deserve. I made the right choice.* He felt a warm flush. It was the feeling of finally finding himself, of being grateful for Suzanne, for these friends, and for his newfound freedom.

Marianne, a successful writer of popular adult romance novels, and her husband, George, approached him.

"What can I get you, Adrian?" George said.

"Just a glass of red wine, thanks."

George, or Professor, as Larry called him, was wearing a sleeveless argyle sweater and a multicolored bow tie clipped to a blue, long sleeve shirt. He often joked his female English Literature majors at Columbia University seemed more interested in his wife's novels than the ones he assigned in his curriculum of books on the Victorian age. Although Adrian liked Marianne for her forthrightness, he found George to be the more intellectual conversationalist.

George took a final gulp of his wine and said," I'll be right back with it."

Adrian looked around the room. Over by the sideboard, he noticed John, a lawyer, dubbed Counselor by Larry, waving his tortoiseshell glasses at Robert, or Doc, an obstetrician, going on about something. Robert stood listening, rubbing his bald head. He wore an oversized sweater covering his girth. From what Adrian had heard from several of his fellow musicians whose wives were seeing him, Robert was well liked and respected. Their wives, Elizabeth, or Lizzie, and Dorothy, a.k.a. Dottie, were in a conversation with Suzanne. Elizabeth, five months pregnant with their third child, was wearing a bright floral dress that made her appear she might deliver momentarily. Dottie, also Robert's nurse in his obstetrics practice, was wearing bright colored clothes and beaded jewelry. She had confided to the group she loved to wear these away from the office, where she dressed in white from head to toe. Adrian was appreciative of Suzanne's more conservative fashion style after observing her with these two women.

Phillip, or Brick, as Larry called him, an architect, walking as tall and straight as one of the buildings he designed, came to Adrian with his wife, Margaret, a.k.a. Maggie, a Broadway set designer. She was dressed in a silk blouse with a family heirloom pin and a pleated skirt. Despite Phillip's rigid appearance, he was very funny, and Maggie was a source of gossip for the group on the shenanigans going on behind the sets of the best Broadway shows.

"Adrian," Phillip said with a grin on his face. "I've got a new one for you. What's the difference between a violin and a viola?"

Adrian had heard the joke from one of his students at Sanfried, but he played along. "I give up. What?"

"They're actually the same size, but the violinist's head is so much bigger," Phillip began laughing, before he finished his joke.

Adrian pretended he hadn't heard the joke. "That's a good one," he said, smiling broadly. "I'll have to tell that to my students."

Adrian felt happy being surrounded by friends who were here to celebrate his engagement to Suzanne, friends he'd known since he started seeing her. Adrian liked them all. They were intelligent and fun to be with.

Claire and Larry returned to the room and announced the first course was ready. "Let's all sit down," Claire said. "We have loads of questions to ask Suzanne and Adrian, don't we, folks?"

When everyone was seated, Elizabeth rubbed her stomach and asked Suzanne, "How did Adrian propose, and where did he get that gorgeous ring?"

Suzanne held the ring up for everyone to see; John leaned over to get a closer look. He turned, winked at Adrian, and said, "I saw a ring just like that being sold by a street vendor on Eighth Avenue."

Adrian looked at John and shook his head. "Damn," he said. "You gave away my secret."

John cupped his lips and pretended to whisper. "Don't worry," he said, "I've been using that same street vendor for years."

Elizabeth waved her husband off. "Don't listen to them, Suzanne. Tell us everything."

"It was simple, really," Suzanne said, about to tell the story she and Adrian rehearsed so as not to give the real story about Otto and how she learned about Adrian's past. "We had a fight. You know how Adrian gets before a concert, how he squirrels himself away."

Adrian's eyes widened. He shrugged his shoulders and raised his hands. "That's why my performances are perfect."

"Well, I lost my temper and hung up on him one night when he cancelled a dinner." Suzanne watched her friends nod their heads in approval.

Adrian covered his ears and grimaced. "She nearly broke my eardrums."

"He called the next day to apologize."

Adrian shrugged his shoulders again. "I hadn't eaten all day. I was hungry." He looked around at everyone. They were enjoying his and Suzanne's little act.

"I played hard to get for two days," Suzanne said. "When he called again, I accepted his invitation to lunch. He proposed at that little Italian restaurant around the corner from Union Hall."

"That dump?" Larry said. "It's noisy as hell in there at lunchtime. I'm surprised you could even hear him propose."

It had been a while since he and Suzanne had been among people who enjoyed each other this much. Adrian felt jubilant being the focus of tonight's surprise, and, from the look on her face, he was sure Suzanne felt the same. He hoped nothing could ever disrupt these friendships.

"When's the wedding?" Claire said. "Will it be big or small?"

"We haven't made plans yet. We've got to work around the symphony's concert schedule," Suzanne said. "Don't worry." Suzanne looked at Adrian hesitantly. "You'll all be the first to know."

Adrian gave a nod to back her up. He felt a pang of guilt deceiving these friends who were being so kind to him and Suzanne.

After their salad course, Larry rubbed his hands and said, "Let's get to that lamb. I've been breathing in that great smell since I got home and can't wait to dig in."

"First the soup," Claire corrected him. "Butternut squash with cinnamon and garlic croutons."

During dinner, they gossiped about other people, and they talked about the movies they'd seen. The men talked about golf and baseball, and Maggie shared the backstage high jinks at the play she was working on due to open in December.

At one point, during the main course, Robert said to Suzanne, "I remember your once telling me your great grandmother was a twin. Twins run in families, you know. It's possible you may have them when you have children."

Adrian looked at Suzanne. "That would be wonderful. I'd love to have two daughters to dote on."

"Honeymoon before children," Claire said. "Have you decided where you'll go?"

"We're not sure when we can plan one, given the busy concert season," Suzanne said. "We may just take a couple of days off after one of the concerts and wait until summer and go up to Cape Cod for a week or so."

When they were nearly finished with the main course, John asked, "What do you think the chances are there will be a draft if we enter the war? Many of the young men at the firm are worried."

"There'll be no talk of war in this house tonight or any night," Claire responded abruptly. She got up from the table, picked up her empty dishes, and carried them to the kitchen.

Larry said apologetically, "She's extremely sensitive about the war. You all know her brother was killed in the last one."

"That's right. I forgot. I'm sorry," John said. "Still, it's a worry for us all."

Larry went into the kitchen and came back with Claire.

"I'm sorry. That's a delicate subject for me," Claire said. "Dessert and coffee will be ready soon. In the meantime, Larry has something to say." She turned to the others. In a lowered voice, a hand covering the side of her mouth, she said, "He's been practicing this since he got home."

Larry stood and cleared his throat. "Thank you dear. It was kind of you to call that to everyone's attention."

"Go ahead, Larry," Robert said. "We're with you."

"Thank you, Doc," Larry said. "I'd like to make a toast." He cleared his throat again. "Over the years, we've grown into a close circle of friends. But you clowns are more than that to me. I'm the only kid of parents who were only kids. I've never had a close family. You've become more than friends to me. You've become like brothers and sisters." Larry rubbed his eyebrows. "Adrian, we've watched you and Suzy grow closer since she first brought you to our clan. We hoped your relationship would lead to this day, aren't I right, folks?"

Their voices expressed agreement.

"To be truly one of us, to be honest to God one of us, you need a nickname."

Suzanne nearly choked on an olive.

"Now what kind of nickname is there for Adrian, I wondered. I asked my men. I won't repeat some of their suggestions in mixed company, but there were two that stood out. One was Andy. The other was Ace. I thought about it. Andy was OK, but Ace seemed right. 'Why?' you ask me."

"Tell us already, for crying out loud," Claire said, interrupting Larry.

"Yes dear. Just give me one more minute of glory." Larry turned to Adrian. "Where was I? Oh, yes. Why Ace? First, as concertmaster, you're the number one violinist, and two, you're our number one choice for Suzy. Larry picked up a butter knife and gently waved it toward Adrian. So, Mr. Adrian Mazurek, from this point on, I dub you Ace."

Larry put down the knife and held up his champagne glass. He asked the others to do the same. "To Suzy and Ace. May you both have a long and happy life together surrounded by family and good friends."

"To Suzy and Ace," the others cheered.

Suzanne shook her head. "That was sweet, Larry." She pinched Adrian's thigh. "Thank you, and Ace thanks you too."

"I do, my friend," Adrian said to Larry. He placed his hand over his heart. "I feel honored and more than a little touched." Adrian stood, still holding his champagne glass. "I'd like to respond." He breathed in deeply to get hold of his emotions. "I, too, have no brothers or sisters, until now." He circled his arm around the table. "You've welcomed me graciously since you've known me. You've no idea how much it means to me that you've accepted me as part of this family. I love you all."

Adrian turned to Suzanne.

"For most of my life music has been my joy, my strength, my religion, my reason for being," he paused. "Until now." He looked down to Suzanne. "You've given me something beyond music." His heart felt tender as he gazed upon her. Her eyes were looking directly into his as if in anticipation of his next words. He reached down and took her hand. "You've brought love and joy into my life, the desire to enjoy the world beyond the stage. You've brought me these friends, my new family, and I love you and plan to make you happy for the rest of my life." He stared into her watery eyes, lifted his glass, and said, "To Suzanne and family."

"To Suzanne and family," their friends toasted joyously.

The room became quiet. Some of the women were dabbing their eyes.

"That was beautiful, Adrian, I mean Ace," Larry said. "You stole my thunder there, didn't you? But I forgive you because of the circumstances. Just don't do it again."

Everyone laughed.

"Let's have dessert and coffee in the living room," Claire suggested. "I'll tell Nellie."

10

THE SHOWSTOPPER

In the living room, Adrian walked toward the sofa to admire the painting Suzanne said had brought Claire and Larry together.

"It's lovely, isn't it," he heard an approaching voice say. It was Marrianne. She was holding a glass of white wine. The multi-layers of bracelets on her wrist jingled as she raised her glass for a sip.

"Yes. It wasn't until this evening that Suzanne told me about its connection between Claire and Larry. It's a beautiful still life. The colors of the flowers are vivid. The heavy strokes bring them to life." He thought that Claire giving Suzanne and him a painting by her would be a treasured wedding gift.

While gathering in the living room, they heard crying. "That must be Larry, Jr.," Claire said, returning from the kitchen. "He's been having bad dreams lately. I'd better see to him."

Claire soon came back carrying her son. He rubbed his eyes as he looked around the room.

"He looks so sweet in that onesie with all those trucks on it. I bet you bought that for him, Larry," Maggie said.

"His grandmother did," Larry answered. "She knows he loves all kinds of trucks. He has a room full of them."

"Come to me," Larry said, reaching for his son. "Say hello to your aunts and uncles." Larry, Jr. hid his face in his father's shoulder.

Adrian watched Larry's gentleness with the boy as he ran his fingers through his son's fine blond hair.

What would it have felt like to have done the same with Simon, to buy him toys and clothes and to teach him to play the violin when he was old enough?

Larry came over to Adrian. "Here," he said, handing over his son. "Give Larry, Jr. a hug good night."

Adrian took the boy and felt the child lay his head on his shoulder. He nuzzled his nose in the child's hair and smelled its shampoo freshness and the sweet talcum someone rubbed on his small body. Adrian had never held a child before except for the two days after Simon's birth. After Chana's death, he never picked up a child again.

The boy called for his daddy, and Larry took him back. "It's time to go beddy-bye." Larry handed his son back to Claire. "Say night-night to your aunts and uncles."

Larry, Jr. rubbed his eyes with one hand and waved with the other. Claire took him back to his room.

"I hope someday soon you'll know the joy of a son," Larry said to Adrian and Suzanne. "I wouldn't give up Larry, Jr. for all the gold in the world."

Adrian forced a smile.

The party ended soon after. Suzanne and Adrian waited for everyone to leave so they could thank Claire and Larry privately.

In the taxi home, Suzanne said, "That was nice of them."

Adrian was quiet.

"You're thinking about what Larry said, aren't you? You're thinking about Simon."

"Yes." Adrian's chin dipped to his chest. He folded his hands tightly as he remembered the day Chana died, how poorly he'd responded, and how he could barely look at his newborn son without feeling profound guilt.

"I was such a foolish young man back then. I felt I had no choice but to abandon him and come to the United States."

Softly, Suzanne said, "If you hadn't, we wouldn't have met. I love you. Don't worry, we'll find him."

Undressing, once they were home, Suzanne said, "I feel bad about not telling them about our wedding plans, especially after Larry's toast."

Adrian kissed Suzanne's cheek. "Don't worry. When they see what we've planned, they'll forgive us,"

Suzanne sighed. "I hope so."

Adrian couldn't sleep thinking about what Larry had said about not giving up his son for all the gold in the world. He felt a hollowness in his chest and needed to get out of bed. He gently pulled the covers off himself, making sure not to wake Suzanne.

He walked to the kitchen without bothering to put on his robe or slippers and started preparing a cup of hot milk. While waiting for the milk to heat, he wondered if the contessa had been successful in finding anyone among her friends to help him locate his family in Poland.

Adrian heard sounds coming from the bathroom. Seconds later, Suzanne appeared in the doorway.

"Are you OK?" she said. Her eyes didn't look fully awake.

"I'm fine. I'm sorry if I woke you. I couldn't sleep. I thought a glass of warm milk might help."

Suzanne sat next to him and leaned in close. "Are you still thinking about what Larry said?"

He nodded. "I can't get it out of my mind. God only knows what kind of trouble I left my son in back in Poland."

Suzanne got up and poured Adrian half a glass of warm milk and handed it to him. She turned off the gas and put the bottle back in the refrigerator.

"Drink your milk and come back to bed. If you're going to worry yourself to death, you need your rest."

After she left the room, Adrian went to a kitchen drawer and pulled out a pencil and small pad Suzanne used to write reminder notes to herself. He wrote a note to Simon to add to his box of cards and notes to his son.

Dear Simon,

A friend gave me a nickname tonight. He called me Ace. I wish you and I had nicknames for each other. I'd love to call you Buddy and muss your hair and laugh along with you when you act funny, and I'd love to walk with you with my arm around your shoulder. Some day that will happen if you let me.

Dad

On the evening of October 8, Suzanne said to Adrian, "My father called this morning. It's all arranged."

"Good," Adrian said, smiling. "Now do your part."

Suzanne's eyes glowed. "I already have."

A month later, the following and similar announcements appeared in gossip columns around New York and the West Coast:

The ending of last night's November 11 performance of the Eleventh State Symphony Orchestra at Union Hall was a showstopper in the truest sense.

Upon completion of the second half, the conductor, Alistair McGowan, asked the audience to remain seated for an encore. The auditorium lights remained dimmed with the stage fully lit. The stage lights lowered as the orchestra began to play Wagner's Wedding March. A spotlight focused on the Very Reverend Father Joseph Mc Leary as he walked to center stage. Adrian Mazurek, the symphony's concertmaster, came forth to meet him. Suzanne Reitman appeared from the right stage curtain wearing an ankle length satin wedding dress and a lace veil. Her father, Marcus Reitman, escorted her to Mr. Mazurek. Miss Reitman is a well-known representative of many prominent artists in the musical world. Marcus Reitman is the symphony's director of development. Mr. Reitman handed his daughter over to Mr. Mazurek. The wedding ceremony was then officiated by Father McLeary. Upon completion of the ceremony, following much applause, the wedding couple hosted a small private reception at a local restaurant for their surprised friends and family.

11

THE PLAZA HOTEL

Adrian arranged a two night stay at the Plaza Hotel with a suite overlooking Central Park.

The morning after the wedding he woke up startled by a dream. He was walking through Central Park. The moon was full. Lamplights lit the way. Crowds of people were singing in the streets of New York, but he couldn't make out the words. Shouts of anger and rebellion rose above the voices. He came to a bandstand where he saw the vague image of a boy playing a warm peaceful melody increasing in intensity on the violin. It was Tchaikovsky's Concerto in D Major.

Adrian interpreted the dream as being about the difference in opinion he was having with his violinists over the bowing for the opening Bach/Mendelssohn concert. They were arguing for free bowing, he for bowing in unison. In his opinion the sound of the string section playing as one created a better tone to these older pieces. Adrian knew he needed to listen to their suggestions before deciding.

The issue was left unsettled until after the wedding when he thought he could persuade them to his side. He was angry with himself for thinking about work. He'd promised Suzanne he would put aside these two days without any thoughts about the symphony. She told him she hadn't scheduled any appointments for the entire week to in order to concentrate on being a dutiful wife. He was amused by her using the word 'dutiful.'

Adrian sat up in bed. Suzanne stirred beside him.

"What's wrong?" she said

"Nothing. "Go back to sleep. We partied a little too much last night. I want you rested for the surprise I have for you later."

"What surprise?" She pulled herself up to sit beside him. A strap from her black satin nightgown fell from her shoulder and briefly distracted Adrian.

"If I told you, it wouldn't be a surprise, would it?"

"Well now that you've got me curious, I can't go back to sleep. Why don't you order breakfast?" She stretched and leaned back into the plush tufted headboard. "Sounds good." Adrian leaned over and kissed her. He looked into her eyes. Softly he said, "Last night was magic."

She returned his kiss. "We surprised everyone, didn't we?"

He poked his finger into the mattress. "I meant what happened afterward, back here."

She smoothed away the hair from his brow. "That too. Adrian ran his fingers down her arm. "How about we test the mattress one more time?"

"Give me a chance to use the bathroom. You order breakfast." She lingered in bed for a few seconds longer. "What time is it?"

Adrian slid off the bed . The room was dark except for light coming in from the edges of the closed curtains. He managed to find the clock.

"It's a little past noon. I'll call room service to see if they have a brunch menu." He picked up the phone and stretched to reach the curtain cord to let in the sunlight. A flash of gold invaded the room. Suzanne closed her eyes.

"I'm sorry dear. I didn't mean to…"

"That's okay. I was about to get out of bed anyway." Suzanne threw her legs over the bed and slid into her slippers. The black lace trim on the bottom of her nightgown fell from her thighs to her ankles as she stood, giving Adrian a quick glance at the curve of her calf. The nightgown swayed with her body as she headed to the bathroom. Adrian held the phone to his chest and watched her walk away. He was wearing only his white silk boxers. His amorous thoughts were interrupted by the pleasant voice of room service asking how he could be helped.

"Do you have a Sunday brunch?" he said.

"We do, Sir. There should be a copy of our menu in your desk drawer."

Adrian found the menu and ordered the Brunch for Two. "Oh yes, and a bottle of champagne." After all they had to drink at the reception last night, he didn't think Suzanne would want any more right now, but, if not, they'd save it for later.

"I ordered the brunch if that's okay," Adrian said to Suzanne when she came out of the bathroom.

"That's fine." She walked to him and placed her arms over his shoulders. "How long did they say it would take?" Her sultry voice tickled his ear.

"About half an hour."

"That gives us just enough time." She pulled Adrian toward the bed.

Half an hour later, they heard a knock at the door announcing room service. Adrian opened the door, and the server entered with a cart containing their meals under silver plated lids and a bottle of champagne on ice. Adrian expressed his satisfaction, tipped the man generously, and walked him to the door. He locked the door behind him.

He and Suzanne hadn't had much to eat at the wedding reception. Adrian pulled out a chair for Suzanne from a small round table near the window. He sat opposite her, and they started their first meal as husband and wife.

Suzanne wiped away a piece of scrambled egg from the corner of her mouth. "We pulled it off better than I'd hoped for. We owe a great debt to my father. It wasn't easy to get the symphony management behind this and to arrange for Father McLeary to perform the ceremony."

"Your father knew it would be great publicity for the symphony, but most importantly, he loves you and would do anything to make you happy. The amazing thing is how he got everyone to keep it a secret."

"Yes, Father always comes through for me. I hope our friends will forgive us for not letting them in on our wedding plans."

"Are you kidding. We've given them something to talk about for years to come. They're in seventh heaven right now."

Suzanne pinched the skin of her throat. "I hope you're right. I'm worried about Claire. We've been best friends for a long time, but I left her out of one of the most important days of my life."

"Our life," Adrian corrected her. Aren't you forgetting about what you told me about her not being able to keep a secret? I hope you're not regretting what we've done." He reached for Suzanne's hand and squeezed it gently.

"No, you're right," Suzanne said with a faint smile."

"Damn right I am." Adrian released her hand. He reached into the pocket of his robe and pulled out a small robin egg blue box wrapped with a white satin ribbon. It bore the logo of Tiffany and Company. He slid it across the table.

Suzanne's eyes widened. "What's this?"

"See for yourself." Adrian leaned forward and placed his hands between his knees.

Suzanne pulled the ribbon from the box and opened it. Inside was a gold heart shaped locket on a gold chain. She looked up at Adrian. "It's beautiful." She held it in her hand and twisted it in the light to watch it shine.

"Turn it over," Adrian said.

On the back was an engraving that read *Suzanne and Adrian, November 11, 1939.*

"Open it."

Inside were pictures of each of them.

Surprised, Suzanne looked up. "Where did you get this picture of me?"

"From Claire. She helped me pick out the locket as a future wedding present before we even set the date for the wedding. I had it engraved later. So you see, Claire was a part of our wedding after all." Adrian got up and clasped the locket around Suzanne's neck.

She pulled his hand around and kissed it. "I love you so very much. He kissed her neck. "I love you too."

Adrian opened the champagne and poured two glasses. He and Suzanne toasted each other, Suzanne's father, and Claire.

Adrian's surprise for Suzanne was a carriage ride through Central Park, the ride which he'd first planned to propose to her weeks ago before she persuaded him to stop by the Three Aces Club. Afterward, they walked hand and hand window shopping along Fifth Avenue before returning to their suite, where they planned to have dinner alone with room service.

Back at the hotel, Adrian pulled two living room chairs together to face the park. They held hands and watched the sun set and the trees cast shadows along the green grass and walkways of Central Park.

After a while, Suzanne broke the silence." Do you think it's true what Robert said?"

"What's that?"

"That because my grandmother was a twin, we might have twins."

"I hope so. That would be wonderful." Adrian stared out the window looking for the Gemini twin stars. He hoped to point them out to Suzanne so they could make a wish on them for twin daughters. He didn't see them. *Another time,* he thought.

Suzanne turned toward Adrian. "Have you thought about Simon?"

"I have, last night before the wedding ceremony. I wish he could have been there with us. I pray wherever he is he's thriving and not caught up in this Nazi craziness." He felt Suzanne squeeze his hand. Adrian turned to face her. "My aunt and uncle are good people. I'm sure they're taking good care of him. I do wonder if he knows about me and what he thinks of me if he does at all. I hope he doesn't hate me for leaving him in possible danger." Adrian made a mental note to take a piece of hotel stationary with him when he and Suzanne checked out. He would use it to write to Simon about the wedding and how he was searching for him. He'd place it in the box of notes and birthday cards he was keeping to give Simon were they ever to meet.

Later, after dinner, they turned on the radio in time to catch Nelson Bryant dish out his weekly gossip. The background music created a sense of urgency and importance. Mr. Bryant delivered the news in his well-known melodious voice.

"Good evening everyone. The marriage last night of two bright stars in New York's classical music scene, that of the concertmaster of the Eleventh State Symphony Orchestra, Adrian Mazurek, to Suzanne Reitman, agent to many of our finest musicians, has produced a brighter and more noticeable star in our skyline. May their union produce a constellation of stars worthy of their talents."

Suzanne's mouth opened. She looked at Adrian. "Are you responsible for that?"

"No. When would I have had the time?" Then he realized and snapped his fingers. "Your father. It must have been your father."

Suzanne placed her hand on Adrian's arm. "We should call him to thank him."

"I think we thanked him enough last night at the reception. I'm sure he knows how grateful we are, and I'm pretty sure he's quite proud and full of himself for orchestrating it, no pun intended.

Adrian rose, took Suzanne's hand, and led her to the bedroom.

12

BROWN PAPER WRAPPED PACKAGES

The day after they returned from their brief honeymoon, Suzanne said to Adrian ,"My father called while you were shaving. He invited himself to dinner. He has a surprise for us."

Adrian kissed Suzanne's cheek. "What, managing to get us mentioned on Bryant Nelson's show wasn't enough? He's managed to get our picture on a postage stamp?"

"No. silly, and you've got shaving cream on your ear." Suzanne used a dish towel to wipe it away.

"Well, I look forward to seeing what more surprises your father can muster up." Adrian wiped his ear to make sure all the shaving cream was gone. He kissed Suzanne goodbye and headed to Union Hall for a meeting with the violinists to talk about the fingering for the Mozart/Haydn concert. He'd listen to their views one more time, but stick to his own conviction on the matter.

Upon arrival, Adrian checked with the switchboard operator to see if he had any messages. There were many notes of congratulations. He stuffed them into his coat pocket to show Suzanne. There were two requests for return calls, one from the contessa, the other from Otto. He asked if his father-in-law was in. Upon learning he wasn't, he went straight to his office. He looked at the message from Otto again and decided not to call back until later. Excited to hear the contessa's reaction to his wedding, he returned her call right away.

"I'm so happy for you, my dear," she said. Your wedding was such a surprise and stunningly beautiful. You've become quite the celebrities du jour. You were in all the papers. Even Nelson Bryant mentioned you on his program Sunday night."

"I'm grateful to you, Rose, for giving me the courage to make it happen. I'm glad you were in there to see it and come to the reception."

"You didn't need me to give you courage. All you needed was an ear to listen to you." The contessa said she'd like to have him and Suzanna for dinner as soon as they could arrange it.

"That would be great. I'll check with her tonight about dates we're available and have her get back to you."

"I'll look forward to hearing from her."

Adrian looked at his watch. It was nearly ten o'clock, time to meet with the violinists. They were waiting for him on stage. He was able to persuade them to his point of view for this concert program. A few of the violinists frowned, but he felt confident about his decision. He was beginning to recognize, however, that many concertmasters were encouraging more virtuoso-style bowings, and he'd need to give this issue more thought.

"He called home later to check that dinner with his father-in-law was still on. He hadn't seen Mr. Reitman all day. Suzanne said that it was and she'd invited her cousin Charlotte and Claire and Larry as well. The mix seemed like a recipe for disaster.

Adrian came home from work a little early to help out. He took a quick shower, threw on a fresh pair of slacks, a clean shirt, and a navy blue pullover sweater. "How can I help?" he asked Suzanne, who was busy in the kitchen with the final touches of fixing dinner.

"You can straighten up the living room and set up the bar."

"Yes ma'am." He saluted her and kicked his heels together before making a military style exit from the kitchen.

At six thirty Mr. Reitman arrived with Charlotte. He was carrying a large package covered with brown paper.

"What's this?" Suzanne said.

"It's the surprise I told you about,"

Just then, the doorbell again. It was Claire and Larry. Larry was awkwardly balancing a larger package on his knee. It was wrapped in brown paper also.

"Quick Ace. Give me a hand with this before I get a hernia."

Adrian grabbed a corner of the package, and they moved from the foyer to the living room. They leaned the package against a nearby chair. Adrian took everyone's coats and hung them in the hall closet.

Once back, Adrian rubbed his hands together and said, "It seems we have two surprises tonight."

"Why don't you open your father's first." Claire said to Suzanne.

"Okay," Mr. Reitman said. "If you insist."

The package was too large to open standing. Suzanne and Adrian sat on the sofa. Larry helped Mr. Reitman bring it to them to unwrap.

Suzanne covered her face once the unwrapping was done. "Oh my God," she said

"Wow!" Adrian said, echoing Suzanne's surprise.

"What is it? Show us," Claire said impatiently.

They turned it around for the others to see. It was a framed two by three foot color photograph of Suzanne and Adrian exchanging wedding vows on the stage of Union Hall in front of the Reverend Father Joseph Mc Leary and the full orchestra.

Mr. Reitman's chest puffed out. "It's going to appear in this weekend's edition of *LIFETIME* magazine."

"This is wonderful, Dad. You outdid yourself. I didn't think that was possible." Adrian said.

"The photographer was proud of this shot," Mr. Reitman responded. "He thanked me for calling him to let him know something special was going to happen and for giving him the scoop. He said it will advance his career. This is going to be a two -page center spread. Isn't that wonderful? He rewarded me with this framed photograph."

"Thank you, Dad." Suzanne stood to kiss her father. "We love it, don't we Adrian?

"It's perfect, Marcus," Adrian said

Mr. Reitman turned to Claire and Larry. "I didn't mean to upstage you. What is it you have there?"

"I don't think it can compare with your gift, Marcus," Claire said. She had called him that for years at his request. "Go on and unwrap it, Adrian."

Suzanne stood by Adrian while he unwrapped the gift. It was an oil painting of him standing on a stage in a tuxedo holding a violin as if he were playing. To his side was a brass music stand with sheet music. The background was a red velvet curtain. The frame of the painting was gilded.

Adrian was speechless. It was as beautiful a present he could ever have hoped to receive

He got his wish, a painting by Claire as a wedding gift. He bit his lip to hold back his emotions. He thought of a photograph taken many years ago. He and Chana were standing in front of the Krakow School of Music. He was holding his violin by his side *Where is that photograph now? Does Simon have the violin I left for him?*

Claire's voice disrupted his reverie. "I painted it from a photo Suzanne took of you a year ago. It's her wedding present to you."

Adrian didn't know who to thank first, Suzanne or Claire. He drew them together and squeezed them both.

"We have two magnificent pieces of art to hang on our walls to remember our wedding from two of our favorite people," Suzanne said.

"Hey, what about me?" Charlotte said. She sounded hurt. "Didn't I find you that fabulous wedding gown, Suzanne?"

Suzanne clasped her hands to her chest. "You did," she said and it will always be memorialized in Dad's wedding photo."

Adrian saw the expression on Claire's face. He could tell she was upset to hear Charlotte knew about the wedding plans and she didn't. He glanced at Suzanne and then at Claire. Suzanne was well ahead of him.

"I'm sorry Claire. I had to tell Charlotte, but she was the only one, I promise. I got the dress at her salon. She kept it open for me after hours with no one else there.

Suzanne fingered her gold locket. "I'll have this to remember my wedding day for as long as I live. Adrian gave it to me the next morning, and I love it. He said you helped pick it out. So, you see, you were part of my wedding."

Suzanne and Claire hugged each other. When they parted, Claire wagged her finger at Suzanne. "your forgiven," she said, "but don't ever do that again."

When Adrian saw this was turning into a tear fest, he called out, "How about a drink before dinner?" Larry helped him take everyone's order and serve.

During dinner everyone wanted to know how Mr. Reitman was able to pull off such a fete without anyone finding out about it in advance.

He held his head back and inhaled deeply. "It took a lot of back slapping mixed with calling in favors, a few threats, and," he laughed, "some contributions to favored charities" He dug his fork into his spaghetti and twirled it around his spoon. With a gleam in his eyes. He looked around the table and thrust the spaghetti into his mouth. He swallowed and wiped his chin with his napkin.

Then he raised his eyebrows and added, "Mostly I depended on good will from people who wanted to do something special for people they liked and from those who wanted to be able to brag afterward that they were a part of it. He looked at his daughter and Adrian and smiled.

"Well, Marcus," Larry said, "I've got to hand it to you. The next time I need a permit from the Housing Bureau to build another project, I'm calling on you for advice." He turned to Suzanne and Adrian. "And you two, are there any other secrets you're holding from us?"

"Holy cow, Larry. We just got married, but when there are, you'll be among the first to know after Grandpa here." He nodded to his father-in-law.

Mr. Reitman looked up toward the ceiling as if it were heaven.

"From your lips to God's ears. But plan this one yourselves. I need a rest."

That got a few chuckles. Larry held up his glass and said, "All kidding aside, Marcus, you're to be congratulated. You're a good man. The attention turned to Charlotte when Claire asked if she was seeing anyone special.

"No, I'm afraid my love life is on hold. This is my busy season with the holidays and the parties. People like to dress up for Christmas and New Years' Eve, you know. I've gotten several new fashion lines which have generated a lot of new business."

Charlotte spoke very properly, having attended an exclusive boarding school in her teen years. Larry had described her speech as 'verry uppah class, don't you know' in his worst British accent. She held a long cigarette holder which she waved as she spoke. She wore false eyelashes and a lot of lipstick, and her hair was always perfectly coiffed.

Suzanne had told Adrian Charlotte was a regular at one of New York's most well-known hair and makeup salons that catered to the rich and famous. There she learned to look naturally elegant despite any false enhancements. Adrian was sure Larry was making fun of Charlotte in his head this very moment.

Charlotte blew out smoke and said, "That's not to say if someone caught my eye, I wouldn't be adverse to taking some time off."

"That little shop of yours is a gold mine, isn't it," Larry blurted out.

"I prefer to think of it as a salon rather than a shop." Charlotte curled her lip.

"We do carry the finest couture and cater to the wealthy. And, yes, I do very well."

"I guess that puts me at the other end of the scale. I cater to people who are poor and who live in units," Larry said. I do well too, but one day I'd like to build a fancy high rise for fancy people to live in."

"Don't give up hope," Charlotte responded. "A new suit and a good haircut can do wonders.

"Anyone for more coffee?" Adrian said quickly before things got heated. He could practically see the steam rising from Larry's head. But it was Larry's fault, he figured. He didn't like Charlotte, and the feeling was mutual. Suzanne knew this. He wondered why she had brought them together this evening.

The evening ended with a lot of hugs and kisses between Suzanne and Adrian and their guests, but not among them.

13

A MATTER OF CIRCUMSTANCE OR CHARACTER

A week after their wedding, Adrian and Suzanne sat on their living room sofa opening wedding gifts and congratulatory cards. Wrapping paper and open and unopened boxes cluttered the room.

"Did I tell you Otto called me?" Adrian said.

Suzanne looked up and tilted her head. "Oh, what did he want?"

"He read about our wedding in the papers and called to congratulate us. He thought he must have said something wrong at the Three Aces Club to upset you. He was glad we were OK."

"What did you say?"

"I told him what had happened. I said I hadn't told you about Simon, and you were shocked when he mentioned him. I told him his revealing it was the best thing that could have happened. It brought us closer together." Adrian reached for Suzanne's hand and kissed it.

"And…?"

"I asked him to keep it to himself until I was ready to share it with others. He promised he would."

"Can you trust him?"

"I hope so. I hardly know him. I hadn't seen him in fourteen years." Adrian rubbed the back of his neck. He remembered things about Otto that gave him a twinge of anxiety. "Oh, and he wanted to know how I'd feel if you represented him."

Suzanne stopped unwrapping and looked up at Adrian. "How

would you feel?"

"I'm not sure." Adrian raised his eyebrows feigning jealousy. "I saw the way you looked at him at the Three Aces Club."

Her chin jutted out. "Like the way you looked at me the first time we met? Isn't that the way you—all men for that matter—size up women?" Suzanne patted his hand. "That was my professional side working. I was 'looking him over,' as you put it, to see if he'd be attractive to an audience and to be able to develop a following."

"Used to size up women," Adrian said, with emphasis on the word "used." He waved his hand in defeat. "That's in the past. Now that I've got you, there are no other women." He took her hand and kissed it. When he let go, Suzanne picked up another gift and started unwrapping it. "Now, tell me more about Otto."

"Like?"

"You know, how you met, where he's from, how he happened to be on that ship with you."

Adrian let out a heavy sigh. "From what I know, he was born in New York. His parents came here from Germany after the World War One. I'm not clear where he got his musical training. He said his parents were poor. He supported himself by playing on ships and in orchestras for silent movies." Adrian remembered Otto had been kind to him when they arrived in New York. "During the week I stayed with him he got me a couple of jobs playing my violin in movie theater orchestras. I was grateful for the extra money. He was popular with the ladies and wanted to fix me up, but I was too wounded from Chana's death to be interested." Adrian leaned back, put his hands behind his neck and yawned. "After I was accepted to Sanfried, I never saw him again until that night at the contessa's. At any rate, I told him to give you a call. After all, you did give him your card."

"Well, I'll wait to see what he has to offer. Isn't there a violinist at the symphony who has a jazz ensemble?'

"Yes, but let's not get ahead of ourselves."

"You're right," Suzanne said. "Let me first see if he calls and gives me a chance to see how good he is. I'll go from there and ask your help if I need it."

"Sounds good." Adrian reached over to pick up the wrappings around their feet.

"Leave it for tomorrow," she said. "I'll take care of it." She pulled him down and leaned closer to him. He kissed her cheek. She turned and kissed his lips. Nature took its course from there.

Adrian had difficulty sleeping that night. He was worried about having Otto back in his life. He and Suzanne were on sound footing. Otto was an unknown who could easily upset the balance between them. He remembered Otto's words when they met at the contessa's. "I've not reached your level of success, my friend..." *Why wasn't Otto successful in his career and his marriage? Was it a matter of circumstances or of character?*

Adrian remembered Otto's behavior on the ship, how he'd gained a reputation among the other musicians as being a ladies' man. There were many nights Otto didn't return to the musicians' quarters when their late-night entertainment ended. He bragged about the number of divorced and widowed passengers he'd seduced, and how, with lipstick taken from them, he'd marked the edges of the keys in the lounge piano to show his conquests. The day before the ship arrived in New York, Otto confided in him he'd been summoned by the ship's captain, rebuked for his behavior, and was told he wouldn't be rehired.

Adrian wondered if he was being fair. Maybe Otto had pulled his life together and was trying to make a living to support his children. Maybe Otto's slip of the tongue at the Three Aces Club was innocent. He couldn't have known he'd been hiding Simon's existence from Suzanne. Perhaps he needed to give Otto the benefit of the doubt until he had reason to feel otherwise.

The next Monday at dinner, Suzanne told Adrian Otto had called. She was meeting with him Thursday morning. That evening during dinner Adrian asked how the meeting went.

"You won't believe it. My cousin Charlotte popped in to see me this morning while Otto was in the waiting room. She just barged into my office and asked who that gorgeous man sitting out there was."

Adrian shook his head. "She's always had a sense of entitlement." He wondered whether he should tell Suzanne to warn Charlotte about Otto's shipboard romances.

"Well, Uncle Gregory treated her like a princess after Aunt Eloise died. Charlotte was only ten and had a slew of governesses doting on her."

"Why did she stop by?" Adrian said buttering a biscuit.

"She wanted me to join her for lunch later. I told her I'd get back to her. Then she got so involved with questions about Otto, I had to ask her to leave. When I went out to the waiting room, she was sitting there talking with him. They seemed quite engaged. I think they may have made plans for lunch. I couldn't reach her after Otto left, and I called her to accept her luncheon invitation.

"I doubt if Otto took her to lunch," Adrian said. "I don't think he can afford the restaurants she's used to."

"Charlotte is not above picking up the check, especially if she's done the inviting and the guy is attractive enough. She's had her share of forgettable liaisons because of her impetuousness."

"Well, we'll see. What did you think of Otto?" Adrian picked up another biscuit. "These are really good, by the way."

"Thank you, sir, but maybe you should go a little easy on the butter."

"I will, on the next one," he said, his mouth full of biscuit.

Suzanne shook her head. "Otto makes a nice impression, better than you at this moment, I might add. He arrived in a nice sport jacket and tie, and there was no biscuit falling out of his mouth."

Adrian swallowed the mouthful. "Yes, yes, yes. We know how good-looking he is. What did you think of his musical talent? Will you represent him?"

"I think I may. Not only does he play the piano well, but he also has a beautiful voice. Did you know he sings?" Adrian looked up. No, I didn't. He never sang on the ship."

"He's self-taught on the piano," Suzanne continued. "His parents didn't have much money, but someone left a piano in the basement of their building when he was a boy, and he went down there to play.

He said he's always liked jazz, but he likes Broadway and popular tunes too." Suzanne cut off a piece of her lamb chop. "I stepped out for a moment, and when I got back, he was at the piano singing. He has a beautifully strong and rich baritone voice that will charm women. With training, I think he will be able to carry his voice up to the higher notes.

"Swell."

"You sound annoyed. Are you still feeling jealous of Otto?

"Do I have any reason to be?"

"Of course not. Besides, I think Charlotte has him locked up for the time being. When I finally reached her later in the afternoon, she told me that not only had she taken Otto to lunch, but afterward she had taken him shopping for new clothes. She charged them to her account."

Adrian shook his head. "Isn't that taking it a little too far for someone she just met?"

"Nothing stops Charlotte when she's in a romantic mood. Besides, he'll make a better impression at auditions if he's dressed nicely. That will help when I'm representing him."

"Sure. Sure," Adrian muttered under his breath. *And it looks like he's already figured out how to take advantage of Charlotte.*

Adrian lifted his glass of water to Suzanne and made a toast. "To you and Otto. May you make him an enormous success." In his head he was thinking, *There's something wrong with a man who lets women pay for his clothes, and God knows what else, after knowing her only a couple of hours.* He had an uneasy feeling about Otto. He wasn't Charlotte's greatest fan, but now she was family. That made a difference to him.

14

THE RISE OF NICK WELLS

Suzanne became actively involved in finding work for Otto. She found him a voice coach who was willing to reduce his fees because he thought Otto had great promise as a popular singer.

One afternoon Suzanne met Adrian at Union Hall, and they taxied to La Casa Nicolo on 36th Street, a hangout for Italian musicians. Suzanne was in the mood for risotto. On their way to their table, they passed Albert Colombo, one of the symphony's trombonists. He was drawing a caricature of a beautiful woman sharing his table, along with the popular Latin band leader, Mateo Pérez.

"Won't you join us?" Mr. Colombo said. When they sat down, he introduced Mr. Pérez, as his cousin from Argentina, and the beautiful woman as his cousin's wife, Ramona.

"You remember Albert, dear," Adrian said to Suzanne. "Besides being one of the symphony's trombone players, he's a master caricaturist. He's very well known for his talent in this area."

"It's wonderful to see you again, Mrs. Mazurek," Mr. Colombo said. "Mateo, his brothers, and his orchestra are appearing at the Galaxy Room on top of the Grecian Hotel. Ramona is their lead singer."

"It's our pleasure to meet you both. Please call me Suzanne."

"And me Adrian."

In his Argentinian accent Mr. Pérez said to Adrian, "We have symphonic music in common. I was once a concert saxophone player, but our talents run in different directions now. I very much admire your classical skills. Me, my brothers, and my wife have found our success with Latin music, especially tango."

Adrian raised his arms and clicked his fingers pretending they were castanets. "From what I hear, you're very successful," he said.

Mr. Pérez smiled. and said, "I'm afraid you're confusing the castanets with flamenco, but you are very amusing for one who plays such serious music."

"Yes, I'm all fun and games, aren't I, Albert?"

"I'll get back to you on that one," Albert, who was busy drawing, said.

"What are you scribbling there, Albert?" Adrian peered over his shoulder.

Albert turned it around for everyone to see. It was a caricature of Adrian with a small violin and an oversized head.

They all laughed, Suzanne the loudest.

"Seriously," Mr. Pérez said looking at his wife. "We would love for you both to be guests at one of our shows. When you can find the time, come one evening. I'll alert the maître d' to be on the look -out for you. Just give your names, and he'll find you a good table."

"That would be great," Adrian said. "May we bring some friends along?"

"Only the ones who like to drink and tango."

"We'll try to make time soon," Adrian said.

Because the others had finished their lunch, Adrian and Suzanne excused themselves and went to another table.

Suzanne spread her napkin on her lap. "That was charming. You were very playful. The Pérezes were quite taken with you."

"Well, thank you Mrs. Mazurek. You were a hoot yourself."

Suzanne kicked him under the table.

"Ouch!" he said.

Suzanne placed her right forefinger on her lower lip. "I think I have an idea where I can find a great engagement for Otto."

"Oh, for heaven's sake," Adrian growled. "I'm hungry. Waiter," he called out. He'd heard enough about Otto for a while.

Two weeks later, Adrian and Suzanne took Charlotte and Otto to the Galaxy Room. Charlotte and Otto had become a couple. There was an ulterior motive to this outing. Suzanne planned to introduce Otto to Mateo Pérez and suggest Otto play for the patrons during one of the band's intermissions. Adrian felt uncomfortable taking advantage of Mr. Pérez's graciousness in inviting them. However, because Suzanne was supportive of his career, he felt he owed her the same.

When they gave the maître d' their names, he greeted them as if they were expected, and he led them to a table close to the stage. The band was finishing its last song in the set before intermission.

Mr. Pérez and his wife came over to greet them. A waiter brought two additional chairs.

"I'm delighted to see you," Mr. Pérez said. "Please introduce me to your friends."

"This is my cousin Charlotte and her friend, Otto Schmidt," Suzanne said. "Otto is my newest client. He plays the piano and has a singing voice that's a gift from God. I'm expecting he'll soon be too big for me to represent. With his good looks and musical ability, Hollywood will be coming for him."

She's really laying it on thick, Adrian thought, watching Otto display a big toothy grin. *Damn, he is more handsome than I remember. Look at that smile on Ramona's face. Charlotte doesn't look too pleased.*

"I'd like to hear you sometime, Mr. Schmidt, if you're as good as Suzanne says you are," Mr. Pérez said. He nodded to his wife. "We're always interested in new talent, aren't we, Ramona?"

Otto gave another toothy smile. "I'd like that. I'd like that very much."

The Pérez's stood to excuse themselves to prepare for their next set. "Stop by tomorrow at eleven, before lunch. We'll see if you fit in. Have fun the rest of the evening folks."

Adrian was impressed. *That was too easy. Nothing happens that quickly. A new violinist with only a stranger's recommendation would have to beg me for a hearing with all the talent out there waiting for a big break. I've got to hand it to Suzanne. She did no pushing. She just put the bait out there to be snagged and reeled in.*

"I'd hoped you might get a chance to sing tonight, but I didn't want to push it," Suzanne said to Otto. "Better it was his idea to see you tomorrow. Don't drink tonight. Save your voice for then. I'll pick you up at ten to bring you here. In the meantime, let's stay for dinner and through the next set and make it an early night."

The next morning, as he was leaving for Union Hall, Adrian asked Suzanne to call him to let him know how the audition went.

"I will. I've got to come up with a better name for him. Otto Schmidt doesn't hit the ear well. See if you can cook up a catchy name, dear."

"Sure, I'll give it some thought." The thought left Adrian's mind as soon as the door closed behind him.

Later, Suzanne called Adrian as promised. "It went great. They're letting him go on tonight between sets. Come with me. It'll be fun. Charlotte's coming too. Oh, and by the way, we've got a new name for Otto: Nick Wells. How's that for a good, all-around American name?"

"It's crisp," Adrian said. "It kind of rolls off the tongue."

Suzanne laughed. "It does, doesn't it? Ramona thought of it. I've got to go now. I want to make some calls to see if I can get a few columnists to cover tonight. I'd like to see headlines about Nick spread across tomorrow's papers. Oh, Adrian, I know I'm babbling, but I'm so excited. See you later, dear. I love you."

Adrian heard the excitement in Suzanne's voice. He was happy for her success. *She's really shown how good an agent she is. I'm glad I got a chance to see her in action. I'll have to do something special for her.* Adrian leaned back in his chair and placed his hands behind his neck. *Well, it looks like Otto is a part of our lives now. I'll have to watch carefully to make sure he doesn't get in the way of our marriage. I hope I can trust him around others with my secret.* He looked down and shook his head.

Otto, now Nick, was a smash hit that night. Before leaving the stage after his first set, Mr. Pérez introduced Otto as Nick Wells, the newly discovered singing sensation whom he was proud to present to his audience for Nick's very first public singing appearance. An employee rolled a piano to the center of the dance floor. The lights dimmed. A spotlight focused on Otto when he appeared in a tuxedo and looking very handsome, Adrian had to admit. He wondered who had paid for it.

Adrian watched Suzanne move to the edge of her seat and twist around, probably looking to see which newspapers were represented to report on Otto tomorrow. Charlotte leaned forward in her seat and placed her elbows on the table. She placed her chin on her gloved hands.

Without speaking, Otto sat at the piano and began to play "Begin the Beguine," the popular Cole Porter song. He started slowly, building up in intensity. Soon he started to sing. His voice was smooth and seductive. He stood and picked up the microphone by the piano and started gliding around the front tables of the room, stopping to sing directly to the women seated there. Even their male companions appeared seduced by Otto's voice.

Normally, patrons ate, ordered more drinks, danced, and enjoyed each other's company between sets. Tonight, the room was quiet. Few voices or sounds were heard above Otto's singing. Patrons waved away waiters when they came to take orders. The audience seemed mesmerized by Otto. Adrian felt Suzanne's hand on his thigh. She looked at him and whispered, "He's a hit." He was happy for her. *Who knew Otto had that much talent?* Adrian thought. *I guess I'll' be seeing more of him than I had hoped to.* Otto sang one more song at the piano, "Body and Soul," before leaving the stage to vigorous applause.

The next day, three papers wrote about Nick Wells, New York's newest singing sensation.

Nelson Bryant mentioned him the following evening in his broadcast. He identified Charlotte, "the owner of one of New York's most fashionable dress salons," as Mr. Wells' companion. He mentioned Suzanne as Nick's agent and representative.

"Are you annoyed Charlotte's name was put above yours?"

Adrian said, after they listened to Bryant's broadcast.

"I did my job. I got him recognized. His success and my ten percent will be my satisfaction." Her voice was sharp.

Adrian let it go, but he was angry enough for the both of them. As much as Suzanne did to help jump start Otto's career, he hadn't so much as thanked her last night or today. *There's something off about Otto*, he thought. He wasn't sure what it was, but he'd find out.

15
ENTER THE FBI

Suzanne and Adrian accepted the contessa's invitation to dinner for the first week in January. She said there were people she wanted them to meet. Adrian speculated they were people of influence who might be able to help him locate Simon. He looked forward to the dinner.

Paul met them in the lobby and rode them up to the contessa's apartment. When they got off the elevator, Paul took their coats and led them into the parlor. A group of six surrounded the contessa. She spotted Adrian and Suzanne and came to greet them.

Adrian had the feeling he'd seen one of the men before, but he couldn't think from where. He didn't recognize the other guests.

The contessa introduced the three couples to Adrian and Suzanne without any explanations as to their positions. The one who looked familiar was Philip Carter. His wife was Amy. The other two couples were Samson Reed, his wife, Eloise, and William Johnston and his wife, Beverly. They were pleasant, but Adrian felt uncomfortable. Suzanne looked less so. *If they were people who could be helpful in locating my family in Poland, the contessa certainly would have told me beforehand*, Adrian thought. He was baffled as to the purpose of this dinner. His mind raced for answers, but he couldn't think of any.

The dinner conversation was light and congenial but uncomfortable for Adrian. He kept wondering why the contessa had pulled this group together. Despite his discomfort, he used his charm to get through the meal.

During dinner, the wife of Samson Reed brought up Suzanne and

Adrian's wedding at Union Hall. "How did you manage that?" she said.

Suzanne smiled, "My father arranged it. He's the Director of Development for the orchestra. He and conductor McGowan thought it would be good publicity for the symphony." Suzanne blushed. "I must admit it was a fairy tale wedding ceremony. I'm very grateful to them."

"I understand you're the agent for Nick Wells," Beverly Johnston said. "He's deliciously handsome and talented."

Adrian heard her husband clear his throat and place his hand on his wife's elbow. His wife looked over to him and bit her lip. The other two gentlemen looked at each other quickly then glanced over at the contessa.

Adrian watched this with curiosity. *What is going on here?*, he wondered.

It wasn't until after dinner that Adrian got his answer.

"If you don't mind, we'd like to meet with you in the contessa's library," Philip Carter said to Adrian and Suzanne.

Adrian and Suzanne looked at each other. *Here it comes*, thought Adrian. *The real reason we're here.* He took Suzanne's hand, and they and the three men followed Paul to the library where a bar was set up. Paul left. A slight chill went through Adrian.

Mr. Carter offered Suzanne and Adrian drinks. At their request, he poured Suzanne a glass of white wine and Adrian a brandy. The others filled their glasses, and they sat in a circle of leather and upholstered chairs.

Mr. Carter unwrapped a fresh cigar. He didn't light it.

"I like to chew on these," he said, directing himself to Suzanne. "I hope you don't mind. My wife says it's a disgusting habit, and she's right, but I can't seem to stop."

Suzanne nodded her approval.

"If you don't mind, I'd like to get right to the point," Mr. Carter said. "I know you must be wondering why we're here tonight and what you have to do with it." He leaned forward. "The mayor has appointed me to lead a commission to root out Nazi American activities in New York. I must ask that that you keep this meeting confidential."

Now Adrian knew why he recognized Mr. Carter. His picture had been in the newspapers with the announcement of this new committee by the mayor.

Adrian and Suzanne looked at each other and back at Mr. Carter. They nodded their agreement.

"Thank you," Mr. Carter said. He jutted his chin toward the other two gentlemen. "Mr. Reed and Mr. Johnston are agents with the New York FBI office. They're helping the commission to investigate and prosecute Nazi sympathizers. We think you can help us."

Adrian paused to look at Suzanne again to gage her reaction. She hunched her shoulders and spread her hands palms up at Adrian.

"How well do you know Otto Schmidt?" Mr. Carter said. "I believe he goes by the name Nick Wells now."

Adrian grinned. "Is Otto what this is about?" he said. Of all the reasons he thought of for being here, he never thought it would be about Otto.

"Yes," Mr. Carter answered.

Mr. Reed leaned back in his chair, rolling his glass in circles. The room was silent except for the quiet tapping of Mr. Johnston's foot on the carpeted floor.

"Why are you asking?" Adrian said.

"I think it's best if you let us ask the questions first. It will become clear to you later," Mr. Reed said.

Adrian didn't like anyone speaking to him like that. It made him feel under attack, and he didn't appreciate anyone putting Suzanne in this position either. He settled back into his chair, pulled his brandy glass closer to his waist in an attempt to relax, and waited to see where this was heading.

Please, we're all friendly here," Mr. Carter said. "The contessa wouldn't have asked you here tonight to be with us if we weren't."

That's probably true, Adrian thought, but he felt anger toward her for putting him and Suzanne in this spot. *She'll have to answer for this. Perhaps I misjudged her and her feelings toward him.* He tried to stop himself from getting carried away by his thoughts.

Adrian attempted to appear relaxed. "I know very little about Otto," he said. He decided it was best, right now, to be polite and cooperative with these men to see where this was leading. "I hadn't seen him in fourteen years until we met on September fourth, when I gave a fundraising concert right here in the contessa's apartment. He was playing background music on the piano during cocktails. We recognized each other, said hello, and that was that." Adrian adjusted himself in his chair careful not to spill his drink. "We met one more time when Suzanne and I went to the Three Aces Club where he was performing with a jazz band." Adrian waved his hand over to Suzanne. "My wife casually gave him her card. She's an agent for musicians, but you probably know that," Adrian said with a bit of sarcasm. He immediately regretted his tone. "He called Suzanne. She found him to be talented, and she got him his first break. That's it."

"What did you talk about?" Mr. Reed said.

"When?" Adrian asked.

"That night here, at the fundraiser."

"Nothing. We just said hello. I was in a hurry to tune my violin."

"I saw him talking with Adrian. I was curious who he was," Suzanne said. "I went up to ask him. He told me he knew Adrian from long ago. I thought it would be a welcome surprise to take Adrian to see Otto perform and reacquaint them."

"When you met him that night at the Three Aces Club you both left in a hurry. You looked upset," Mr. Reed said.

Suzanne leaned forward. Her voice rose. "Were you there watching us?"

"We've been watching Mr. Schmidt and other members of the Nazi party here in New York for a while now," Mr. Reed said.

"What was your relationship with Otto fourteen years ago?" Mr. Carter said to Adrian.

Adrian twisted in his chair. "Look. This is getting ridiculous."

He was becoming impatient to know where this was leading.

"Just bear with me for a few more minutes," Mr. Carter said.

Adrian looked at Mr. Johnston, who had remained quiet this entire time. Mr. Johnston nodded at him and said, "This is important, Adrian. Just be patient with us, please."

Adrian took a deep breath and exhaled. He explained how he and Otto berthed together while entertaining on a ship to the United States, and he'd spent a week sharing space in Otto's apartment until he was accepted into Sanfried. He hadn't seen nor heard from Otto again until September fourth at the contessa's fundraiser and three nights later at the Three Aces Club. In November, Otto called asking Suzanne to represent him.

Adrian caught his breath and said, "Now will you tell us what this is about?"

"Just a couple more questions, please. Have you ever heard Otto speak any other languages?"

Adrian looked at Suzanne. "When we were on the ship to the United States we communicated in German and Polish, but not since then," he answered.

"Neither have I," Suzanne said.

"Did either of you see Otto stay behind during Adrian's performance at the contessa's fundraiser?" Mr. Carter said.

They both said they hadn't.

Mr. Carter looked at Adrian. "We understand you came back to retrieve your violin and may have overheard a conversation in a room off the foyer."

Adrian wondered how they knew that. He was sure no one saw him. *Paul. It had to be Paul who told them. Were they suspecting Otto was one of the people in that room?*

"Paul is very loyal to the contessa. He's an observant and protective servant. One may not always know he's around," Mr. Carter said. "He did see the count let other people into the apartment while guests were leaving, and he never saw Otto leave after cocktails. Other surveillance supports this."

If the contessa had tricked us into coming tonight, Adrian thought, *at least she hadn't meant to. She herself may have been a victim of the count and been unwittingly drawn into this scrutiny.* Adrian felt sure the men had asked the contessa not to tell him and Suzanne about the purpose of tonight's dinner. He now felt sorry for her, knowing how awful she must feel having been asked to deceive them.

"What is it you want from us?" Adrian said.

"We'd like you to keep a very close eye on Mr. Schmidt, or Mr. Wells, I guess we should now call him," Mr. Carter said. "We suspect he's involved with the American Nazi Bund in New York and may lead us to others. You'd be doing an important service to your country if he and others are helping to spread Nazi propaganda here and helping the Nazis in Germany."

Adrian looked at Suzanne. He guessed what she was thinking. Not only would she be worrying about the ethical concerns of deceiving her client and taking money from him, and the potential damage to her reputation, but she'd also be angry at herself for getting Charlotte involved with a possible Nazi sympathizer. Charlotte's own reputation as a successful businesswoman could be damaged as well. He decided to let Suzanne speak first.

Suzanne was quiet. She looked pensive. Then, she looked back and forth among the men and said, "Do we have to do this?"

"We're asking you to do this as your patriotic duty," Mr. Carter said.

Adrian saw her flinch. He could read her mind. No one could accuse her of being unpatriotic. She wouldn't take that remark lightly.

"I understand your concerns," Mr. Carter said.

Suzanne shifted in her chair and tugged at her dress. "I'm not sure you do," she said. "You're asking me to spy on my family and a client, to deceive them. My cousin is currently romantically involved with Nick."

"They'll never have to know. We'll see you're not exposed," Mr. Reed said reassuringly.

"But I'll be exposing my cousin and my family to someone who can hurt them, embarrass them," She looked at Adrian.

He knew she was right. They were asking her to make Charlotte a pawn in this scheme. She couldn't do this to her own family.

"Your cousin is already exposed," Mr. Reed said. "She's seeing him. If you keep an eye on him, you may be able to protect her. Do you think if you told your cousin about our suspicions, she'd believe you and stop seeing Nick?"

Suzanne hesitated. She started to say yes, then shook her head.

Adrian knew Charlotte never took anyone's advice about her unscrupulous lovers. She'd accuse Suzanne of being envious of her happiness, or she'd say Suzanne was interfering with Nick's career for Suzanne's own selfish benefit.

"Then maybe you can see this as your way of either making sure she is in a safe relationship or helping to remove her from a harmful one," Mr. Carter said.

This man is clever, thought Adrian. *He doesn't give up*. That last argument seemed to get Suzanne's attention, and it got his, as well. There was truth to what Carter was saying. Adrian hoped Suzanne might calm down enough to see this.

Mr. Carter had the last word. "We've managed to make a strong foothold in these American Nazi organizations. With the arrest and conviction of their leader in New York we've freed our city from many Nazi sympathizers." He looked back and forth at Adrian and Suzanne. "With your help, we may be able to do more. All we ask is you both think about it."

Adrian felt impotent he'd been unable to find a way to contact Simon to know if he was safe. He realized there would be little, if anything, he could do. If he spied on a suspected Nazi sympathizer, he wouldn't be helping Simon directly, but it would give him the satisfaction of feeling he was doing something to hurt Nazis. He decided not to dismiss the idea too quickly. He'd discuss it more with Suzanne later.

The contessa asked Adrian and Suzanne to stay after the others left. She apologized for putting them in an uncomfortable position.

She explained she had called Mr. Carter when Paul told her of the count's involvement in raising money for the German war effort. Their investigation led to Otto when they learned he had played the piano the night of the fundraiser and had stayed behind and later left with a group of uninvited guests. Paul had heard the group's pleas for money for the Nazi cause.

"He suspected you did too, Adrian, when you came back for your violin," she said.

Adrian lowered his gaze. He wished now he had told the contessa back then what he had heard that night. It would have been the honest thing to do between friends. He hoped she didn't hold it against him.

"Later," the contessa continued, "Mr. Carter discovered both of your connections to Otto and asked me to set up this dinner. I didn't want to do it secretly, but he insisted." She wrung her hands. "I'm so sorry if I put you in an awkward situation."

It was difficult for Adrian to see the contessa so distressed as she told the story. He and Suzanne assured her they understood.

When they got home, Adrian and Suzanne discussed the meeting while getting ready for bed. "You were quiet on the way home. What are you thinking?" Adrian said.

"I don't like it, Adrian. I resent even being asked."

"We might never have been if you hadn't taken me to the Three Aces Club rather than coming with me on a carriage ride. They might not have connected us to Otto." He regretted saying this as soon as the words left his mouth.

"So, you're blaming me?" Suzanne fumed. She grabbed a corner of the bed cover and yanked it back with such strength a pillow fell to the floor.

"No. Of course not." Adrian stood still, not sure how to deal with the force of her anger.

"You are. You just did. If you hadn't kept your past a secret, maybe I wouldn't have taken you there." Suzanne glared at Adrian.

"Calm down. Let's talk this through."

"You calm down." She picked up the pillow and threw it back on the bed as hard as she could. "You're enjoying this, aren't you? You can't get Simon out of Poland, so you need to find a way to ease your conscience about leaving him there by fighting the Nazis here."

God, she's smart. She reads me like a book. "Look, we don't have to do this if you don't want to."

"Don't put this on me. You make it sound like it's all up to me. That says to me you're OK with it."

"I'm not totally against it," he said, with an unease that only made her angrier.

Suzanne faced him. Her nostrils were flaring. "How would my family feel if they found out and it backfires, and if they got hurt?"

"If it did work out, you'd be a hero."

"You mean you'd be a hero," she spat back.

This was their first fight, and it was a big one. He tried to bring the temperature down. "Let's not talk about it anymore. We're both tired, and it's a major decision. Let's let it settle and talk about it tomorrow."

"OK, but I won't feel any better about it then." She turned and headed toward the bathroom. They went to bed sleeping far apart.

Adrian and Suzanne resumed their discussion at dinner the next evening.

"Charlotte called me this morning," Suzanne said.

"Oh. What did she have to say?"

"Nick has invited her to spend next weekend in Yaphank." There was a slight edge to her voice.

"Long Island?" Adrian put his spoon back into his soup bowl. "Whatever for?" He kept his voice tight, but he knew what was coming.

"She said his family has a cabin there, and he's going to ready it for spring."

"Are they going alone?" He started flexing his fingers. He knew this area was known as a camp for Nazi sympathizers.

"She said he told her there'd be other people there doing the same thing."

"Has she decided to go?"

"It sounds like she's considering it. She seemed excited Nick had asked her to go away with him."

Adrian couldn't control his temper anymore. "Does she have any idea what she'd be getting herself into?" He tossed his napkin on the table, pushed his chair back, and got up and paced the kitchen.

"I'm not sure, Adrian. I'm not sure." Suzanne crossed her arms and stared down at her plate, biting her lip.

"Doesn't she know that's a Bund compound, for Christ's sake?"

"Please don't curse, Adrian. You know I don't like that tone. I'm worried."

"I'm sorry. I'm worried, too." He patted Suzanne's shoulder and sat back down. Although he wasn't that fond of Charlotte, he knew she and Suzanne were close. He didn't want to see Charlotte get hurt. "I think we should contact Mr. Carter and get on board with him to see how we can protect Charlotte."

Suzanne shook her head. "I hate to say so, but maybe you're right."

"He gave me his card. It has his private number. Let's call him after dinner and see what he says."

They waited for a reasonable time to call Mr. Carter. Adrian explained the situation. Mr. Carter told them to see if there was a legitimate way to persuade Charlotte not to go away with Nick. If they can't, they shouldn't worry. There'd be undercover FBI agents observing the compound to protect her if something were to put her in danger.

Three days later, Charlotte told Suzanne she had to cancel her weekend with Nick. Her manager had broken her leg and would be out for ten days. Charlotte had to cover for her.

"Actually, I think Charlotte sounded relieved," Suzanne said. "I think she's beginning to see some things in Nick she's starting to question."

"Really," Adrian's eyes perked up. "Such as?"

"She's been hinting about his drinking. To be honest, I've been worried about that too. I've seen clients of mine who work in cabarets and dance halls drink too much. It's become a problem for them. I've gotten calls from employers and have had to speak with some clients about it."

"Have you gotten complaints about Nick?"

"No. He's too new and still able to cover it up, but sometimes I've smelled it on his breath and wondered."

"What else has she said about Nick?"

"It sounds like he's been rude to her sometimes, has said unpleasant things to her in front of others. I've seen this with other men Charlotte's dated. They end up resenting her money and how she supports them."

"I'm sorry to hear this." Adrian felt sympathy for Charlotte. He could see the unhappiness under her veneer of self-confidence. "I'm glad we don't have to worry about her going away next weekend with Nick to Yaphank."

They'd escaped one possible threatening situation. *What others lie ahead?* Adrian wondered.

16

THE BROOCH

In early April, the contessa invited Suzanne, Adrian, and Charlotte to lunch at The Lady Liberty Room at the Hudson View Hotel. Nick was in Philadelphia for the opening of a new nightclub. The contessa told Suzanne and Adrian she wanted to see what was going on with Nick through Charlotte and report back to Mr. Carter. She'd arranged for a quiet table in the back.

"That's a lovely brooch you're wearing, Charlotte," the contessa commented. "Is it a family heirloom?"

Charlotte's face lit up. "It's a gift from Nick. He said it's a family piece brought over by his mother when they immigrated to the United States."

The contessa leaned closer to Charlotte to get a better look at the brooch. It was a large golden filigree circular pin set with sapphires, emeralds, and diamonds. "It looks quite valuable. They must have come from a wealthy family," the contessa said.

"Not how he tells it," Charlotte said. "He did say this was the one piece his mother refused to sell to help meet their needs once they settled here. Nick said it's cursed. His mother didn't want to pass it on to anyone."

"Cursed?" Suzanne said. "What did he mean?"

Charlotte reached into her purse and pulled out her cigarette holder and a cigarette. "Nick's mother passed it down to each of the brides of Nick's five older brothers when they married. It was supposed to bring good luck so they'd have sons to carry on the family name."

Charlotte fumbled through her purse again and pulled out a gold lighter. She lit her cigarette, placed the lighter back into her purse, and inhaled deeply. After shooing away the exhaled smoke she continued her story. "All five brothers had daughters only. The pin became a cursed piece to the family, and each brother gave it back to Nick's mother. She refused to give Nick's bride the pin when he married. She gave it to Nick's wife only after she gave birth to their son. He took it back after his divorce."

"All I know is he said I've been good to him, and he wanted me to have it. Don't you think it looks good with the red suit I'm wearing?" Charlotte turned her body so everyone could see the brooch.

"Well, it is lovely. He seems very taken with you. Are you happy, my dear?" the contessa said.

Charlotte looked at Suzanne. "I'm very happy," she answered.

Adrian knew Charlotte wasn't telling the truth. Suzanne had tried to convince Charlotte to break up with Nick, but Charlotte ignored her advice.

When Charlotte excused herself to go to the restroom, the contessa leaned over and whispered to Adrian and Suzanne. "That's my brooch she's wearing; I'm positive. I've been looking for it for weeks. It's registered with my insurance company. They have pictures of all my jewelry. If Nick gave it to her, the count must have stolen it from me to give to the Bund the night of the fundraiser. I'll bet Nick was the person who collected the jewelry and took it home and hid it away somewhere, maybe in that cabin in Yaphank."

Adrian looked at Suzanne and shook his head. She placed her elbow on the table and shielded her face.

They saw Charlotte heading back to their table and stopped talking.

Later, when they separated from Charlotte, the contessa told Adrian and Suzanne she'd have to call Mr. Carter about the brooch. She told them he would likely contact Mr. Reed and Mr. Johnston who would go talk with Charlotte.

"She'll be terribly upset," Suzanne said. "She's not as tough as she appears. She's sensitive about her reputation and what people think of her. My uncle will be upset, too, and this will trickle down to my father." Her voice wavered. "I knew it was a mistake for us to get involved."

"I assure you I'll keep you and Charlotte out of this," the contessa said. "I'll take full responsibility for this, and no one will ever know you and she are involved."

The following week, Charlotte called Suzanne and Adrian. "The FBI is here. Please come over quickly."

When they arrived at Charlotte's apartment, the FBI agents had left. Charlotte was crying. Adrian and Suzanne sat with Charlotte in her living room while she told them what had happened.

"They appeared out of nowhere. There was a knock on the door, and there they were." Charlotte blew her nose into her handkerchief. "They told me they'd been investigating Nick secretly for months. The contessa reported I was wearing a pin of hers that was missing. She suspected Nick had stolen it. They told me she thinks the count took it and gave it to Nick as a contribution to the Bund. They accused Nick of being a Nazi sympathizer."

Suzanne moved closer to Charlotte on the sofa and took her hand.

"They raided Nick's apartment and his family's house on Long Island," Charlotte said. "They found a box of jewelry, and they were able to trace much of it to people they'd suspected to be Nazi supporters. They've arrested Nick, and they're trying to find out who else the jewelry belongs to."

Adrian paced the room thinking about what to do. This could become a scandal that could adversely affect everyone in his new family through guilt by association. The public could falsely brand Charlotte, Suzanne, and Adrian as Bund supporters through their relationships with Nick. Suzanne's father and uncle could be embarrassed publicly by this. Charlotte's business could be adversely affected, and they could all be openly shamed and ostracized.

Charlotte wept into her handkerchief. "I'll be ruined. I'll never be able to hold my head up again."

"Let me make a call," Adrian said. He went to the phone on the desk in the corner of the living room and phoned the contessa. Paul answered and went to bring the contessa to the phone. Adrian stood bouncing on his knees while he waited. He was too agitated to sit on the chair by the desk.

"Tell Charlotte not to worry," the contessa said. "Her name will not be involved. I've asked Mr. Carter not to implicate her, nor you and Suzanne, for that matter, in this. He assured me it will be handled discreetly. They've made it known to Nick that if he cooperates, he'll get off easier. He has no reason to involve Charlotte nor you. You haven't done anything wrong."

Adrian let out a large breath. He flopped into the desk chair and waved the thumbs up sign to Suzanne and Charlotte.

"I know Charlotte's upset. Her relationship with Nick has hurt her," the contessa said. "I can relate to that. Tell her I'm on her side and to stay strong."

Adrian thanked her and told Suzanne and Charlotte about his conversation with the contessa.

That calmed them. Suzanne cancelled a meeting to stay with Charlotte. Adrian went to Union Hall to prepare for a weekend concert in Philadelphia, where he was guest soloist. The FBI's investigation wouldn't really harm Charlotte, apart from her hurt feelings about Nick. Adrian was relieved, but bringing Nick down hadn't done anything to assuage his guilt over his abandonment of Simon.

17

THE ARTICLE

Nick managed to give an interview to a persistent reporter from *KNOW,* a New York weekly gossip magazine. The reporter was intent on getting the dirt on Nick's story, and Nick was angry enough to oblige despite warnings from the FBI to stay quiet.

The article said Nick insisted he was innocent and had been set up. He admitted Count Uberti had hired him to play the piano at his and the contessa's apartment during a fundraiser, but he had no other connection with the count nor the Bund. With the count out of the country, his story couldn't be verified.

He blamed Suzanne and Adrian for his current troubles. He said they were trying to discredit him because he knew about Adrian's long hidden secret, which Adrian and Suzanne were afraid he'd reveal. Adrian had a fourteen-year-old son he'd deserted in Poland when he came to the United States.

Adrian was initially shocked and angry when the article appeared. He worried how people would react to the article, what they would think of him, and how it would affect his career and personal relationships.

When Adrian arrived at Union Hall the morning after the article became public, he was handed a pile of messages by the switchboard operator. He took them from her and told her to hold all other calls unless they were from conductor McGowan and Mr. Reitman. He went to his office and closed the door. He sat there thinking. *I should have discouraged Suzanne from becoming Otto's agent. If she hadn't set up that first appointment to meet with him, he wouldn't have met Charlotte, and Otto wouldn't have become a part of our world. The FBI wouldn't have involved me and Suzanne and none of this would have happened.*

There was a knock on the door. "Who is it?" Adrian asked.

"It's Alistair, Adrian. May I come in?"

Adrian had been waiting for the conductor's visit. He was prepared for the worst.

"Of course, Alistair. I've been expecting you."

The conductor entered, and Adrian motioned for him to sit in a chair opposite his desk.

"You look especially low spirited, or drumly, as we Scots say." The conductor scrunched his lips and told Adrian he'd seen the article in *KNOW* and asked if he wanted to talk about it.

Adrian felt he owed the conductor an explanation and told him how he'd dropped out of Simon's life when he came to America to study.

"I've hidden this secret because I've been ashamed I abandoned my son, especially now," Adrian said. He looked down at his hands. He didn't want to see the conductor's expressions of disappointment and disapproval of him. "His mother was Jewish, and he may be in danger with the Nazis having invaded Poland. I've made it my life's goal to find him. Susanne is with me on that." He waited, in the moment of silence that followed, to hear the conductor's response.

"We all have our secrets and feelings of shame, Adrian. We're human beings, not gods." The conductor rubbed his chin. "I would venture to say there's not a member of our orchestra who hasn't done something he regrets or feels ashamed of. Take me, for example. My first wife sued me for adultery before I came to America. Our marriage was not a happy one, and I'd been unfaithful. Can you imagine the sadness and humiliation I felt about my part in breaking up that relationship, and how I felt knowing people gossiped about us?"

Adrian looked up at McGowan. The conductor pressed his lips together, as if he were reliving those days.

McGowan leaned forward, raised his arm, and snapped his thumb and middle finger. "Now I'm married to Francine," he smiled, "and the past is in the past. My public and those friends I hold dear have forgiven me. But, Adrian, the first person I needed to forgive me was myself." He leaned back and crossed one leg over his knee. "You're a good person. People admire and like you. I recommend you own up to your story. The orchestra and board will understand your situation and will be sympathetic. So will your friends and the public." He waited a few seconds and pulled himself out of his chair. "Now, if you'll please excuse me, I've got to prepare for our rehearsal. I'll see you there." McGowan got up and left.

The conductor's words heartened Adrian, but his apprehension wasn't relieved. He needed reassurances by more than the maestro. Until he received them, he knew he'd be ruminating about the harm that might have been done to his reputation and the effect this would have on his relationships with others.

The *KNOW* article spread quickly. Adrian told Suzanne and her father about his talk with McGowan. They decided to take the conductor's advice to take control and to tell the truth. Adrian met with the board of directors of the symphony and members of the orchestra. When he told his story, they were more supportive than he had hoped.

Adrian and Suzanne's greatest concern was how their circle of friends would react. Would they feel betrayed? Would they think Adrian lied to them and deceived Suzanne? Adrian and Suzanne gathered their closest circle of friends at their home to tell them the whole story.

"What the hell is wrong with you, Ace?" Larry's said, breaking the silence when Adrian finished. "Don't you know how we feel about you? You could have trusted us. Come here you big idiot. Give me a hug." With that, the others came to him reassuring him of their friendship, no matter what.

Adrian found it hard to speak. He felt an unexpected release of all tension and a desire to be still and let the relief sink in.

After telling their friends, Adrian and Suzanne gave a radio interview to Nelson Bryant, who, among others, was well known for his denouncement of the Nazi rally that took place at Madison Square Garden the previous February. They were prepared for

Bryant's first question.

"Nick Wells is accusing you both of being responsible for his troubles, saying you cooperated with the FBI to expose him as an American Nazi sympathizer. Care to respond?"

Adrian spoke for them both. "No, Nelson There is nothing we did to contribute to Nick Wells' arrest. The credit fully goes to Contessa Uberti. From what we understand, the FBI found Mr. Wells to be in possession of a piece of the contessa's missing jewelry. She reported it to her insurance company, and an investigation led to him. We were as surprised as anyone of his connection to the American Nazi organization." He said nothing else.

Mr. Bryant said, "OK then. Let's move on," and he asked Adrian about his son in Poland.

Adrian let himself talk about his personal agony over not being able to reunite with Simon and his fears for him, given the war. Suzanne stood by his side and promised she would help bring his son home to them. Together, they won the public's sympathy.

18

"CALL ME IZZY."

Adrian found a stack of messages waiting for him when he came back from lunch in late April 1940. One was from Isidore Waxman, a recruiter for the Three M Studio in Hollywood, California. Adrian had read about this new studio started by three Jewish brothers, and he'd heard Nelson Bryant mention them on his broadcast one evening. The studio was looking for a music director.

Out of curiosity, he returned the call.

A cheery operator connected him with a man with a high-pitched voice. "Mr. Mazurek. Thank you for calling back. How's it there in New York?"

"It's cloudy with a chance of rain, typical April weather here," Adrian said. "How about where you are?"

"Sunny. Sunny and beautiful, like heaven on earth, Adrian. May I call you Adrian?"

"Sure."

"Good. Call me Izzy."

Adrian hesitated, waiting for Izzy to continue.

"I've heard good things about you, Adrian. No, wonderful things. I represent Three M Studio, a new one by Hollywood standards, formed by three young brothers determined to make a success of it. They're looking for someone of your caliber to both select and score music for their films. They've asked me to talk with you about being that man. Would you be willing to come out here next week to discuss it?"

The invitation caught Adrian by surprise. His and Suzanne's lives had settled down after the scandal created by Otto had subsided. The offer flattered him, but he was reluctant to make any major changes in their life right now.

Adrian was cautious in his response. "I don't know. The symphony has a tight schedule, and I've got upcoming commitments to prepare for."

"Yes, I'm sure a man of your prominence is busy. I'll tell you what. I'm coming to New York in two weeks. Can we set up something then?" He suggested a day and time.

Adrian reached for his calendar and thumbed through it. "That sounds good." He wasn't sure how he felt, however. The call came out of the blue. He'd never considered doing anything that didn't take place in a symphony hall or in front of a live orchestra. He had no idea what it would be like to produce music for movies. On the other hand, the more he thought about the call, the more intrigued he became. He couldn't wait to talk with Suzanne about it.

That night after supper, in the living room, Adrian told her about Mr. Waxman's call.

"We'd have to leave New York," Suzanne said.

"Yes. I know. It would be hard to leave your father and our friends." Adrian waited to hear her reaction.

"I don't know. I need to think about it. What would I do about my clients?" She leaned back into the sofa and let out a sigh.

"You can pick up new ones in Hollywood. Look at the talent there and the people trying to break into the movies. They're looking for agents like you to get them started."

"It's crazy," she said. She folded her arms and looked down.

He could see he'd thrown her something too big to digest in one night, something that was too dramatic of a change to make impulsively. "Look," he said. "Maybe nothing will come of this. Why don't we wait to hear what they have to say? Let's not jump the gun."

"OK," Suzanne said. "That sounds like the wise thing to do."

There was something about the tone of her voice. Something was bothering her. He assumed it had to do with what they'd just discussed. He decided not to pursue it until determining if the job had any merit.

Adrian met with Isadore Waxman. The job sounded intriguing. As the studio's music director, he'd have, within budget, sole responsibility for hiring musicians and composers. He'd use his own compositions for original scores and select existing works that would fit in with the characters and do justice to a film. He'd have complete artistic discretion, with a two-year renewable contract at the studio's consideration.

Adrian tried not to display too much enthusiasm with Izzy. He wasn't sure whether the studio was considering others. Until he was offered the position, he didn't want to raise his hopes or put pressure on Suzanne. It would be too big a decision to make without a specific offer.

The next week Izzy called to say the studio wanted him for the job at a significant increase over his current salary and at the terms he mentioned earlier at their meeting in New York.

Adrian became both nervous and excited. It would be a momentous change, but he felt ready to tackle this. He hoped Suzanne would feel the same.

When he told Suzanne about the call, she expressed excitement. However, he sensed she was holding back.

"Are you afraid you'll miss your family and friends?" he said, thinking that would be the main spoiler.

"Let's wait for the contract and see what it says. I've seen too many people become excited before contracts arrive, only to see holes in them when they do."

Three nights later, a messenger delivered the contract.

"Let me look it over, and we'll discuss it when I finish,"

"It looks good," she said, after reading it, "but before you sign it, I think you'd better have my uncle study it."

Adrian raised his eyebrows. "If he says it's a tight contract, what do you think?"

"I guess California would be a good place to raise our girls," she said.

It took a few seconds for the words to sink in. He looked at her while watching him. Her eyes were wide and lustrous. She was biting her lower lip. He looked down at her hands cradling her belly. She nodded her head and held up two fingers. His own eyes widened, and his heart swelled as he went to her and wrapped his arms around her.

That, he realized, was what had been holding her back.

PART TWO
HOLLYWOOD

19

A SENSE OF APPFREHENSION

On September 1, 1940, Adrian and Suzanne boarded a DC-3 to California. From the window seat of the plane, Adrian watched Mr. Reitman, Charlotte, and Claire wave them off. Farewell parties and dinners with friends and colleagues had filled the weeks before their departure. They'd even taken driving lessons.

For a moment, during takeoff, a sense of apprehension fell over Adrian. Was he doing the right thing? He looked over at Suzanne and thought how eerily similar this journey was to the one in his past. He was taking the woman he loved, who had lived in the city of her birth surrounded by her family and friends, to a strange place for the sake of his career, just as he had removed Chana from a life of love and security. Instead of a horse drawn carriage on rugged roads to Krakow, they were traveling through the sky in a luxurious plane to Hollywood, the city of dreams. He and Chana had dreams. Those dreams had not turned out well. His chest tightened. He promised himself no tragedy would come from this new beginning. He'd make sure of that.

They arrived in California at the Glendale Airport at 8 a.m. Pacific Time. A shiny black Cadillac was waiting to take them to their hotel. The driver introduced himself as Rudy and said he worked for Martin Marcus, the studio's executive director. On the way to their hotel Adrian asked Rudy to drive by the Los Angeles Odeum Center, one of California's most famous venues for opera, ballet, and symphony orchestra performances. Its Romanesque architecture, inside and out, created a magnificent setting, which, despite its many columns, boasted there were no obstructing views. It was a landmark that visitors to the area did not want to miss.

Adrian hoped one day he'd have the privilege of performing there.

When they arrived at their hotel, Rudy took out their bags, and a bellhop took them inside.

"Mr. Martin asked me to remind you of your meeting at 8 a.m. tomorrow," Rudy said. "I'll pick you up at 7:30 to take you to the studio."

"I'll be in the lobby waiting," Adrian said.

A real estate agent, Molly Furrows, had left a message for Suzanne at the front desk saying she'd be at the hotel the following morning at ten to show her houses. She left a number to call if that wasn't convenient. A bellhop led them to a spacious and airy room. A bowl of fruit and a vase of flowers stood on a table with a note from the studio welcoming them.

After freshening up, they ate breakfast at a restaurant facing the hotel pool. Suzanne ordered the Breakfast Supreme, Adrian just coffee, two scrambled eggs, and toast.

Suzanne ate heartily. Adrian nibbled at his food.

"What's wrong?" Suzanne said.

"I was thinking about something."

"Tell me."

"No. You'll think I'm silly." Adrian stirred his coffee meaninglessly.

Suzanne put down her fork. "No, I won't. Please, tell me."

Adrian told her about the thoughts he had on the plane. "I made a mess of things back then. I don't want to do that again."

"That was long ago," Suzanne said. "A lifetime ago."

Adrian shook his head. "I know, but I can't help but see the similarities. I'm afraid I'll screw things up." He took his spoon out of his coffee cup and put it in the cup's saucer. "You know how involved I get in my work. You've grown used to it in New York. You had your family and friends and your clients to keep you busy. Here you don't know anybody. I'm afraid you'll get homesick and resent me."

Suzanne reached for Adrian's hand. "I'm not Chana, Adrian."

Her tone was gentle. "She was half my age. She didn't know herself or what she wanted, but I do." Suzanne rubbed Adrian's knuckles and looked deeply into his eyes. "I want you and a life with you. I know your faults, and I can live with them. Haven't I proven that to you?"

Adrian kissed Suzanne's hand. "Promise you won't hate me if I get too involved in this job, and you'll tell me if you need more of me when you do."

"I promise." They released their hands. "You know, when the twins are born, I'll be too busy to even know you're not around," Suzanne said.

"Oh no. Those girls are going to get plenty of my attention. They'll know who their father is."

Feeling better, Adrian finished his breakfast.

The next morning Rudy drove Adrian through the entrance of the Three M Studio without fanfare. There wasn't a gate or guard, only a sign designating the studio. He pulled up in front of a one-story stucco building.

"Here we are," Rudy said. Inside he announced to a woman sitting at a typewriter that Mr. Mazurek was here to see Mr. Marcus.

The office was drab and sparingly furnished with cheap metal furniture. The floor was tiled in a checkerboard pattern of blue and gray. One window with a Venetian blind let in the morning light.

The woman picked up her phone, pushed a button, and announced Adrian had arrived. She ushered Adrian into a room unlike the spare front office. Martin's domain was furnished with rich mahogany furniture and with seating covered in brown leather. A brilliantly colored oriental rug was spread out across the floor. Pleated curtains in a hue that picked up the pale blue in the carpet covered two large windows.

Martin came around his desk with an outstretched hand to greet Adrian. He wore a black pinstripe suit, a white shirt, and a silk silver and gray polka dot tie tied in a Windsor knot. Adrian was glad Suzanne had suggested he wear a suit and tie for this meeting. Martin's chestnut brown hair was curly with strands of gray. His eyes were dark brown, his nose straight, his lips full. Adrian liked his smile. It seemed genuine.

"It's good to meet you, Adrian. I've been looking forward to it." He pointed to one of the leather chairs in front of his desk. "Come, sit down. Can I get you something? Orange juice? Coffee?"

"Coffee would be fine," Adrian said.

Martin went to a sideboard where a coffee service was set and poured a cup. "Do you take cream or sugar?"

"Black, please."

Martin came back with Adrian's coffee. They sat opposite each other. Adrian sipped his coffee.

Martin started right in. "Tell me, Adrian, how do you feel about the war?"

Adrian looked up. "I'm not sure what you mean."

"Do you feel the United States should get involved?"

"Well, as you know, I have a son in Poland. Suzanne and I are dedicated to bringing him to the United States."

Martin sat back and crossed his legs. "Then you think we should enter the war?"

"I'm conflicted," Adrian said. "I don't know how I'd feel if it weren't for my son. You're aware, from the publicity Suzanne and I received in New York, he's Jewish and is living in Krakow with relatives. I can't help but worry about what he might be going through." Adrian shook his head. "I hope our allies can win the war without our help, but if it comes to the point we need to get involved, I guess I'd support it."

"My parents have relatives in Europe who are suffering because of Hitler," Martin said. "My mother has two sisters. My father has a brother, a sister, and three nephews. They'd like to bring them to the United States, but they're having trouble getting the necessary papers. My parents are worried about them. I can understand how you must feel about your son." The tone of his voice was gentle.

Adrian wondered where this was going. He stared at the portraits behind Martin's desk and waited for Martin's lead.

Martin uncrossed his legs and leaned his elbows on the armrests of his chair. "I guess you're wondering why I brought this up."

Adrian shifted sideways, careful to balance his coffee cup. "I am," he said.

"Fair enough." I guess I should get to the point. What I'm getting at is, I want you to understand what my brothers and I want to achieve with our studio. I know Izzy went over this with you in detail, but it's worth repeating." He licked his lips. "We want our studio to stand up for our American values. I want us to stand up against Hitler and his Nazism, and Stalinism, and all the other "isms" out there that want to destroy us. There's been too much shilly-shallying in Hollywood about how to deal with Germany under Hitler. At first, some studios felt they shouldn't deal with anything but entertainment. 'People go to the movies for enjoyment, not politics. The newsreels will take care of that,' seemed to be the consensus."

Martin pulled his chair closer to Adrian. "When the Los Angeles Bund started attacking the Hollywood Jews and everyone with close ties to the movie industry, some of the executives woke up. But not all were convinced." Martin shook his head. "I don't know. Maybe Jews didn't want to call attention to themselves as Jews. There was and is a lot of discrimination against us." Martin looked Adrian in the eyes and nodded. "My feeling is it was economic. Some studio executives feared financial losses if the Nazis wouldn't show their films that reflected poorly on them, so they gave in to the bastards."

Martin stood and walked to the sideboard.

"I'm afraid I'm letting my feelings get the best of me. Joanne, my wife, says I let myself get too excited, that movie making should be fun. I hope I'm not upsetting you, Adrian. How about a glass of water?"

Adrian needed time to absorb what he'd heard so far, and he needed to stretch his legs. He followed his new boss to the sideboard. "Water would be fine. Let me help." He took his empty coffee cup with him and placed it on the sideboard.

"By the way, my close friends and colleagues call me Martin. I'd be pleased if you'd do the same."

"Martin it is," Adrian said.

Martin poured two glasses of water. He told Adrian about some of the pictures above the sideboard. Many were of his family. Martin showed pride in his two children, Mark, eight, and Rebecca, ten.

"Did I hear correctly that you and Suzanne are expecting twins?"

Adrian smiled proudly. "Yes, in December."

"Exciting. If you need help with them, let me know. I'll tell Joanne. She'll know good people. Twins will be a handful." Martin motioned for them to return to their chairs.

Adrian couldn't help noticing the portraits behind Martin's desk. "Are they your parents?"

"Yes, they are. They live in Pasadena, outside of Los Angeles. My father owns a food company. They helped fund my brothers and me so we could start this studio. We owe a great deal to them. They're looking forward to meeting you."

Adrian felt a lump in his throat as Martin spoke about his parents. He thought about his mother and wondered how she was faring under the conditions of war.

Back in their chairs, Martin took a deep breath and returned to his earlier thoughts. "The President is remaining neutral in this war. Some of the studios are following his lead. They don't want to make films that will offend the Germans. My brothers and I have opposite goals. We want Americans to know what's going on in Europe. We want the United States to join the fight."

Adrian felt a thrill of excitement, the same feeling he'd had when he'd been asked by Philip Carter and the New York FBI office to help eradicate Nazi sympathizers in that city. This was a way for him to do something to make up for his feelings of impotence in helping Simon. He shifted in his chair. *I made a good decision in leaving New York to come work with this studio.*

"I've almost finished my diatribe, but I want you to understand what my brothers and I want our studio to be. We think Hollywood is coming more to grips with America's neutrality in the war. Roosevelt is calling for the country to stay out of the fight, but he knows not everyone agrees. The studio needs to make money to survive, so we'll make pictures that appeal to the public, like musicals and love stories. As we can afford, we'll also make movies to expose Hitler and to sensitize the public here so they'll see the importance of entering the conflict."

"It all sounds great," Adrian said rubbing his hands together. "I'd like to meet your brothers."

"They're looking forward to meeting you. Max isn't here right now. He's out talking with theater owners to persuade them to show our latest film."

"How many do you have in the works?" Adrian asked.

"We've finished one, except for the final editing, and the music, of course. There's the one Manus is currently filming and two he's screenwriting. He's incredibly talented. He has an eye and an ear for a good story. He's also a capable writer. You'll enjoy collaborating with him." Martin put down his glass and got to his feet. "Let's go to the set. If they're not too involved with filming, you can meet Manus."

On the way out, Martin introduced Adrian to Sophie, the secretary for the three brothers. She looked to be in her mid-sixties. She combed her black hair straight back in a bun. She wore a black cardigan, a black skirt, and a pea green blouse. A pair of black spangled, horn-rimmed glasses hung from a chain around her neck. Sophie greeted Adrian and said she looked forward to working with him. Adrian wondered if her raspy voice was natural or if she had a cold.

Out of her hearing range, Martin said, "She's very efficient and sharp as a tack. Stay on her good side and your life here will be very pleasant." They walked to a two-story brick building a short distance from Martin's office. The outside was deceptive. Inside, the building was one tall story.

"We were lucky to find this. We're renting it from another studio. Their last two films earned them enough to move to a larger building. God willing, we'll have the same good fortune. The previous studio converted the building from a factory to a soundstage. It's large enough to shoot two pictures at a time once we hit it big and can afford to do so. Right now, we're operating with a limited staff."

They walked to an area where it looked like filming had been going on but had stopped. Up ahead, two men were arguing.

Martin whispered, "The one flailing his arms is my brother, Manus. The one with his hands on his hips is our director, Rodney Sample. The pretty brunette off to the side putting on lipstick is Cora Hart, the film's main actress. We'd better stay back 'til this plays out."

"The man is hammered Manus said, loud enough for them to hear. "He can't remember his goddamn lines. Get him sobered up. Quick!"

The director removed his hands from his hips and walked off in response to the demand.

Cora walked up to Manus. "I'm not letting that man put his lips on me. His breath stinks."

"You will if you want to stay on this film, Cora," Manus said. He said more to Cora that Adrian couldn't hear.

Cora gave Manus a look of frustration and disappeared behind a nearby door.

Manus threw up his arms. "Actors," he said, 'they're a pain in the ass."

"Well, it looks like we walked into a fire storm," Martin said to Adrian.

What have I gotten myself into? This is crazy. These people can't control their employees. He was glad Suzanne hadn't seen the fight. She'd want to get on the next plane back to New York.

They walked over to Manus. Martin introduced Adrian to his older brother. The brothers bore a slight resemblance. Both had upturned eyes and full lips. Manus wore his straight hair combed back. He was slimmer than Martin and shorter. The sleeves of his white dress shirt were rolled up to his elbows. He wore casual but expensive looking trousers.

Manus gave Adrian an apologetic look and shook his hand. "Sorry you had to see that."

"What's going on?" Martin said, his voice calm.

"Bradley had a blowout with his wife last night. He came in drunk. I told him I'd give him a pass this time, but if he pulled it once more, I'd spread the word he was unreliable, and he wouldn't work in Hollywood again. I sent him to my office to cool off and told him to be back on the set in twenty minutes."

Martin turned to Adrian. "Bradley Stevens is the actor." He turned back to Manus. "What about Cora?"

"I think I've got her calmed down. I told her this picture would skyrocket her career and to put up with Bradley until it's finished, to think about herself, not that she doesn't every minute of every day." Manus scrunched his face. "Sometimes I think we need to consider hiring a psychiatrist on the set."

Martin laughed and shook his head. "God bless you, brother. You're better in dealing with these temperamental people than I could ever be."

Adrian liked the interaction between the two.

Manus turned to him, grinning. "Do you have any training in psychiatry, Adrian?"

"Afraid not. From what I see, you seem to be managing things well."

Manus shook his head and turned back to Martin. "We're almost finished shooting this picture. I'm anxious to get started on the next one." He rubbed his forehead. "We're going to look at the rushes from today and tomorrow at four tomorrow. That will give Adrian a chance to get his head around the more recent takes and get a feel for the movie."

"How about it, Adrian?" Martin said.

Adrian rubbed his hands together. "I can't wait to see them."

"Great." Martin winked at his brother. "We'll leave you now to deal with your 'patients'. I want to show Adrian his studio."

Manus shook Adrian's hand again. "Welcome aboard. I look forward to seeing you tomorrow."

On the way out, they approached a man leaning against a

triangular ladder taking a swig from a soft drink bottle. A large camera sat by his feet. His curly hair was peppered in black and gray, and he needed a haircut. He was wearing blue jeans and an untucked yellow plaid shirt. Martin introduced them. "Elliot is our cinematographer. He's got a great eye with the camera," Martin said, patting Elliot on the shoulder. "You two will be working together closely," he said to Adrian.

Elliot gave Adrian a perfunctory nod and took a sip from his bottle.

Martin walked Adrian to a small white stucco building with a red wooden door. He unlocked it, and they went in. "I'm sure it's not what you've been used to, but I hope you can turn it into what suits your needs."

The inside had been thoroughly cleaned and set up for him. A wooden desk had a phone and typewriter. A swivel desk chair and two other small chairs graced the desk. In the corner were a file cabinet and a polished brass music stand. Adrian's eyes were drawn to the Victor radio phonograph console. He walked over to it and ran his hand across the smooth wood.

"This is fantastic. Whoever pulled this room together deserves a big hug."

Martin smiled. "That was my wife, Joanne. I'll give her the hug for you if you don't mind." He paused to look around. "Feel free to change anything. Joanne left the floor concrete, but she had it painted this color blue. Someone told her a concrete floor was best for a music studio, but if you'd prefer carpeting…"

"No, she was right. The color's fine. Please thank her for me."

"You can tell her yourself. My parents want to arrange a party to introduce you and Suzanne to our community. My mother will be calling Suzanne. You'll meet Joanne there."

"That sounds great. I'll let Suzanne know tonight."

"Good," Martin said. He turned and motioned to a set of doors in the back far corner of the studio. "There's a small washroom behind there and a supply closet next to it. The boxes you sent ahead are in there. Joanne didn't do more than the basics in case Suzanne wanted to come in and help you decorate. Your desk has supplies. Ask Sophie for whatever else you need."

Adrian was delighted. "You've made me feel quite welcome. I'm looking forward to seeing those rushes tomorrow, and you said there's a film finished except for the editing and music. When will I be able to see that?" His creative juices had started to flow.

"I'll talk with Manus and ask him to work that out with you. I'm sure he'll want you to get started on it right away."

Adrian nodded.

"There's not much more I can think of for you today." Martin said, "I'm sure you'll want to see Suzanne about the properties Molly showed her. I'll have Sophie call you as soon as Rudy is ready to take you back to the hotel. In the meantime, get familiar with your studio." Before he left, he handed Adrian a key to his studio and said, "Sophie has a duplicate if you need it."

Martin reached out to shake hands. He smiled widely. "I'm glad you're here, Adrian. I look forward to our collaboration."

When Martin left, Adrian walked around his studio touching everything and feeling pleased. The morning had gone well. Martin and Manus seemed intelligent, well bred, and determined to make a success of their company. Admittedly, the small staff might be a worry and, likewise, the behavior he'd seen on the set, but Adrian decided this was the nature of working with temperamental actors, not too unlike musicians, at times.

On the drive back to the hotel with Rudy, Adrian thought again about how the Marcus brothers wanted to raise the consciousness of Americans about what was happening overseas. He was eager to help them. He couldn't wait to begin. He'd start thinking about what music would stir the hearts of moviegoers.

20

HOLLYWOODERS OR HOLLYWOODIANS?

Adrian got to their room at 2:30. Suzanne wasn't back. He was curious if she'd found a house she liked. He was leaving the decision to her. His only requirement was to have a private office where he wouldn't interfere with the babies' routines when he played his violin or recordings.

Suzanne arrived not long after looking exhausted.

"Are you OK?" He led her to a chair. "Here, sit down." He walked to the bathroom and returned with a glass of water.

"I'm all right. Just let me catch my breath."

"Drink this and let me take off your shoes." She drank half the water and handed the glass back to Adrian. He placed it on the windowsill and knelt, removed her shoes, and waited until she was ready to talk.

"Molly is a go getter. She was ready with four houses for me to see, all beautiful. I had to beg off on the fourth. All that getting in and out of the car and going over every detail of each house was wearing. Not that I didn't appreciate it, but I'm not sure the twins did."

"She probably gave you special treatment because of the Marcus's. The way Martin treated me today, he may have made her think you were Queen Elizabeth."

"If so, she lived up to their expectation. Two of the houses were palaces." Suzanne smiled at him. "It sounds as if you had a good day, or half a day it seems. I wasn't expecting you until five or six."

"Tomorrow I'll be later. We're having a four o'clock look at today's and tomorrow's rushes."

"Rushes?" Suzanne bent to rub her feet. "Remind me not to wear heels when I go out with Molly again."

"Here, let me rub them for you." Adrian pulled up a chair opposite her, and she rested her feet on his knees. He explained. "Rushes are viewings of recently shot scenes."

"Shot? Listen to you. You're talking like you've been in the movie business for years."

He pinched her toe.

Suzanne squirmed. "Ouch."

"That's for making fun of me."

Suzanne covered a yawn with her forearm. Her eyes were beginning to cloud over.

"I'll tell you what," Adrian said. "Let me help you get undressed, and then you take a nap. Sleep for as long as you need. We'll discuss all this tonight at dinner. We can eat downstairs or order room service, whatever you want."

"Bless you, Adrian. That's just what the girls and I need."

He helped her out of her dress and into bed. Her eyes closed as soon as her head hit the pillow. He pulled a blanket over her, closed the curtains, and turned off the light. Then he went to one of the hotel's restaurants for a light lunch so he wouldn't spoil their dinner together.

Later, Suzanne decided she was feeling up to eating in the hotel's dining room. They dressed for dinner and took the elevator to the lobby.

After they ordered, Suzanne said she was going to cancel tomorrow's appointment with Molly to look at other properties. She knew which house she wanted.

Adrian leaned into the table. "Tell me."

Suzanne gave a wide smile. "It's a four bedroom, three bath Spanish style bungalow set back on a beautiful street. It sits on half an acre with lush gardens and a pool. The inside is roomy and beautifully furnished. The half basement is perfect for you to use as a studio."

"It sounds nice." He wrinkled his brow. "Can we afford it?" With two incomes in New York, they'd gotten along well. Now with one income and two babies on the way, Adrian worried about the expense of keeping up such a house.

"Rental prices here are comparable to those in New York.," Suzanne said. "With the income we're getting from the brownstone and your income, we should break even. We always have my grandmother's trust if we need more.

Adrian covered his mouth with his napkin to hide a frown. "Don't forget to add in the maintenance on the grounds and pool." His mind was counting expenses and how much this would add to their costs.

"The rental cost includes furniture, and a house cleaner who comes in two days a week. The owner is an engineer who's working on a project in Argentina. He plans to move back into the house in two years. The real estate firm is providing maintenance for the owner so the house is in undamaged condition when he returns. All we need to do is move in."

"Will we be able to hang Claire's portrait of me and your father's wedding picture?"

"Let them try and stop us. I've had them professionally wrapped for their shipment here. We'll find prominent places to display them."

Adrian couldn't resist her enthusiasm. "It sounds perfect. If we're going to live in Hollywood, we should live like Hollywooders, or is it Hollywoodians?"

"I know you're being flip, Adrian. You're still worried about the money, aren't you?"

He scratched his head. "Honestly, yes."

"I understand how you feel about taking income from my grandmother's trust. She left it to me to have a comfortable life. She'd want us to use it, especially now that we're going to have children." Suzanne took the last bite of her salad. "Just consider it as you would our income if I were working. You're asking me to live on your income, so why can't you accept my being able to contribute from the trust?"

Adrian was quiet for a moment. He didn't have the right to deprive her of what was hers. He looked at her and said, "You're right. I'm being selfish. I'd say the same to you if the situation were reversed."

Suzanne reached and put her hand over his. "Thank you, Adrian. I'm so happy. I'll call Emily in the morning and tell her to prepare the papers."

"There's another decision to make," Adrian said.

"What's that?"

"I'm going to need a car and quickly."

"Do we have to buy one, or can we rent one?"

"Good thinking. I'll ask Martin about that tomorrow."

Their entrées arrived, and Suzanne began asking Adrian about his day. He told her how gracious Martin had been and how he and his brothers planned to grow and expand. He left out the part about wanting to make anti-Nazi movies.

"My studio is a small, but separate, Spanish style one room building with a half bath. Joanne, Martin's wife, furnished it. They were ready for me. They made me feel special."

Suzanne reached under the table to squeeze his knee. "You are special. I'm happy they made you feel so welcome."

"Martin said his mother will be calling you. She wants to give a party in our honor at their home. Are you up to it?"

"Of course. I wouldn't let you down. Molly told me a lot about the family. She's quite a gossip. One needs to be careful what one shares with her."

"What did she tell you?"

"The Marcus family is wealthy. Mr. Marcus started a wholesale food distributing business soon after he and his wife were married. He's built into an extremely successful enterprise. His sons worked for him for several years. When they persuaded their father their hearts were in the movie industry, he set them up with a substantial draw from the same bank where your two-year guaranteed salary is set up. The brothers have two sisters whose husbands help run the business. According to Molly, the family is charitable in Jewish and cultural organizations."

Adrian was pleased to learn the studio was on sound footing. "All I can say is class shows. I think you'll enjoy meeting them."

Later that evening, Suzanne received a call from the senior Mrs. Marcus inviting them to a welcoming party in their honor for the first Saturday in October. Suzanne accepted graciously.

21
A MEMORABLE TITLE

R udy picked Adrian up at 7:30 the next morning. Adrian asked Rudy to let him out at Martin's office.

"Good morning, Sophie. How are you?" Adrian greeted her.

"I'm fit as a fiddle. I'm looking forward to hearing you play."

Adrian indulged himself at her pun. "That tugs at my heart strings."

"I like your at-*etude*, Mr. Mazurek."

Adrian couldn't help laughing. "I could string you along for a while, Sophie, but I need to see Mr. Marcus."

Sophie picked up the phone. "I'll let him know you're here." After a moment, she looked at Adrian. "He says to go in."

As soon as Adrian walked in, Martin got up and held out his hand. "Good morning, Adrian."

Adrian shook Martin's hand. "We've found a house," he said. "Once we sign the papers, we can move in. Now I need a car. Suzanne suggested I rent one. I think that's a good idea. We also need to get our California driver's licenses."

"Sure. I'll get on the car rental this morning, and I'll ask Sophie to check out what's required to transfer your New York licenses. You're fast workers. I appreciate that."

"I have to give credit to Suzanne for the house, and Miss Furrows too."

"Joanne tells me you're coming to my parents' party. We can't wait to show you off. Mother is preparing the guest list now."

"I feel like a prized cocker spaniel. I'll make sure I'm clipped and shampooed."

Martin laughed. "Better add a fancy bow. It will be formal."

"I'll see what I can find. I'm looking forward to seeing the rushes later," he said, changing the subject. "Right now, I'm going to head to my office and get my vinyl and sheet music collection organized."

"I'll get on that car rental and have Sophie call you."

In twenty-five minutes, Adrian was in a new Cadillac Sixteen on the way to the rental place. He resisted the rental manager's efforts to put him in a Cadillac and chose a beautiful 1939 Ford Deluxe Station Wagon in perfect condition. He figured it would be more useful after the girls arrived. He was sure Suzanne would approve of his selection.

The rental agency said they'd have the car serviced and washed and delivered to him at the Studio. He called Suzanne to tell her the news. She said he'd made the right choice. By two o'clock a bright polished wagon was waiting outside his studio.

At four o'clock Adrian walked into the filming studio. Martin waved him over. "Adrian, this is my brother, Max." They shook hands. Max was the youngest of the three brothers. He was short and pudgy. He combed his thinning hair to the side. Adrian thought he resembled his mother, based on the portraits hanging behind Martin's desk, and his brothers more their father.

Max removed his wire rimmed glasses and wiped them with a red silk handkerchief he pulled out of the breast pocket of his expensive looking gray suit. "It's a pleasure to meet you, Adrian. My wife and I are looking forward to officially welcoming you and Suzanne at my parent's gathering in your honor." His manner was exceedingly friendly. Adrian saw why he worked in the public relations side of their venture.

After brief pleasantries, Martin said there'd been a change of plans.

"Max says two theater owners are interested in the movie that's finished except for the editing and music. We wanted to show it to you for your ideas." They led him to a room set with metal chairs, a screen, and a projector. Elliot was there to show the film.

The movie, not yet titled, was a story about two college students who fell in love. The girl came from a privileged background, the boy from a blue-collar family. The girl's father didn't approve of the young man and forced the couple apart. She married a man of prominence but never forgot her college sweetheart. He married and became a successful lawyer. He never forgot the girl. Later in life they met and found happiness together. There was a line early in the film when the boy said to the girl: "I'm nickel. You're gold. Your family will never approve of me."

Adrian thought it was a tender story. Its themes of coming of age, love, prejudice, and the individual versus society inspired him immediately. The tale reminded him of his relationship with Chana.

"What do you think, Adrian?" Martin said.

Adrian cleared his throat. He wanted to be careful how he answered. This was his first important meeting with the group, and he wanted to make a favorable impression.

"It's a sweet film," he said. "The actors are attractive, and the audience will fall for them. The story is sad but has a happy ending. I'm impressed." Adrian stood to stretch his legs. He turned to Manus. "There was a line early in the film that caught my attention."

Manus tilted his body forward. "Which one?" he said, raising his eyebrows.

"The one when Richard tells Abigail he's nickel and she's gold." He decided to run with the idea that had come into his head. "How would you feel about naming the movie *Nickel and Gold*? We could write a love song to that title. I'll take care of the music. You just need to provide a lyricist."

Adrian looked around for reactions.

"Go on," Manus said. "Let's hear more."

"We could use the song during the opening credits and then use the tune as theme music throughout the film." Using his limited knowledge of Yiddish to get their attention, Adrian continued. "We could schmaltz it up with lots of string music to give it a classical sound at appropriate times We'd repeat the song during the closing credits, so the audience goes home humming it, or at least has it on their minds."

He added another idea. "If the studio gets the rights to publish the song, has it recorded and releases it to the public it might bring more people into the theatres and earn royalties through record sales. He saw Martin's eyes catch those of his brothers.

Adrian stopped and looked around.

Martin turned to his brother. "What do you think, Manus?"

Manus grinned widely and clapped his hands. "I like it. I think it's spot on. *Nickel and Gold* makes a memorable title. It's the essence of the film. Adrian's idea for the theme song is fantastic. I'll leave the additional musicians needed up to him, within budget, of course. If we all agree, I'll find a lyricist."

"I like it, too," Martin said. "What about you, Max?"

Max gave a thumbs up, "I say, let's get it rolling."

Manus asked Rodney how soon he could proceed.

"There's some editing I'd like to go over with Elliot," Rodney said. "But we can do that while Adrian works on the music. Then we can get together to synchronize the music with the film. I'd like to get on it right away." Rodney turned to Elliot and said, "Prepare for some overtime. We've got to finish our current filming and complete this at the same time, but I've got a feeling we've got a hit on our hands."

That evening, Adrian drove the Ford wagon to the hotel. He and Suzanne decided to move into the new house on Friday. Suzanne told Adrian the trunks they'd forwarded had arrived, and she'd arrange to have them delivered to the house. Adrian told Suzanne about his day. He was so excited she had to slow him down.

"I knew they'd fall in love with you. I never doubted it for a moment."

Adrian rubbed his hands together. "I can't wait to get started on the music to *Nickel and Gold*. My juices are flowing. I've got so many ideas. I hope they find a lyricist soon."

"I know you," Suzanne said. "You won't be able to sit still until you start writing the words and music yourself. I bet you were working on them on the way here."

He put his arms around her and kissed her. "You think you know me so well, don't you?"

"Calm down. You've had a long day. I bet you haven't had a bite to eat."

"I had a candy bar at the car rental," Adrian said.

"Maybe that's why you're so hyper, Nothing else?"

"I washed it down with a cola."

"Why don't we order room service and get some real food in you?"

"You order while I shower."

In the shower Adrian found himself humming a tune for "Nickle and Gold." The words for the love song seemed to fall into his head. He wanted to hurry and write them down before he forgot. He got out of the shower, ran into the bedroom naked and wet, and searched for a pen and paper in the desk. Just then, room service arrived. Adrian reached for the hotel's menu and covered himself.

Suzanne burst into laughter. "Really, Adrian. You shocked the poor man. We're going to get a bad reputation in Hollywood before our first week is over."

That night, Adrian couldn't sleep. Tunes and words ran through his head. He took a hotel pad and pen into the bathroom and worked behind a closed door so he wouldn't disturb Suzanne.

By 3 a.m. he'd made enough progress to suit himself and went to bed. He fell asleep at once. Suzanne's gentle tugs woke him up at seven.

That morning, he drove to work singing the words to the tune he'd jotted down overnight. They needed refinement, but he looked forward to running them by Manus. He took his violin to the Studio to continue working on the music. Manus was in conference with his brothers, so Adrian went to his studio to work. Later, Sophie called Adrian to tell him Manus was on his way over to his studio.

"My brothers and I can't wait to get you started on *Nickel and*

Gold," Manus said. Adrian smiled. He'd put his first mark on this movie. He felt proud, but he didn't want to overestimate his first achievement. He needed to produce a successful score.

"Like Rodney said, this is going to involve a lot of overtime for you, Rodney, Elliot, and myself to review the film several times so you can decide where the music fits in. We're setting a six-week time limit. Max wants to get the film finished for distribution before Thanksgiving. The independent theater owner Max is working with needs a film by then. He'll sign a contract if we can guarantee it."

"I'll give it my all," Adrian said, but he was worried about what this would mean for Suzanne. *She's in a new state without anyone she knows, and she's pregnant. This will be hard on her. I'll have to get her help. Maybe one of our friends can come and stay for a while. I'll talk it over with her tonight.*

"As a matter of fact," Adrian said, "I started working on the theme last night. I brought my violin in case you'd want to hear it."

Manus gave a quick glance at his watch and said, "Sure. I'd love to."

Adrian played the music he'd composed for the movie. Manus' face brightened. "I like it. I've got a few ideas about a lyricist and a singer. I'll get back to you about that and overtime schedules. Right now, I've got to get back to the set." He was gone in a flash.

Adrian gave a satisfied smile. He'd quickly impressed his new bosses. He went to his closet, took out a few pages of blank sheet paper and transferred to them the notes and words he'd jotted down last night.

That evening, Adrian told Suzanne about his conversation with Manus. She expressed her happiness for him. "Don't be concerned about the overtime," she said. "I don't have to worry about maintenance or cleaning, so I'll be able to enjoy the pool and catch up on my reading. Plus, Joanne called me and said she'd be happy to show me around Hollywood. She's even given me the name of her obstetrician. We're getting together for lunch tomorrow. So, you see, I'm getting all the attention I need. I'll hardly notice you're gone."

Adrian gave her a peck on the cheek. "I'm planning to set up my home studio on Friday morning when we move into the house and then start working in the afternoon with the songwriter Manus has found, a young man named Jonny Richards."

"Who is he?" Suzanne said. "Has he written anything we know?"

"He's a graduate of The Emmitt Walker School of Music in Los Angeles. He's the son of a friend of a friend of Manus. He graduated top in his class three years ago, and, aside from his classical training, he likes jazz and swing." Adrian swayed his hips and swung his shoulders and arms. He stopped when Suzanne shook her head and rolled her eyes. "A bonus is he knows past and current students who can help copy the music and who'd be willing to play just for the recognition if we need more musicians. He's written songs, but he's not had any published. Max said he works in the Mexican theater scene here."

"If you're going to fill the house with young people, we'd better up that food budget for the next few weeks," Suzanne said.

Thursday morning Adrian met with Jonny Richards in his studio. The first thing Adrian noticed about this young man was his easy smile and cordial manner. Jonny was the first to offer his hand with a firm shake. Like Adrian, he was tall, but with a full head of thick, black hair, parted and neatly trimmed. Dressed in pressed denim jeans and a lightweight gray jacket over a blue long-sleeved shirt, he presented himself as a modern young artist. They soon spoke on a first name basis. Adrian told Jonny in detail the story of the film. Jonny listened carefully as Adrian played the theme he'd composed and sang the lyrics he'd written.

"I've got some more ideas floating around in my head," Adrian said, "but I want to hear what you come up with. Tomorrow, my wife and I are moving into our rented house. It has a grand piano for you to play. I'd like us to work there if you want to take this on. It's going to take a commitment of two weeks or thereabouts."

Jonny's eyes sparkled. "I understand. I'm prepared to do that. This is a big opportunity for me. I'll give it my all."

"Fine," Adrian said. "Come at one." He wrote down his address and his home and office phone numbers. "One more question,

Jonny. Have you ever been in love?" He wanted to know if a man this age had had enough experience with love and loss to write about it.

Jonny smiled as he tucked the address and phone numbers into his wallet. "Yes, sir, and spurned. My last girlfriend's father thought I had no future as a musician. I intend to prove him wrong."

"I hope I didn't offend you," Adrian said.

"Not at all. I'm grateful for the chance to work with you."

The next morning Adrian loaded the Ford wagon with their suitcases, and he and Suzanne moved from the hotel to their rented house. Adrian found the house lived up to Suzanne's description. She'd made a smart choice, but he didn't feel he could enjoy it just yet. He had to finish the title song and scoring for the film. He'd never taken on a project like this before. He was going to be in inner turmoil for a while. He hoped Suzanne would understand, despite her reassurances she would.

At one o'clock, Adrian heard the roaring sound of a motorcycle pulling up the driveway. He opened the front door to see Jonny balancing the cycle with the kickstand.

Suzanne appeared at the door next to him. She looked at Adrian incredulously. "Is that your Jonny?

Adrian flexed his eyebrows. "It's not the milkman."

Suzanne greeted Jonny and told the two of them there was cola in the refrigerator and snacks laid out on the kitchen table. Then she left them alone.

Jonny and Adrian went into the living room. "I've revised some of your lyrics," Jonny said. "I think they'll work better with the melody and follow more closely with the storyline." He strolled over to the piano with his shoulders back and his chest out. "They're not perfect. We'll need to work on them."

Adrian couldn't wait to hear what Jonny had.

Jonny played Adrian's tune and sang the revised lyrics, a blend of his own and Adrian's. Adrian grabbed his violin and joined in. They worked together for three hours tweaking each syllable in the lyrics to every musical note until satisfied they'd created a beautiful ballad. Adrian felt that with additional instruments, he'd be able to use the basic melody to create different moods for the movie's scenes and characters. They transcribed the music and lyrics onto sheet music and stopped for the day.

Adrian told Jonny how pleased he was with their work together, and he'd set up a meeting with Manus on Monday for them to play the song to him to get his reaction. "Stand by for my call," he said.

Suzanne came into the living room soon after Johnny's motorcycle pulled away. "How did it go?' she said.

"Splendidly." Adrian caught Suzanne around the waist and started to waltz her around the room. Not wanting to tire her out, he sat her on the piano bench with him and plunked the keys as best he knew how and sang the song he and Jonny had written.

"We were friends 'til love got in the way.
It sprouted wings and flew us to the moon.
I loved you more than I could ever say,
But the seeds of doubt got in your way,
When you were told, I was nickel, and you were gold.

My friends said I was a fool to love you.
They said a love like ours could never be,
But in my heart, I knew you loved me too.
There was nothing you'd ever let them do,
When they told you, I was nickel, and you were gold.

Why can't they understand just how we feel?
That this love of ours will never go away.
Our broken hearts will never truly heal,
Even though they tell you it's not real,
That it's not right to mix pure nickel with pure gold.

We will show them, though it may not be right now,
That the future will prove them to be wrong.
I don't know when, where, or even how,
Someday we'll be together, that's a vow.
They will no longer say I am nickel to your gold.

Suzanne's started to hum along as Adrian played and sang. Adrian saw her eyes light up with enthusiasm. She patted Adrian's bottom, and said, "You're at your best when you're naked and hopping in and out of the shower."

On Monday, Adrian set up a meeting with Manus for 11:00. He called Jonny and asked him to be there.

Manus was thrilled with the song. He caught Adrian by the shoulder and shook his hand heartily. He did the same to Jonny. He stood back and admired them.

"Congratulations," he said. "That was faster than I expected."

"Jonny and I worked well together," Adrian said. "He's got determination and talent. He's going to make it as a songwriter and pianist." Out of the corner of his eye he saw Jonny duck his head to hide a grin.

"That's high praise from a man who knows, Jonny," Manus said. "I'll be sure to tell my brothers." Then he glanced at his watch. "Look, I've got to run, but I have a singer in mind. His name is Eddie Barnes. I'll set up a meeting at a nearby recording studio, hopefully tomorrow. I want you both there to go over this with him. Adrian, take your violin. Jonny, there'll be a piano there. Work together until you think it's right. Adrian, whatever music you want to add you can do it soon after. When you're happy, we'll get it recorded. Remember, we're on a deadline. Work quickly." Before he left, Manus pulled Adrian aside. "I've made a schedule for you, Rodney, and Elliot to review the screening so you can finish your ideas on scoring. I left it with Sophie. Got to run. Catch you later. Really good work, men, really good."

Still recovering from the Manus whirlwind, but smiling to himself, Adrian saw Jonny off. They agreed Jonny would look for other musicians to back up the song and to play in other parts of the score.

From there, everything moved quickly. Manus's singer, Eddie Barnes, was a young man, also from The Walker School. After three sessions, the single, "Nickel and Gold," got recorded. The Studio arranged for it for mass produced and available for distribution right after the first Hollywood showing.

Adrian spent four weeks preparing and recording the soundtrack for the full movie. Jonny found recent graduates from the Walker school for Adrian to help augment the music. Immediately after he finished the work, Adrian began reviewing the rushes for the Studio's next film, nearly completed. The Studio wanted to release it soon after the premiere of *Nickel and Gold.*

Adrian could have claimed part credit for the lyrics to "Nickel and Gold," but he gave Jonny full credit in the film and on the record. When he told Jonny this, the young man looked stunned. "I don't know what to say, Adrian."

"Don't say anything. There are people who gave me breaks, who helped me become what I am. This is my gift to you. When you become successful, help someone else by giving them their first break."

Jonny shook Adrian's hand and pressed it tightly. "You're a real gentleman. I'll do that. I promise you." Adrian felt a warm glow come over him then fade to sadness. He hoped one day he'd feel such admiration and appreciation from Simon.

22

A MILLIONAIRE'S ROW WELCOME

On the first Saturday evening of October, Adrian and Suzanne drove to the Tudor-style mansion on Millionaire's Row in Pasadena. They were greeted by the Marcus clan in a sizable foyer reminiscent of the contessa's. Martin and Joanne escorted Adrian and Suzanne into the opulent ballroom which was lit by rows of glittering crystal chandeliers. An orchestra played on a raised platform while guests mingled and danced. The men wore black formal wear, the women stylish, colorful gowns. Suzanne leaned into Adrian and said she was glad she listened to Charlotte, who insisted she take a maternity gown to Hollywood for such occasions. Her emerald-green gown had an olive bodice laced with gold sequins. Adrian admired how the color set off her hair and eyes.

Martin and Joanne began introducing their guests of honor to the others there to welcome them.. They met Arthur Silverman, Stanley Fisher, and their wives, longtime friends of Martin's parents, who were patrons of the Los Angeles Odeum Center. Mr. Silverman was the music director of the Odeum Philharmonic. Mr. Fisher was on the Board of Directors of "The Center," as it was called by Californians.

"Maybe one day we'll have the honor of your performing there," Mr. Fisher said.

"Now, now Stanley," Martin said. "Adrian's only been with us for five weeks. We worked hard to steal him away from New York. Don't try to get your claws in him so soon."

Mr. Silverman slapped Martin on the back and said, "Don't

worry, my friend. We're booked for this season and into the next." He then looked at Adrian and winked. "We'd be happy to talk with you in the future." Adrian felt a thrill of excitement.

Martin excused themselves to introduce Adrian and Suzanne to other guests. He presented them to influential Californians, including lawyers, educators, people in the film industry, notable personnel from The Emmitt Walker School of Music, and more friends of the family, all who, Suzanne whispered in Adrian's ear, were the muckety-mucks of Los Angeles and its surrounds.

After a while, Joanne said to Martin, "Let's not wear Suzanne out. Let me take her to the library to rest."

"Of course," Martin agreed. "You two go along. I'll take care of Adrian." Martin placed his hand on Adrian's elbow. "Come with me."

After further introductions, Martin said to Adrian, "That's enough chit-chat for now. My mother just gave me the signal it's time to formally introduce you and Suzanne. Let's go find her."

Suzanne and Joanne were waiting with the Marcus family in the foyer. The senior Marcus's walked Adrian and Suzanne to the orchestra. After the men assisted their wives onto the orchestra platform, Mr. Marcus tapped the microphone and asked for everyone's attention. Guests who were on the veranda by the pool came inside.

"Louise and I and our family welcome you to our home," the elder Mr. Marcus began. "We have special guests tonight we wanted you to meet: Suzanne and Adrian Mazurek." As he lifted his hand to them, a polite scatter of applause ran through the room. "Adrian, as you know, was the previous concertmaster of The Eleventh State Symphony Orchestra in New York City. He has performed as a violinist in the greatest concert halls on the east coast, not only the works of others, but compositions of his own. It is a great honor he accepted our sons' invitation to be the Music Director of their new Three M Studio. Only five weeks here, Adrian is near completion of the score for their first film, scheduled for release on Thanksgiving. His beautiful wife, Suzanne, has her own production scheduled for release in December."

Mr. Marcus stopped for laughter and a wave of applause before continuing.

"Suzanne, in her own right, has gained prominence as the manager for some of the finest musicians in New York," He turned to face Adrian and Suzanne. "Look at them. What a handsome couple they are. Their twins will be grateful to inherit their good looks and talent." Mr. Marcus started clapping. "Please welcome them to Hollywood and greater California."

Such a welcome made Adrian feel proud, not only for his professional achievements that brought him here tonight, but also because he had pulled his personal life together and had the prospects of the family with Suzanne he had wanted. He took the microphone and motioned to Suzanne to join him. He took her hand, and when the applause quieted, he said, "We left the Big Apple behind for the Big Orange. Right now, we'd likely be fighting our way through the cold and snow. The Marcus family has given us the warmest reception we could have imagined." He looked out upon the smiles on the faces of the guests. "If you are a sample of California hospitality, California must be melting hearts all year round. We so appreciate all of you for coming here tonight to welcome us. Thank you very much."

During the renewed applause, Suzanne whispered to Adrian, "You've charmed them, sweetheart, as usual. Good work."

Adrian was glad his long training in performance enabled him to feel comfortable meeting famous people and giving impromptu speeches like this one. "They're applauding my good taste in wives. The men's eyes were on you, not me," he said to Suzanne.

"Well, I noticed where the women's eyes were, and they weren't on your bow tie. They were a little north of that, on that swelled head of yours," Suzanne said.

Adrian patted her hand. "Did our marriage vows include 'and to always keep him humble' after 'to love and to cherish'"?

Suzanne nodded. "Come let's go meet your devotees."

After a few more introductions, Martin took Adrian aside. He jutted his chin to a corner of the room and whispered, "See that woman over there, the one in the wheelchair with the two bodyguards by her side and the ridiculous blond wig? That's Pricilla Ward. Despite her handicap, she has the influence to make or destroy the success of a film through her gossip column and radio broadcasts. Let's see if we can entice her to premiere the theme song of *Nickel and Gold* on one of her upcoming programs." Martin tugged at Adrian's elbow, and, as if it were a second thought, he said, "Try not to stare at her hair."

Adrian nodded, put on his best smile, and walked with Martin, who introduced him to Miss Ward. She was an attractive looking woman underneath her blond wig. Her hazel eyes had flecks of blue and she looked somewhere between her late fifties and early sixties. She was gracious to Adrian, but he sensed behind her friendly smile was a tenacious woman who knew what she wanted and how to get it.

Back home, long after Suzanne had gone to bed, Adrian stayed up reviewing the evening, the people they met, and his future in Hollywood. *The Marcus brothers have lived up to their promise. The Marcus family designed the party to introduce me to everyone they know who can help me, not only with my job at the studio, but who can help make me feel welcome in the classical music community.* Adrian was impressed. *What's more, they've taken care of Suzanne with their kindness to her and with her burgeoning friendship with Joanne. Life is going to be good to us here. What privileges I could provide Simon with if he were here with me.*

On Monday morning, Adrian was back on his roller coaster schedule.

The Studio was nearly ready to wrap up the production of *Nickel and Gold*. They would make their target of premiering it on Thanksgiving.

Sophie called Adrian in his office. "Priscilla Ward called while you were with Rodney and Elliot. She'd like you to call her back."

Adrian returned the call immediately.

"It was delightful meeting you at the Marcus's party," Miss Ward said. "How is your lovely wife?"

"She's well. Thank you for asking."

"I'll get to the point. I know you're busy. I'd like you to be on my broadcast this weekend. It would be a wonderful opportunity to plug the studio's new film with your first scoring assignment."

Adrian accepted graciously. Martin clapped his hands when Adrian told him. Although the studio wasn't planning to release the song until after the premiere, Martin and his brothers spoke and decided to release the recording of "Nickle and Gold" on Miss Ward's program. They agreed it would give the public a chance to have an advance hearing of the song and create anticipation among the public to want to see the film when it opened.

The next day Adrian came home for an early dinner. Afterward, he called the contessa. He learned she wasn't feeling well. "The doctor told me I have a heart arrythmia and need to curtail my activities and rest. I tire easily," she said.

Adrian felt bad he hadn't called her sooner. It was hard to imagine her tired and not up to her usual busy life. "You'll always be welcome to visit with us, Rose," he said. "We've rented a lovely home with plenty of room. Suzanne could use the company." In the background, Suzanne nodded. "I'm at work so much. The weather here is perfect. I'm sure it's bitter in New York. It would be good for you and for us to have you come."

"Thank you, dear, but I'm not sure I can manage a cross country trip just now." Adrian could hear she was having difficulty breathing.

That shook him. If he'd been in New York, he would have gone to see her or would have called her every day. He hated being so far away knowing how much he'd neglected her lately. "Whenever you can," he said. "We'd love to have you. You know that don't you? Any time," he said for emphasis.

"Yes, dear," she answered. Adrian heard laughter behind the words and felt better.

"Listen," he said, knowing she would like to hear this. "I'm going to be a guest on Pricilla Ward's show Sunday. I'm giving a preview of our new movie and its theme song. I wrote the music."

"I'll make sure to listen."

"I'll put Suzanne on now. Please take care of yourself, Rose. You mean so much to me." He hoped she understood that.

When Suzanne ended the call with the contessa, Adrian knew she felt as concerned as he did. "We'll stay more in touch with her," Suzanne said. "I'll make sure my father keeps close tabs on her and lets us know how she's doing."

23

SUCCEEDING, JUST BARELY

Adrian's interview with Miss Ward was good for his ego. She described him as handsome as any movie star in Hollywood and asked him why he'd come out west when he had a brilliant career in New York. He explained he'd always been intrigued by movie making, and he had grown impressed with the scores written by prominent musicians, many of them with classical backgrounds like himself.

Miss Ward gave her listeners the details of the film's opening on Thanksgiving Day. "Tell me briefly about it," she said to Adrian. He gave a summary of the film's plot without spoiling the ending.

Adrian told her he'd written the music to the song as well as the score to the film. "We found a talented song writer named Jonny Richards, a young graduate from The Emmitt Walker School of Music, to put words to the music, and a new, up and coming singer, Eddie Barnes, to record the vocals. I brought a copy of the title song for you to play," he said. "You and your listeners will be the first to hear it."

Miss Ward leaned into her microphone from her wheelchair. "It's wonderful you're giving young newcomers such opportunities," she said to Adrian. "Let's listen, everybody."

When the recording finished, Miss Ward praised the song, its music, lyrics, and the singer. "I'm sure we'll be hearing more from these young men," she said to her audience. She ended the interview repeating the details of the Thanksgiving showing. Adrian slipped away at the prompting of the show's producer while Miss Ward

158

reported gossip of the day. He left the studio feeling pleased his appearance on this show had given him a recognizable presence in Hollywood.

On premiere night, *Nickle and Gold* received glowing reviews according to the notes left in boxes in the lobby for the theatergoers to give their comments. Given the attendance and reviews, Buddy Saxon, the theater owner, agreed to extend the showing of the film at this theater and to show it at his other ten movie houses throughout California, Arizona, and Nevada.

The successes of the film and the song brought quick recognition and acclaim to the Marcus brothers and their studio. With those came a sense of pride and encouragement among the brothers that they could make a success of their venture. Everyone connected with the studio benefited. Adrian felt proud his suggestions for the movie's title and the title song contributed to the studio's success.

The Monday after Thanksgiving, Adrian was right back at his desk at the Studio preparing the soundtrack for their next movie, *Crossing Jordan,* the film the studio had put aside to concentrate on *Nickel and Gold.* The film, starring Mona and Bradley, focused on their two characters. Mona played Rebecca, who ran away from a small town in Minnesota and made her way to Minneapolis to escape her husband, an abusive fanatical evangelist. Bradley played Philip, the lawyer who represented Rebecca after she killed her husband when he came searching for her. The two characters fell in love. The studio felt confident the movie's tearjerker ending of a priest escorting Rebecca to her execution to the background music of "Crossing Over Jordan" would draw women to the theaters and, with them, their husbands and boyfriends.

Adrian was determined *Crossing Jordan* would be his next triumph. On many nights he left Suzanne alone while he sat with Rodney, Elliot, and Manus, reviewing the film, and taking notes. He went to the studio early in the mornings to complete his selections. He wanted to finish the scoring before Suzanne gave birth to the twins.

He succeeded, just barely. Two days after they finished recording the film's score Suzanne woke him up to take her to the hospital.

She delivered the twins on the afternoon of December 14. The proud parents named the girls Gabriela, after Adrian's mother, and Elinore after Suzanne's. They gave each of them the middle name Rose, after the contessa. When notified, the contessa sent each of the girls two gifts: a silver engraved rattle to use as soon as they were able to hold them and gold engraved crosses on gold chains for each to have in the future. Adrianne brought Suzanne and the twins home a week later. Suzanne had hired Inga, a middle-aged Swedish woman recommended by Joanne, to come help after the birth of the twins. Inga helped with the laundry, bathing the girls, and changing their diapers. She also kept close track of the amount of time visitors spent with Suzanne and the twins. She'd chase them out when she saw Suzanne fading and the girls getting cranky.

Adrian did his best to help, but he, as well as Suzanne, was becoming sleep deprived. The girls were staying in his and Suzanne's bedroom, and his sleep was frequently interrupted. Sometimes he'd get snappy with Suzanne and feel guilty about it. Suzanne would feel hurt. Inga would see them both pouting. "Don't worry," she'd assure them. "Just take a deep breath. Soon life will be better than you could ever imagine." Later, Adrian found that to be true.

Two days before Christmas, Suzanne's father came to stay with his newly expanded family. He brought a gift of two christening gowns preserved by his wife, one worn at the christening of Suzanne's mother, the other worn at the christening of Suzanne's grandmother.

Mr. Reitman and Adrian vied for the attention of the girls. It was lucky there was one for each. Mr. Reitman saw how tired Suzanne and Adrian were. He helped relieve Adrian of his chores so he and Suzanne could take their naps together to refresh themselves simultaneously to take the pressure off their relationship.

Adrian returned to work the first day after the new year. Mr. Reitman had flown back to New York after Christmas, but said he'd be back for the twins' christening in February. Charlotte had arrived for a two week visit after Mr. Reitman left.

Adrian told Charlotte he wished he could stay home for the

remainder of her visit, but Martin had called to say he and his brothers were anxious to get started on another film. Before he left, he peeked into his daughters' cribs and said, "Charlotte and Inga will take loving care of you, my sweets. Be good and let your mommy rest today. Daddy will see you later." When he reached the bedroom door to leave, he heard gurgling sounds. He paused and turned back toward the cribs. He would have sworn they were saying goodbye to him. He smiled as he carried that thought with him on the drive to the studio. He thought of all the sounds Simon would have made as an infant that might have given him such pleasure if he'd only given his son the chance. *How are you, son? Are your aunt and uncle keeping you safe?*

24

BEST SONG CATEGORY

Martin's enthusiasm about starting a new project, yet unknown to Adrian, had Adrian curious. He was tired on his first day back at the studio and found himself having trouble concentrating. He was letting out a full yawn when Martin came to Adrian's office to greet him upon his return.

"How's it going?" Martin said. "You look a little peaked under those eyes."

Adrian sighed and shook his head. "I haven't been getting much sleep. I'd hoped Suzanne's cousin, Charlotte, would be more helpful during her visit, but she's been spending all her time by the pool reading fashion magazines."

Adrian shook his head. "Thank God," he said, "or I should say, thank Joanne, for sending us Inga. She's been a lifesaver. Inga says Charlotte is more needy and demanding than the twins. I've been trying to appease her by helping more with folding laundry, changing diapers, and feedings. It's a relief to get back to work. I'm sure Inga and I will both feel better when Charlotte heads back to New York." He sat up in his chair and rubbed his hands together. "At any rate, it's good to be back."

Martin reached out and handed Adrian a thickly bound bundle of paper. "Maybe this will get your juices flowing."

Adrian looked at the package and back at Martin. "What's this?"

"It's the proposed screenplay for our next film, *The Andersons and the Steins*." It's by a new writer, a twenty-two-year-old by the name of Arthur Goldberg. Manus had seen a play of his at the

162

Federal Theater Project a year ago and was impressed with his writing.

"My brothers and I have been looking for a vehicle ever since Congress created the Selective Service Training Act this past September. You remember the conversation you and I had in my office your first day, how the studio wants to get our citizens thinking about the United States' role in the war? Well, we think the president's having signed that act says he is becoming more proactive, and it has everyone talking. Now that we've finished our other two movies, we think it's the right time for us to consider making a film that speaks to the people's concerns about the possibility of entering the conflict. Manus asked Mr. Goldberg to present us with a manuscript for our consideration. If we all agree, we'll purchase the rights from Mr. Goldberg and hire him to work on the screenplay with Manus."

Adrian remembered discussing the draft registration with Suzanne when Congress passed the act, and the president signed it not long after their arrival in California. It required all men between the ages of twenty-one and thirty-five to register for the draft. She was upset, but there was little they could do about it. Adrian tried to soothe Suzanne's concerns by telling her that the draft was based on a national lottery system which made it unlikely he'd be called. He'd doubted he'd be considered, anyway, having to support two infant children and a wife.

With so many changes in their life to which they needed to adjust and so many things for them to do, Suzanne seemed to have become distracted from this worry. In fact, she hadn't brought it up since their talk. He decided to leave any further discussion alone unless she raised the subject.

Adrian started reading the script to *The Andersons and the Steins* as soon as Martin left his office. A brief synopsis on the first page gave the essence of the story. It centered on two families, one Christian, the other Jewish. Each family had a son in his early twenties. The two young men were friends at college. The father of each son served in WWI. The fathers had strongly opposite feelings about the possibility of their sons serving in a second war. The parents in the Catholic family were strong neutralists. The Jewish parents were interventionists. Each son took the opposite side of his family.

Adrian was well into the story when Sophie called saying Martin wanted to see him in his office. When he arrived, Sophie announced him and told him to enter. The three Marcus brothers stood before him with champagne glasses held high. "Congratulations," they shouted in unison.

Adrian held up his palms and shrugged. "What's this about?"

"Apparently, you haven't been listening to your radio," Martin said. "The Academy has announced its nominations for their 1940 awards. They've named 'Nickel and Gold' in the best song category."

Martin handed Adrian a glass of champagne, and the three brothers toasted Adrian for his accomplishment on behalf of the studio. Martin went to his desk and pulled out a bottle of champagne. He gave it to Adrian and said, "Take this for you to celebrate with Suzanne." To his brothers he said, "Let's all get together at Mom and Dad's tonight to share this success with them."

Adrian thanked the three and went to his office to call Suzanne and share the news. "That's wonderful," she said. "I can't wait to see you. I've got another surprise. Charlotte is on her way back to New York. Hollywood was too dull for her."

Adrian laughed. "She'll be sorry not to be in on the excitement." Before heading home, he wrote a note to Simon about his song receiving an Academy Award nomination. He wrote an apology for not being in Poland to celebrate his son's achievements over the years. He put the note in the breast pocket of his suit coat to later place it in the box of other notes in his home study intended for Simon.

Suzanne prepared a special dinner that evening to celebrate. Later, after dinner, while Suzanne and Inga bathed the girls and got them ready for bed, Adrian sat on the living room sofa to continue reading Arthur Goldberg's manuscript. He was still reading the story when Suzanne came to him and said the twins were ready for him to say good night. He went to their cribs and gave them each a quick kiss and went back to the living room to continue reading the proposed work.

Suzanne joined him on the sofa. "You practically ignored the girls. What's got you so distracted?"

Adrian held up the manuscript. The title on the cover wouldn't give the story or theme away. He didn't want the subject matter to raise Suzanne's concerns.

"Martin asked me to read this. It's a script written by a young author. The brothers are considering filming it. It's surprisingly good. The young man is a talented writer. I can already hear sounds in my head giving me ideas for the score."

Adrian stayed up late reading the manuscript. The next morning, he told Martin he thought it would make a movie that would appeal to a wide audience.

The following week the studio team agreed this was a film they wanted to make. They set a timetable to have it completed by the end of March, just three months away. Adrian met with Manus, Rodney, and Elliot to discuss their ideas about the film's themes. The script had scenes of high tension, drama, and turbulence between each son and his parents as well as conflicting reactions between the young men and their sweethearts over the prospect of their being drafted. Manus and Rodney wanted a score that would reflect these conflicts. They left it to Adrian to come back with ideas while they concentrated on the actors and the settings.

On the first Sunday of February 1941, Father Joseph McAvoy christened Gabriela Rose and Elinore Rose at the Blessed Church of the Holy Sacrament. Each was wearing one of the christening gowns their grandfather had brought. Claire and Larry were there as godparents. Mr. Reitman beamed as he stood by listening to the priest perform the rituals. Suzanne and Adrian had invited everyone from the studio back to their house for a celebration. Jonny and Eddie were there touch with these young men, especially Jonny. Eddie had recently married and was more preoccupied. Later that evening, Adrian sat by the pool thinking about Simon. Had he had a christening? He was sure he would have. His aunt and uncle were religious and had promised to raise him Catholic. He wrote a note to

Simon. *Your sisters had their christening today. I wish you could have been there. I'm sorry I wasn't there for yours. I hope you'll forgive me. I'll make sure your sisters know you're their brother.* He went downstairs to his study and placed the note in the box he kept for Simon. The next day he returned to the studio to work on the score for *The Andersons and the Steins*.

Adrian had listened to works by Tchaikovsky, Puccini, Beethoven, and Debussy before completing his music. He developed a strong theme that he could use throughout the film at different intensities, depending upon the strength and need of each scene. He selected from more recent romantic songs, including "Body and Soul," "Embraceable You," and "I'll Never Smile Again," for possible inclusion in the film during its tender moments. He attended the daily rushes and made his final choices after going over them with Rodney and Elliot. They had pieced the score together by the time they completed the shooting of the film. Now all they needed to do was to match the soundtrack with the film. There was little doubt the studio would complete the film and have it ready for distribution by Easter. Max was making the rounds looking for theater owners who wanted a new film for that season.

25

FUTURE GOALS

On February 27, 1941, The Motion Picture Academy held its 12th Academy Awards ceremony honoring film achievements in 1940. The Studio bought a table for the three brothers, their wives, Adrian, and Suzanne, the senior Mr. and Mr. Marcus, Jonny and his guest, and Eddie and his wife. The winning song was "Over the Rainbow." The Marcus party applauded gracefully, though they were disappointed. However, Adrian now had an Oscar nomination under his belt. *That's not bad for my first attempt*, he thought. He felt good for Jonny and Eddie who, as young beginners, each also had an early success.

When the ladies excused themselves to go to the powder room and the others left, Martin turned to his brothers and Adrian. "We've reached far beyond where we expected to be by now," *Nickel and Gold* was our make or break moment, the chance to show our father we could succeed in the movie business, to make him proud of us.

He focused on Adrian. "Your talent and suggestions helped us do that. The Academy nominating your song has brought additional recognition to our film and, thereby, to our studio. You've become an integral part of our success, and we're grateful."

Adrian placed a hand on his chest. "Thank you, gentlemen, for giving me the opportunity. I can't think of a nicer family I'd like to work with."

"To Adrian," Martin said. "Here to a long and fruitful collaboration." They all drank to the toast.

Warmth radiated through Adrian's body. He had worked hard for

167

these men and deserved their praise. It felt good working for people who were able to express their appreciation so generously.

Later that evening, while Suzanne was preparing for bed, Adrian sat by the pool thinking about the past six months. He'd become accepted as part of the Los Angeles professional scene as a respected musician. He lunched with other studio music directors and exchanged ideas with them about film scoring. He and Suzanne had been invited to parties given by prominent California classical musicians, some who either knew him from their shared days at the Sanfried school or his reputation as concertmaster of The Eleventh State Symphony Orchestra.

Adrian had hoped to achieve two goals during his first year in Hollywood. One was to be asked to perform at the Los Angeles Odeum Center in its next season. The other was to finish composing a concerto for the violin. He'd started working on the concerto while still in New York and had planned to complete it by the end of his first year in Hollywood. It looked as if his busy schedule at the studio would interfere with meeting either of these goals this year.

Composing a concerto was important to him. Music was his life and for what he' been trained. His education had given him an understanding of music theory, including harmony, melody, rhythm, and counterpoint. His creative emotions were so urgent they cried out for them to be expressed. It was imperative for a man of his education and talent to do so, an obligation to God for giving him this gift. He had composed two sonatas and a short chamber music piece, but these were not important enough to satisfy his need to showcase his skills. His work for Three M Studio satisfied some of his expressive desires. It wasn't enough, however. He need something apart from his works for the Studio, something that was his own. He was intuitive enough to perceive it was the guilt and shame he felt over the misdeeds in his earlier years that contributed to this. Creating something of his own beyond which he was paid to create, something that would last beyond his lifetime, a gift to the world by which people would remember him with regard and respect and whereby he'd redeem himself from his past mistakes was what was behind this obsession. These thoughts hovered in the back of his mind and came forth whenever there was a release of tension from the strains of daily life.

In early March 1941, Congress passed the Lend-Lease Act authorizing the president to provide Great Britain with ships, planes, weapons, and ammunitions needed to fight Nazi Germany. Soon after, *The Andersons and the Steins* was ready for release.

The Gallup poll showed 67 percent of the country agreed with the president's action. The country was coming closer to war. So far, Adrian had been lucky the armed forces hadn't picked his draft number, although he felt it was probable that, as a married man with children, he'd be deferred. He was now thirty-five. Suzanne still hadn't expressed any concern. He thought it best to continue to leave this subject undiscussed. He didn't want to take away her happiness over their new family life.

In mid-March, the Studio released *The Andersons and the Steins*. The Studio knew it had produced an important motion picture by ticket sales and the response of critics. There was early talk about Academy recognition in all aspects of its filming.

26
QUIET PLANS

Adrian was feeling tired but satisfied. He'd worked on and completed the scores for three films in seven months. Fortunately, he and Suzanne were getting more sleep, thanks to Inga, who suggested to Suzanne that the girls take shorter naps during the day, and she or their parents put them to bed later. This resulted in fewer disruptions for him and Suzanne during the night.

Suzanne was more rested and enjoyed discussing the girls' progress with him when he arrived home from work. Her enthusiasm in reporting their milestones brought them closer together.

The girls were rolling over in their cribs and sitting with little support. Adrian brought home balls and rolling toys they could push along the floor. He loved to sit with them on the living carpet and take turns holding hands and bouncing their upper bodies to music. In spite of their occasional tantrums, Adrian found them a delight to be around.

Adrian held Simon dearer in his heart now that he had these two precious girls. He wished he had read to and played with his son and had paid him the attention he had with his daughters. Sometimes, alone at night, when he couldn't sleep, he sat by the pool and thought about where Simon might be and what his life was like. He renewed his vow to never give up his quest to find his son and to make things right between them. He wrote notes to Simon about his sisters and about things in his and Suzanne's life he thought would interest him. He added them to the box in his study. On March 19,

Simon's sixteenth birthday, Adrian placed another birthday card in the growing pile.

On Easter Sunday, April 13, 1941, Adrian called the contessa to wish her a happy Easter. He'd made it a point to call her every Sunday at five. Her illness had kept her home, and her outside activities with the symphony and her other institutions and charities had virtually stopped.

"Thank you for the Easter bouquet, Adrian," the contessa started. "Let me thank Suzanne too."

Adrian handed Suzanne the phone. The contessa thanked Suzanne for the flowers. "You're welcome. I hope you didn't spend Easter alone," Suzanne responded.

"Your father stopped by, but other than that I wasn't much up for company."

"I'm so sorry. I'm trying to persuade Adrian to bring the girls to New York for Thanksgiving to spend a week visiting our family and friends, you among them, of course. Please stay well for our visit."

"I'll look forward to it, dear. My love to you all."

"Our love to you, as well," Suzanne said. She handed the phone back to Adrian.

Adrian put the phone near the twins' mouths so the contessa might hear them wish her a happy Easter, as he had rehearsed with them to do. The contessa laughed at their voices and stopped to drink water.

"They sound adorable, Adrian. I can't wait to see them at Thanksgiving," the contessa said, coughing and breathing heavily. It worried Adrian to hear her sound this ill.

Adrian, Suzanne, and the girls flew to New York the week before Thanksgiving, 1941. By then, Adrian had scored two more films, comedies titled *Two by Two* and *Three by Three.* They followed the lives of two young recently married couples, each of whom was the offspring of highly emotional Italian families and whose lives intertwined. *Two by Two* became a summer blockbuster. The posters showed each couple standing side by side in their wedding regalia. The posters for *Three by Three,* when it was scheduled for release around Christmas, would again show the young couples standing side by side, but this time, with their newborn babies. Both films dealt with the stresses placed upon the young couples and their families with the prospects of the United States entering the war and the possibilities of the young men being drafted.

Adrian and Suzanne planned to stay in New York through the Monday after the holiday. Mr. Reitman and Claire greeted them at the airport. Each of them immediately grabbed one of the twins.

They had quiet plans for their visit. Adrian looked forward to a low-key schedule. Suzanne said she hadn't been feeling well the week prior to the flight. She attributed it to the stress of getting ready for the trip while tending to eleven-month-old twins. Plus, the flight was difficult. The girls hadn't taken well to their parents' confining them on the plane, and they were cranky. Both Suzanne and Adrian struggled to maintain a good relationship with the crew and passengers by trying to contain the girls.

They visited the contessa on the Friday after their arrival and were surprised to find Eleanor Roosevelt had stopped by also.

"It's an honor to meet you," Adrian said to Mrs. Roosevelt. He was set back being in the presence of someone he admired so, but he managed to keep his surprise hidden.

Mrs. Roosevelt offered her hand and gave Adrian a wide smile. "The pleasure is mine. Rose has spoken of you both often. I feel I know you well." Her face turned serious. "I'm sorry I haven't been of any assistance in connecting you with your son." She shook her head. "There are so many refugees who have escaped the Nazis but can't find their way here. I promise to continue to lobby my husband for greater immigration reform to accomplish this." Adrian hoped Simon was one of those people who had escaped the clutches of the Nazis and would find his way to him.

Adrian and Suzanne showed off the twins, and the contessa and Mrs. Roosevelt fussed over them. Paul had laid out a wide blanket on the floor with toys, picture books, and a basket of stuffed animals. The girls played, showing each other what they were looking at in their books. Periodically, they interrupted their parents to show them a page in one of the books or an animal from the basket. Suzanne smiled apologetically for the interruptions. Their antics brought chuckles to the contessa and Mrs. Roosevelt. Mrs. Roosevelt said she had raised six children and appreciated what Adrian and Suzanne were going through. "Enjoy them while they're young," she said.

After a while, Mrs. Roosevelt excused herself. "I've got a committee meeting to attend." She kissed the contessa on the cheek and said, "Take care of yourself, dear." Adrian walked Mrs. Roosevelt to the door. He shook her extended hand.

"I cannot tell you how much I've enjoyed meeting you and your family. I'll keep trying to persuade Congress and the president to loosen our immigration laws," she said before Paul took her down to the lobby.

Adrian and Suzanne spent another hour with the contessa. She didn't talk about her health, but Adrian could see she wasn't well. Her face was thin and pale, and her clothes were ill-fitting. While Suzanne took the girls to use the potty, the contessa spoke with Adrian.

"My days are numbered," she said. "I've had a good life and can't complain." She laid a hand against her chest and took a shallow breath. "I want you to know I've made provisions for you in my will."

"Don't talk that way, Rose. You have years ahead of you," Adrian said, but he realized his words only denied that with which she was trying to come to terms. After they left the apartment and reached the lobby, Adrian put Suzanne and the girls in a cab and went back upstairs. He sat with the contessa and told her he felt bad for not allowing her to speak freely about her health.

She took his hands in hers. "Don't worry about me. You have a fine new family to take care of. It gives me much pleasure to see you so happy." Before he left, Adrian spoke with Paul, asking him to keep him informed. He gave Paul the phone numbers where he could reach him in California. Adrian pulled himself together enough to not let his worries about the contessa be a drag at Thanksgiving dinner with Suzanne's family.

The highlight of their visit was the dinner party at Claire and

Larry's. All their New York friends were there. They oohed and aahed over pictures of the twins and asked question after question about Adrian's work. Claire pulled out sheet music to "Nickel and Gold." She began playing it on the piano. "Adrian, and the rest of you, sing along with me," she insisted.

When they sat for dinner, Adrian looked around the table. He felt a warm glow. He and Suzanne were back among their dearest friends. It seemed as though little time had passed. They'd picked up right where they had left off before he and Suzanne had moved. He remembered how worried he'd been they'd reject him once they found out about his past and thought how wrong he'd been.

During dinner Adrian felt Suzanne's hand on his. "I feel sick. I need to get to the bathroom."

He got up to help her. The sudden disruption frightened him. He held on to her waist to hold her steady. Claire came around the table to take her.

Adrian saw the worried looks on the faces of their friends. "She didn't feel well the week before we left California, but she's seemed fine since we've been here," he said to them.

Claire came back and asked Dottie to stay with Suzanne for a while. Adrian kept his eyes on the direction Suzanne had gone.

His friends tried to distract him, but he couldn't listen. He debated with himself whether he should go to Suzanne.

Soon Dottie and Suzanne returned. "Adrian, you'd better make sure Suzanne gets to her obstetrician when you get back to California," Dottie said. "I think she may be pregnant."

Adrian looked at Suzanne. He took her hand. With a dazed look, he asked, "Could it be true?"

She shrugged her shoulders.

Adrian didn't know how to respond. This was too big of a surprise if it were true. They were just beginning to feel some relief with the twins getting older. They hadn't planned to have another child until the girls were at least three.

The men laughed at Dottie's advice to Adrian, and Larry stood and made a toast. "To Suzy and Ace, may they be fruitful and multiply…again."

On the plane home, the girls were no less difficult to manage than on the flight to New York. While attempting to keep the girls still during dinner, Suzanne said, "I don't think we can plan on another trip to New York until the girls are older."

Adrian shook his head and breathed out a soft sigh. "If there is another child on the way, New York will have to come to us."

Adrian was back at the studio on Tuesday morning, December 2, 1941, after his and Suzanne's visit to New York. Martin called a meeting of the brothers, Rodney, Elliot, and Adrian to discuss the pre-release publicity for *Three by Three* and to talk about other films in the pipeline. Manus summarized scripts he'd been considering, and the others expressed their thoughts. Everything seemed to run on course. But then, on Sunday, December 7, everyone woke up to the news that the Japanese had attacked Pearl Harbor. The next day the United States declared war on Japan. Four days later, Nazi Germany declared war on the United States. Hours after, the United States Congress and Senate unanimously declared war on Germany. Everything was about to change.

27

ENTRY INTO WAR

Entry into the war brought home to Suzanne Adrian's possible eligibility for the draft. The night the United States declared war, after they had settled into bed, Suzanne leaned into Adrian and said, "I'm afraid you may be enlisted."

Adrian heard the unease in her voice. He tried to reassure her. "Don't worry. They're not drafting married men right now. The Selective Services Act has raised the upper draft registration age from thirty-five to sixty-four. There's less chance of their calling me."

She laid her head on his chest. "But they'll be calling more men now," she said, softly.

Her point is well taken, Adrian thought. He too was worried about changing policy that might result in his being drafted and the effect this would have on his family, if there were to be revisions. Right now, however, enough men were volunteering for the draft to meet the need.

Adrian had no idea how the war was affecting Simon. After the attack on Pearl Harbor and America's declaration of war with Japan, the Pacific conflict had become a greater concern than the war in Europe. American soldiers were fighting Germany because Germany had allied itself with the Japanese.

Newspapers and newsreels focused on the battles of the war. There was little mention of atrocities toward Jews on the front pages. Articles concentrated on refugee rescue efforts. Newspapers placed any mention of atrocities associated with Jewish people on pages inside the papers where they'd likely be missed. Nevertheless, Adrian found his thoughts more distracted by his worries about Simon. He feared the Nazis would, if they hadn't already, discover his son's Jewish heritage. He remembered how much prejudice there was against the Jews when he lived in Poland. He continued to hope his uncle's German heritage was protecting Simon and his family.

Adrian thought about his first meeting with Martin and of Martin's expressed passion for making films that would get people interested in supporting America's entry into the war in Europe. He wondered whether the studio had any additional films in the pipeline that would speak to America's role in it. *The Andersons and the Steins* and the lighter *Two by Two* and *Three by Three* were a start, but in his mind they were not enough.

His answer came when Martin called another meeting on Friday, December 12.

"My brothers and I have come to a decision, given the new world circumstances."

The others looked at him with rapt attention.

"We have two films we want to make to influence Americans to come to grips with the war, and to serve as propaganda to boost patriotism. One is to add a third film to the *Two by Two* series showing the families' reactions to their young men's enlistment into the Armed Services. The second is a follow-up to *The Andersons and the Steins* showing how each son and his family responds to the country's entry into the war and to the reality of the army drafting the two sons.

"I've talked with Arthur Goldberg about writing the script for the latter, and he's excited about it," Martin said to his crew.

"I like the idea," Rodney said. Elliot agreed.

"In the meantime, Max will continue working on the publicity for *Three by Three*, due out in thirteen days," Martin said.

Adrian felt excited. The prospect of making films that centered on the war lessened Adrian's restlessness about where he was heading with the studio. He felt stimulated by the challenge of scoring the two films.

On December 18, Suzanne called Adrian at work. "My obstetrician has confirmed the news. I'm two months pregnant and due in mid-July."

"How many?" he asked.

Suzanne chuckled. "Only one."

Adrian was relieved Suzanne's condition wasn't related to an illness. He had let the contessa's condition bring all sorts of exaggerated thoughts into his mind about Suzanne's symptoms, though he knew them to be unlikely. *But having another child? This will mean going through all the struggles of having another baby in the house.* The thought wasn't pleasant, but he tried to be cheerful.

"I'll bring home ice cream and pickles, and we'll have our own little party in bed tonight. Do the twins know yet?"

Suzanne laughed. "I don't think they're quite ready to understand."

"What about Claire? You know she's waiting to hear." He thought how excited Claire would be. This bit of normalcy in sharing such news with friends brought cheer to Adrian.

"I will have to tell her, but I'll swear her to secrecy."

"Good luck with that. When can I tell Martin?"

"Let's not jinx it. Let's wait a month."

"It'll be hard, but OK. You're the boss, but do you still want pickles and ice cream tonight?"

"How about just the ice cream. I bought two jars of pickles after I left the doctor's office." Suzanne then aroused his interest by saying, "I have a surprise for you when you get home."

"What's that?"

"You'll see. I don't want to spoil it for you."

As soon as Adrian got off the phone, Sophie called to tell him Martin wanted to see him, Manus, Rodney, and Elliot at two o'clock.

"I've arranged something unique for you gentlemen that will get you prepared for the next two films we discussed," Martin said when they met. "I've cleared it with the Governor, who's cleared it with the local Army Draft Center in Los Angeles. You're going to volunteer for the draft. Soon after, you'll spend a day at the Army's Desert Training Center, where you'll get an opportunity to experience what new inductees go through. The draft center has agreed to do it as part of the propaganda effort for the war."

Martin paused for dramatic effect, then saluted, smiled broadly, and said, "The army is going to recruit you. Good luck."

The four other men stared at each other opened mouthed.

Manus was the first to speak. "What the hell are you talking about, Martin?"

Martin thrust his fist at them and said, "If we're going to make war movies, we've got to know what war is like."

Manus spoke up. "Don't you think you should have cleared this with us, dear brother? This could get us drafted before our numbers actually get selected, if, in fact, they ever do."

"Don't worry. You'll all have false identities. The recruitment officers and the basic training officers at the camp will know we're making a film and will be cooperating."

Rodney shook his head. "I don't like this at all. Are you sure this is legal? Why can't we just visit and observe or get army uniforms and act like we're there officially?"

"Look, gentlemen. I've gotten permission, verbal and in writing. Don't ask me any more questions. If it is illegal, those who granted permission will be at fault, not us. You'll fit in just like the hundreds of others at these centers. Disguise yourselves if you want. Wear eyeglasses, part your hair on the wrong side, don't shave the week before. This needs to be authentic. If you're going to produce and direct the films, you need to experience firsthand what our men go through."

"That's bullshit," Rodney said. "Do you think Nevin Brooks took dancing lessons to direct *Star Dancing*? Did Timothy Lewis have to enter a mental institution before directing *Self Loathing*?"

"Why does Adrian need to be included?" Manus asked.

Adrian was glad someone spoke up for him. He was both taken aback by the proposal and intrigued. Adrian agreed with the others, however. It felt risky. Suzanne had expressed her worry about his being drafted, and he'd assured her it was unlikely. Now that they were about to have another baby, she'd never let him go along with such an idea. Just the thought of him being near draft and training centers would place a strain on her and on the pregnancy. He knew she'd immediately reject the idea.

"I thought it might help Adrian get the feel of what these experiences are like to give him ideas for the soundtrack," Martin said. "Look, if you're all that concerned, suppose I join you in this? I figure it will take two or three days out of our lives. Then maybe we can gain access to filming army life scenes just being ourselves, ordinary citizens. Think it over tonight. Let's meet again tomorrow morning."

The room quieted. Adrian looked around. Everyone seemed to be in deep thought. The room emptied into Sophie's office.

"Why so glum, fellas?" Sophie said. "You all look like you've just gotten your draft notices."

That evening, both Suzanne and Adrian had surprises. Hers was showing him how the twins were starting to take their first steps. He was in awe. He and Suzanne each took one of the girls to help them walk around the living room."

Later, in bed, Suzanne told Adrian about her call to Claire and of Claire's excitement and her promise to keep their secret. He found the courage to tell her about Martin's idea. He braced himself for her vehement objection.

After a moment passed, she said, "It sounds very clever. Can he really conceal your identities?"

Adrian nodded. "He says he can."

"Promise me it will only be for two nonconsecutive days, and I'll go along with it."

"I've got to say, Suzanne, I am surprised you're accepting this." Adrian was relieved she was taking this so easily.

She bit into a pickle. "Me, too."

The next morning in Martin's office, the consensus was to accept

Martin's idea, provided he participated. Martin said he'd set it in motion right after the new year.

28

THE PHYSICAL

Three by Three was the holiday success the Studio had hoped for. Arthur Goldberg started on writing the sequel to *The Andersons and the Steins* right after Christmas.

The day for their draft physical was Wednesday, January 13. Martin, Manus, Rodney, Elliot, and Adrian arrived at the Los Angeles Draft Center at 9 a.m. Adrian saw men of all ages forming a double line around the block. Some were older than he had expected, but most looked like college-age boys.

"I guess this is the army's first test, seeing how long we can stand in line," Rodney said.

"With a line this long outside, I'm sure our patience will be tested by similar lines inside," Martin responded.

Manus gave Martin a look. "Don't complain, my brother. We're on army time now. You're the one who got us into this."

It took an hour and fifteen minutes before they entered the double front doors. Once inside, they reached a counter and were handed drawstring cloth bags to hang around their necks to hold their personal items. Next, a recruiter sent them to an area where they were told to strip down to their shorts. When undressed, they were handed cups and sent to an area to leave urine samples. Next, another soldier in uniform divided them into groups and sent them to doctors for physicals. The Studio men were placed in a group together. The doctor told the men to drop their shorts to receive hernia exams.

The rest of the physical proceeded with less personal exposure.

Other army physicians inspected their eyes, ears, and mouths, took chest x-rays, and drew blood for testing. They met individually with psychiatrists who asked them brief questions, including their relationships with members of the opposite sex. Adrian felt he was in good enough shape to pass this physical, but in the back of his mind he wished the doctors had found something wrong with him, something minor, that would make him ineligible for service.

Afterward, they sat in a nearby coffee shop waiting for Rudy to take them back to the studio.

"Let's talk about what we saw today," Martin said, "and how it can help us make our films."

Great, Adrian thought. He wanted to hear what the others observed and learned that would make their films more relevant.

"The country's scared and tired," Martin started. "People remember the ravages of the Great War, and the Depression is still on their minds. Now the government is asking them to face another war, to give up their way of living, to postpone their dreams and aspirations for more years of hardship, and to send their children off to war."

Adrian leaned forward and listened closely to Martin.

Martin slapped his fingers against the rim of the table. "Our films must give people a feeling that we're fighting for what we believe in, that we're all in this together, and give them hope we'll get through this and be better for it." He waved his hand in the air. "You saw the line we stood in to get into the building. Men of all ages are standing in line in front of draft and induction centers, some because they've been forced to, others who've volunteered for different reasons. They have loved ones at home worrying about them, what could happen to them, how their lives will be affected. This is happening across America." Martin stopped to look at the other men.

Manus smiled, reached over, and gently placed his hand on his brother's forearm. "Martin," he said. "I love your enthusiasm. And everything you say is true. But it's been a long day, and I, for one, am tired. What do you say we go home, take warm showers, and enjoy our families? Rodney and I can get together tomorrow to talk about how we can use today's experiences in our films. You're welcome to join us."

Putting aside Martin's almost pompous tone, Adrian knew he had excellent points, but because of his own experience today he couldn't stop thinking about Simon. He quickly tallied the boy's age in his head. Simon was just shy of seventeen, now a young man. He could well be eligible for military service in Poland, if, in fact, he was still there. *Is he in a draft line somewhere stripping for a physical exam?* Adrian thought of his own discomfort under the doctor's eyes and imagined his son's body exposed and vulnerable. He tried not to let himself think further, but the images came anyway: Simon the soldier, in active duty, on a battlefield. *Was Simon's life hanging in the balance? Was the son he'd never known still alive?*

Martin pushed his chair back. The noise of it scraping on the floor pulled Adrian out of his thoughts. "I want you to remember the looks on the faces of those in line with us," he said. "Think about what they were feeling. Some were scared. Others were looking forward to the fight, even knowing what it might cost." Martin's eyes moved from one face to another around the table. "Think about their families when they realize they might lose their sons, their husbands, their fathers." He looked at Manus and added, "and their brothers."

Before Manus could respond, Rodney jumped in. "We've got a pretty good idea about our characters from the previous films and how they'll react." Adrian could hear him biting back irritation. He didn't much like Martin's lecture.

"Yes and no," Manus jumped in. "What Martin means is, we can give our characters more depth. Take the *Two* by *Two* series. The next one could be more than a light comedy. The audience needs to see our characters, especially our young soldiers, as real people with thoughts and feelings of their own. We need to show them as individuals they can relate to."

Rudy walked in the door to take them back to the studio.

Adrian liked the idea the studio's films could make a real difference to their audiences and make a statement about the war. He thought ahead quickly. He needed to plan for his absence with Suzanne. "When do we get to the next step, the introduction to basic training?" he asked Martin.

"I'm working on that," Martin said. "I'll let you know soon. Before we finish here, one more thing. We need to remind our audiences why we're fighting this war at the very start of both films." He turned to Manus. "We can use newsreels. Suppose at the very beginning of the third *Two by Two* film, we have the young couples in a movie theater viewing a news reel showing who our enemies are in this war and why we're fighting. We can show their parents watching a similar newsreel in another theater. The same idea may influence the reluctant young man in our *The Andersons and the Steins* sequel."

When they got back to the Studio, Adrian pulled Martin aside and told him about Suzanne's pregnancy.

"It's important I know in advance when the visit to the induction center is scheduled."

"Congratulations." Martin said, holding out his hand to shake Adrian's. "I'll get back to you soon."

Adrian asked Martin not to tell anyone about the pregnancy. Suzanne wanted to wait another month. Martin slapped him on the back and said he understood.

Two days later, Martin notified the team that the induction center scheduled them to appear Monday morning, February 2, into the morning of February 3.

"February second is your birthday," Suzanne said disappointedly. They were sitting at the dinner table watching the twins struggling to eat with spoons. Adrian and Suzanne sat with additional spoons to get food into them.

"You weren't planning a surprise party for me, were you?"

"No, I'm not up to that, but I thought you might like to go out to dinner. I asked Inga to keep the evening free."

"I'll tell you what. Ask her for the following Saturday evening, and you can take me to the Chrysanthemum Room."

"I'll check with her tomorrow. She should be available."

"Thanks for understanding," Adrian said. "It's an overnight at the army base. We'll take the bus up in the morning with the new recruits, sleep there, and come home the next day. We just want to get a taste of a recruit's first day."

"You'd better get in a little better shape before then. I hear it's rough. I don't want you coming home with anything broken."

Adrian lifted his hand to his chest. "The only thing that will be broken will be my heart from spending a night away from you."

Suzanne swatted him with the back of her hand. "You've been hanging around movie people too long. That sounds like a corny line from a B movie."

"Really? I made it up myself. I thought it was rather good."

Suzanne reached over and dumped a spoon full of Elinor's dinner on his head.

29

EVERY PROFANITY POSSIBLE

Early on the morning of February 2, the Studio guys hopped on a bus with fifty-six new recruits and traveled to the Army Desert Training Center. Ten other buses pulled up behind them when they arrived. Drill sergeants greeted each bus. By the time everyone disembarked and lined up in groups, two hours had passed. The drill sergeants led the recruits into a building for their medical exams. Army doctors told the men to strip to their skin. The physicians left no orifice untouched. The Studio men observed, but didn't receive, the series of shots given to authentic recruits, nor did they have their fingerprints taken. They posed, however, for ID cards that, by arrangement, the army would allow them to take home. The induction center would be sending fingerprints and IDs for healthy recruits to Washington, D.C., where they would be filed in the Office of the Adjunct General.

Next, an army barber closely shaved the men's heads. The men from the Three M Studio laughed hard when they saw each other's scalps. They rubbed the stubble on their heads and shook their fists at Martin, but they'd made a pact to take every aspect of the experience seriously, except for the fingerprinting and inoculations.

Wait until Suzanne sees me, Adrian thought. He hadn't prepared her for this. She'll be upset. She loved his healthy head of blond hair. She had said she wished it were hers, and she'd hoped their children would inherit this characteristic. He thought about how she had told him how sexy he looked when his hair bounced with the music when he performed at concerts. He wondered how long it would take for his hair to grow back.

187

Soon, another soldier led the new inductees into a large room with rows of desks. There they were given an exam to assess their skills and determine their assignments. A session followed in which interviewers asked each inductee what assignment he'd prefer and made note of it. Then, a fresh-faced young soldier escorted them for more paperwork for payroll and other business things. Afterward, he took them to get fitted for their uniforms.

At one o'clock another soldier walked them to a large hall for lunch. They were hungry. Cafeteria staff served the men a meal that was tasteless but heartily eaten.

The next stop was to their assigned barracks. There, their drill sergeant greeted them. The Studio men shared the barracks with fifty-four others. There were thirty bunk beds, fifteen on each side of the barracks separated by a wide aisle. Next to each set of beds was a place for storage. Each bed had two sheets, two blankets and a pillow on top of a thin, but firm, mattress.

The drill sergeant had selected an earlier inductee to show the new recruits how to make their beds for inspection every morning. He then directed the men to prepare their beds. The sergeant ripped apart any bed he determined wasn't made according to army specifications. When every recruit had complied to his satisfaction, the drill sergeant showed the new recruits the barracks shower and bathroom areas. He told them they had no more than three minutes each night to use the bathroom and shower before lights out at nine sharp.

As a young man living in close quarters among the students at The Krakow School of Music, and later at The Sanfried School of Music in New York, Adrian had been used to living like this. However, he'd now become accustomed to greater comforts. Were the army to induct him, a life like this would be a strain.

The drill sergeant led his barracks to dinner at six o'clock. Afterward they had time to wander around the base. This gave the Studio men time to and talk with real inductees.

"Today was a hell of a way to celebrate my birthday," Adrian said to Elliot at 8:30, when the men were preparing for bed.

"Today's your birthday, huh?" Elliot turned to the others and called out loudly. "Hey men. Today is this man's birthday. Let's give him a real party."

Before Adrian knew what was happening, the entire barracks surrounded him. Four recruits lifted him into the air and took him to the showers. Elliot turned on a shower head. The men holding Adrian let him down and pushed him under. Adrian stood dripping wet and shivering in his clothes, while the others sang "Happy Birthday," riotously clapping and waving their arms and fists. Their raucous singing echoed off the shower walls and made Adrian's head spin.

The men headed for their beds, patting Adrian on the back as they went. He knew he had to accept the hazing as an act of friendship.

Adrian shook his fist at Elliot. "Thanks, buddy. I'll get you for that." At the same time, he thought to tell Manus what the men had done to him might make a great scene in one of the two films they'd be making.

While lying in his upper bunk, Adrian reviewed the day. He thought about the instant camaraderie that had developed among men who didn't know one another, who wouldn't ordinarily have met and shared a day. *Part of that camaraderie,* he thought, *is the result of a common sense of anxiety about the unknowns they were about to face and the need for fellowship with which to share that unease.*

Adrian had heard a new inductee confide to another his worry he wouldn't pass muster, that he wouldn't be able to keep up with his peers and they'd ridicule him. Another was already writing a letter to his girl saying how much he missed her. There were those who he assumed were frightened they might be injured or killed, and there were those he judged to be strong and confident and couldn't wait to prove themselves.

The recalling of these expressions caused Adrian to think more about what he'd heard and observed and how they might influence his scoring of the next films. *A very few won't be able to stand the rigors of boot camp, but the army will train those who are to look out for each other, no matter what they were dealing with privately.*

Despite the tensions that may result among the recruits because of their different backgrounds, the army will build their spirits and draw them together by a common purpose, fighting the enemy for a higher goal. These new recruits are going to learn what it means to be a unit and to cover each other's backs. The army will train them to come together like a fine-tuned orchestra playing a symphony on a concert stage. A range of music will be needed to help audiences identify with human emotions and the realities of war.

Adrian listened to the sounds around him: the snoring of those who fell asleep quickly, the tossing and turning of those trying to adjust to their new beds, the sounds of footsteps and of toilets flushing. He lay on his back, his hands behind his head, until he was tired enough to roll over and fall asleep.

The next morning, their drill sergeant woke them at five shouting, "Get up!" He used every profanity possible to wake them and get them prepared for the day. He ordered them to be dressed in their uniforms and standing by their perfectly made beds for inspection in thirty minutes.

Rudy was there at nine to drive the men back to the Studio. When Rudy saw them in uniforms and with their heads shaved, he bent over and slapped his knees laughing. On the way, they stopped at a roadside restaurant for breakfast and told Rudy what a day in the army was like. The brothers, Rodney, and Elliot talked about what staging and props they'd need for filming. They discussed what they'd need to film basic training scenes and actual war settings. Martin said he'd try to obtain government cooperation to get films for background use.

When the bill arrived, they realized they hadn't brought any money with them. The owner tore it up saying breakfast was on the house. His son had left for his first day in the army the day before. Breakfast was in his son's honor.

Adrian took note of the name of the restaurant, and once home he sent the owner a letter thanking him for his kindness and wishing his son well. He enclosed money to cover their bill, and extra for his son. He signed the letter, "your five broke soldiers." Doing little things like this helped him feel closer to Simon. He hoped someone, somewhere, would return similar acts of kindness to his son.

Suzanne was stunned to see Adrian's haircut and to see him in uniform. She stared at his head. "I'm never letting the studio take you on another trip without me. Get out of that uniform and put on civilian clothes. It makes me nervous to see you like that."

When he came back in his own clothes, Adrian said, "It was fun play-acting, Suzanne, but I wouldn't want to do that for real. It was a relief knowing Rudy would be there to pick us up this morning."

At dinner he told her about his experience.

"Are you sure you didn't leave anything behind for them to send to the Adjunct General?" she said.

"All I have to remember the day is my ID card in my wallet."

"Go get it."

He knew better than to argue.

When he came back and handed it to her, she cut it into pieces with scissors and threw them into the trash basket. Her face told him how scared she'd been. They didn't talk about that day again.

Through the rest of February and March the Studio prepared for the filming of its yet-to-be-titled follow-ups to *Three by Three* and *The Andersons and the Steins*. Adrian hired an associate, Albert White, an accomplished classically trained cellist, to work with him on the scoring of the two films. Martin told the crew he had learned the government, under FDR, was setting up an Office of Information and a Bureau of Motion Pictures that would work with the studios to provide scenes for their films. Adrian hoped this would eliminate any more of Martin's ideas for him to visit military sites. He admitted, however, the experiences had given him a feel for the emotional reactions of men to their introduction to the service and had helped him with ideas for scoring.

30

A FEW MINUTES ALONE

By April 2, 1942, the Studio was ready to begin filming the two new projects. That morning at six o'clock, Adrian received a call from Paul saying the contessa was in the hospital. The doctors didn't expect her to live more than another two or three days.

Adrian took the first available plane to New York. He arrived at 10 a.m. His worrying whether he'd make it to the hospital in time made the flight stressful. He prayed the contessa wouldn't die until he had the chance to tell her how much she meant to him.

Mr. Reitman met Adrian at the airport to drive him to the hospital.

"How is she, Dad?" Adrian asked.

"She's hanging in there. She's waiting for you."

They arrived to find the contessa's priest, Father Kerran, waiting for them. He pulled them aside and told them the doctor said she had only hours to live. He'd performed the last rites.

Father Kerran left Adrian alone with the contessa. He stood by her bedside. Her eyes were closed. Adrian touched her knee. He felt relieved when her eyes opened halfway, and she gave him a weak smile of recognition. She looked frail. Her skin was pale and wrinkled. Her hair was flattened from lying on her back. A blanket covered her up to her shoulders. She loosened her blanket enough to free her hand. Adrian reached for it. It felt cold and boney.

Adrian fought back tears. "Stay still. I'm here. I came as soon as Paul called," he managed to get out in an uneven voice.

192

She struggled for breath to answer, but Adrian said, "Don't speak. Let me talk." He bent down to face her. "I want you to know how much you've meant to me and how grateful I am for the opportunities you've given me." Tears filled his eyes. "You've been like a mother to me. I'll miss you more than I can say."

He kissed her forehead. She tried to touch his cheek but couldn't lift her arm high enough.

"I love you too," she whispered. "You've been like a son to me. You've given me so much joy." Her eyes closed. Adrian felt her breath quietly leave her for the last time.

She's gone. Adrian could barely understand it yet, but he offered a silent prayer. *God, look after her.* He wanted a few minutes alone with her, but a nurse came into the room and felt her pulse. She confirmed what he already knew.

Adrian joined his father-in-law and Father Kerran in the hallway. They discussed the funeral.

Adrian called Suzanne from his father-in-law's apartment "I got here just in time to say goodbye," he said. "I'm quite sure she waited for me. I'll miss her, Suzanne, I'll really miss her."

Adrian heard Suzanne sniffling. "I know, sweetheart, I know. She was wonderful to you, and she knew how much she meant to you." Her words were gentle. "Get a good night's sleep. Call me in the morning to let me know how you are."

Adrian didn't sleep well that night. He thought about how he had learned the contessa had supported him through Sanfried without his knowledge until after he had graduated and how she had followed his career. He thought about their experience with the Bund and her separation from the count, how much that had hurt her, and how they had worked secretly together to dismantle Bund activities in New York. She had helped and supported so many people, but for Adrian, what mattered most was the love she had for him. Nothing could replace that.

Adrian arrived back in California on Thursday afternoon, two days after the contessa's funeral. The intervening time had felt like a haze of faces, shadowed by the cloud of sadness that never left him.

From home, he called the Studio to let them know he'd be there the next morning. He spent the afternoon with the twins, who helped bring him back to himself. The girls weren't just taking baby steps anymore. They were walking at warp speed.

When Suzanne put the girls down for a nap, Adrian told Suzanne in detail about his time in New York. As they were talking, the phone rang. Adrian went to pick it up. Suzanne watched, looking curious to know who was calling. Adrian's mouth opened wide, and his head turned toward her with an incredulous stare. Suzanne got up off the sofa and walked to him. He covered the mouthpiece of the phone and whispered to her it was good news. After a few minutes, he said, "Thank you," and hung up.

Adrian took Suzanne's arm and led her back to the sofa. He could hardly speak.

"What?" she said. "Tell me."

Adrian caught his breath. "That was Rose's lawyer. She's left me one hundred thousand dollars." He shook his head. "I can't believe it, Suzanne. That's a fortune. She told me she was leaving me money, but I never dreamed…" his voice trailed off.

Suzanne took hold of Adrian's hands. "Oh, Adrian," she said. "That's wonderful. I know you would have been happy with just your memories of her, but this is such a show of love. I'm so happy for you."

"There's more," Adrian said. She's left pieces of jewelry for you and for each of the girls to remember her by."

"That was sweet of her. I'll wear mine with great affection." Her voice broke. "Oh Adrian, I think I'm going to cry."

Adrian wrapped his arm around her and waited until Suzanne composed herself. "The jewelry and a letter to me from Rose will arrive by special mail. I'll have to provide our bank account number to the lawyer to have the money transferred here. He's sending me forms to fill out."

Suzanne wiped her eyes and looked around the room. "You know, Adrian, we don't have a single photograph of Rose. You should ask the lawyer to send us one, the nicest one he can. That will be worth more than all the jewelry she could possibly have given us."

"What a wonderful idea. Thank you. You're right. That would be a gift we could look at and treasure every day. We could hang it between our wedding picture and Claire's portrait of me.

Three days later, the letter from the lawyer arrived confirming the contessa's gifts to Adrian, Suzanne, and the twins.

The envelope also contained an enclosure from the contessa.

Dear Adrian,

I remember the first day I saw you. It was at a reception for new students at the home of the Sanfrieds. As president of the board of directors I was there to welcome all of you. You looked like a fish out of water, so I came over to say hello. It was then I discovered that your lack of knowledge of English had caused your discomfort. Fortunately, I knew a little German, and tried to make you feel comfortable by using what I remembered. When I got tangled up in my German, I pounded my head with my palm and called myself a "dummkopf" not knowing it was a harsh swear word in German. You looked at me and burst out laughing. I turned bright red when you leaned in and told me what that harsher meaning was. I grabbed your arm and laughed with you. We bonded right there.

I arranged for you to have an English tutor who knew fluent Polish. I kept tabs on you and learned how quickly you caught on. I followed your progress and was told by your professors you were a gifted student. I saw that for myself when I attended your recitals and invited you to my home to play at my gatherings. In a short time, we developed a close relationship that has continued throughout my life and has given me much pleasure.

I may have played a part in your education, but I want you to know and believe I never played a part in influencing your career. You achieved your success on your own through your own talent. You became not only a fine violinist, but, also, a fine man.

The Lord never blessed me with children, but for some unexplained reason, He brought you to me. For all the happiness you've brought into my life, I want you to be free to become whatever you want to be. That is one of the reasons I'm leaving you this money, so you are free to choose your own course in this world on your own terms, to not be obliged to or be influenced by anyone. The other reason is plain and simple. I love you as a son.

I must admit, and perhaps it is not my place to say, I was surprised when you went to Hollywood for the position you did. I'm aware of your success, but I worry you may neglect the gift God gave you, to be one of the greatest violinists of our time. Please don't forget your gift. Remember how far back your desire goes, all the way to when you were a young boy in Poland and when you were a student at The Krakow School of Music. Even if you choose not to pursue a career as a concert violinist, keep up with your skills. Whatever you do, you and Suzanne and the children be happy. I'll be watching from above.

With my love,
Rose

Adrian became overcome by emotion. Feeling he had brought misery into the lives of others back in Poland, Adrian felt he had made up for it, in some part, by bringing happiness to the contessa, a woman whom he'd come to love as a mother The lines in the letter, the words he would treasure most, were that he'd become not only a fine violinist but a fine man, and that she had loved him as a son.

Suzanne found him sitting by the pool, the letter dangling from his hand. Without saying a word, he handed it to her. She sat in a chair beside him and read it.

Suzanne looked up with tears in her eyes when she said, "Oh, Adrian, this is so beautiful. She loved you so, and it's a blessing she knew you loved her too."

She was right. Adrian tried to pull his scattered thoughts together. "I do wish Rose could have had more time with us." He paused, then said with a catch in his voice, "This letter brings back all those memories and sad feelings about how I dishonored my real mother. I'm carrying that grief with me right now, too."

Suzanne got up and sat on Adrian's lap. She put her arms around him. "I'm a lucky girl," she said. "Not every man would share such deep feelings. You telling me this makes me love you even more." She rested her head on his shoulder. They sat quietly in each other's arms.

Suzanne asked Adrian what he thought about the last paragraph in the contessa's letter. He said he had thought about it, even before receiving the letter. He was having fun at the Three M Studio. It was a challenge, and his contribution to the studio's success had rewarded him. These were all good things, but he was beginning to feel he was missing his past career. His contract with Three M was up in five months. He decided it was time to start thinking about where he wanted to be in his career by then. Thanks to the contessa he could be anything he wanted.

"Keep in mind, dear," Suzanne said, "our lease for the house expires in September. We need to seriously discuss what you want to do and where you want to be. We'll have three young children then. Moving won't be as easy as it was when we came here."

"You're right. Keep pushing me."

Adrian knew he'd soon be writing the scores for two new films. This would consume his time, especially since he wanted to finish the work before the new baby came, but he mustn't lose sight of the future.

31

SO OBVIOUS AND PERFECT

On a Saturday morning in mid-April Adrian was sitting at the piano in his living room pounding keys, trying out sounds for a scene he was reading in the script of the newest in the *Two by Two* series, still untitled. He heard the roar of a motorcycle in the driveway and went out to find Jonny kicking down the kickstand.

"Hi, Adrian."

"Jonny, so good to see you. It's been a while. Come on in. How about a Coke?"

"Sure."

Adrian went to the kitchen and came back with a bottle and handed it to Jonny.

"I hope I'm not interrupting," Jonny said.

"Not at all. It's great to see you. How are you?"

"A little nervous."

Adrian could see that now that he looked at Jonny more closely. "What's going on? Tell me what's bothering you."

"I got my Greetings letter. I'm due at the draft office next week. I heard you and the crew at the Studio were there. Eddie said he saw you standing in line outside when he drove by a while back."

Adrian gave an understanding nod. "That was work, my friend. We went there to get firsthand experience before we started filming."

Jonny was bouncing up and down on his toes. "My folks are really besides themselves. I'm their only child. I'm uptight about it

198

too. I thought you could tell me what to expect."

"Sure. Let's go sit by the pool. It'll be more comfortable there. Want another Coke?"

Jonny's hand shook as he held up his bottle. "No thanks. I'm good."

Adrian told Jonny about his experiences at the draft and training centers.

"What I can tell you, Jonny, is that just about everyone at both places was scared. What impressed me most at the induction center was no matter whether the inductees wanted to be there or not, they quickly bonded. Their common fears, anxiety, whatever you want to call it, united them." Adrian leaned forward. "I know you're facing something scary, but you're not alone. You'll have plenty of company, and you and the others will get through it together."

Jonny's toes tapped rapidly on the ground as he listened to Adrian.

"I know you can't see that now, but if you're inducted, you'll find that out."

"If you say so, Adrian. I hope that's true, but you're right about one thing. I can't see that now."

Adrian nodded. "I know, Jonny. I know." He wished he could say something better to take away Jonny's anxiety.

Jonny took a sip of his Coke and wiped his mouth with the back of his hand. "Where's the studio with its follow up to *Three by Three*?" Jonny said, changing the subject. "What's the new title?"

"No one's come up with a good one yet. Got any ideas?"

Jonny laughed. "Well, the obvious is *Four by Four*, isn't it?"

"Of course," Adrian said. "That would give it instant recognition. But the question is, who or what is the 'Four' for?"

"That's simple. It would be their drill sergeants. Make a poster of each young family of three with a drill sergeant hovering over them."

It was so obvious and perfect. Adrian couldn't believe no one had thought of it. "Jonny, you're a genius. You were made to work in the entertainment industry. Do you mind if I tell the Studio your idea?"

"No, sir. Just give me the credit."

"Of course." Adrian raised an eyebrow. "And why are you suddenly calling me 'Sir'"?

Jonny saluted. "Just practicing," he said.

Adrian laughed. He placed his arm around the young man's shoulder and walked him out. "Let me know how it goes," he said to Jonny before he got on his motorcycle.

"You bet."

Adrian watched Jonny ride off. He wondered if, someday, Simon would look up to him and seek out his advice the way Jonny had. He wanted to think so. He thought about his relationship with the contessa, how she had always been in the background cheering for him without his knowing until he was a grown man on his own. He hoped Simon would learn one day that he'd always been there, thinking about him, searching for him, wishing they'd been together instead of strangers.

Adrian told the Marcus brothers and Rodney about Jonny's idea. The sequel to *Three by Three* became titled *Four by Four.*

Together, Adrian and Albert White worked on the scores for *Four by Four* and the sequel to *The Andersons and the Steins,* now titled *Private Anderson and Seaman Stein.* Adrian and Albert made a good team. They chose lighthearted hits like "Boogie Woogie Bugle Boy" for the more upbeat *Four by Four,* and darker classical works for the solemn *Private Anderson.* Phillip proved to be a smart, knowledgeable musician. If Adrian were to decide to leave the Three M Studio, he felt Albert would make a good replacement. If he stayed, Albert would make a valuable Associate Music Director.

One evening, a month later, Adrian came home to find a letter from Jonny. He went to the kitchen to read it to Suzanne. "Jonny's in Georgia, at Fort Benning," he told her. "He's in basic training."

Suzanne bit her lip. "Poor Jonny," she said, "How's he doing?"

Adrian scanned the letter. "He's had his hair shaved off, and he says basic training is hell. He has a drill instructor whom he swears must have been brought up in a brothel. He yells at the men all day long and only knows how to curse. The man hasn't spoken a word that has more than four letters." Adrian recalled how he and the other studio men had been awakened that morning at the training center. He couldn't imagine going through that every day.

Suzanne shook her head. "That beautiful head of hair," she said. "What a shame. What else?"

"He says the army treats them like they're a bunch of useless men who need to be turned into fighting machines." He read further. "Jonny says I was right. The guys he's met have a sense of camaraderie and are loyal to one another. He's made a lot of friends. The training is exhausting and is weeding out those who can't cut it. So far, he says he's bearing up." Adrian looked up. "He says to say 'hi' to you and the kids."

Suzanne patted Adrian's shoulder. "When you write back, be sure to send him my love."

Adrian thought about Jonny's letter as he was preparing for bed. He wondered if Simon were going through military training also and whether he was bearing up.

32

"I FEEL A 'BUT' COMING."

The individual crew and casts worked hard to meet their deadline for their two new films. In 1942 nearly four million men and women served in the US military, and war movies had become a powerful release and inspiration to the country. The studio released their two sequels on July 15 to wide success.

On July 18, Suzanne delivered a seven-pound, eight-ounce boy. They named him Dominik, after Adrian's father. Adrian was happy to have a son. He'd pretended with Suzanne it didn't matter whether the baby was a boy or girl, but he had prayed for a son. He wanted someone to continue the family name, but more importantly, he wanted to believe that in being a good father to this boy he could make up for his neglect of his firstborn.

Meanwhile, the Studio's two new films were such successes, the Marcus brothers talked about expanding. There were even rumors of a merger with a larger studio.

Adrian thought about what that might mean. He'd done excellent work for the Marcus brothers. Whispers already hinted that the score for *Private Anderson and Seaman Stein* might be up for an Academy Award. A merger meant a change of a kind Adrian couldn't predict.

One night, when they were lying in bed in the quiet after a long day, Suzanne brought up the question of Adrian's career. He was glad to talk.

"I've got several options in mind," he said. "I'm thinking I might stay with Three M no more than another year. I've been successful there, and I'm enjoying it."

"I feel a 'but' coming," Suzanne said.

He told her what had been most on his mind. "There have been rumors of a merger between Three M and a larger studio. I don't know whether there'll be room for me."

Adrian felt the mattress shift as Suzanne lifted herself and looked down on him. "How long have you known this?"

He saw her concern for him in her eyes. She was going to think he felt the Marcus brothers had betrayed him.

"Just a few days," he said. "Don't worry about it, Suzanne. I'm not. In fact, I've been thinking about getting back to my classical roots and looking for a position as a concertmaster when my contract expires." He had enough ties in the classical music world that this felt feasible. "Or I could take time off to teach for a while and work on finishing my concerto. I've been so busy with the last two films I haven't had time nor energy to work on it. Before I make any decisions, I plan to have a frank talk with Martin about the brothers' plans for the Studio."

Adrian met with Martin to discuss the rumors about a merger. He needed to know where he stood if there were to be one. Their lease on the house was expiring September 7, although Nancy hinted the lease might be available for extension.

"I'm sorry for not letting you in on what's going on," Martin said. "It's true a major picture studio has approached us to discuss the possibility of a merger. My brothers and I and our lawyer are negotiating the details. Our lawyer said to keep it quiet 'til it's settled one way or another. I guess the rumor mill has gotten ahead of us."

Adrian was annoyed Martin hadn't told him sooner. He'd been important to the studio beyond his position as its Music Director. His imagination and his name recognition had helped the studio achieve its current success. He realized he had no right to feel this way. He wasn't a founder of the studio, not a Marcus. This had nothing to do with him. This was a business decision, but it still stuck in his craw.

Adrian tried not to let his true feelings show. In truth, he felt ambivalent. He wasn't sure if his irritation wasn't caused more by his sense of pride rather than a resentment of not being told about the merger talk.

"It will take a few more months before, and if, anything is agreed upon," Martin said. "Even if there were to be a merger, we'll continue making films, but under the name of the other studio. There'd still be room for you." Martin sounded apologetic. "My brothers and I want you to continue with us, Adrian, but right now we can only offer you an additional one-year contract."

Adrian tried not to sound hurt. "I'll talk it over with Suzanne." He forced a smile. "Let me see how she feels about it."

Adrian could see Suzanne was upset about the news, but she tried to put a good spin on it. "This might be a blessing in disguise. You've been talking about getting back to your classical roots. This may be just the impetus to do that."

He and Suzanne decided that whatever happened, they wanted to stay in California. Only if a full-time position as concertmaster became available would they consider a move. Financially they were sound. If Adrian decided to continue with the studio, it would be with the provision he'd work on only three films that year, be free to teach, be able to accept guest appearances at symphonies across the United States, and be given time to compose on his own.

In late July 1942 reports had begun to surface in the newspapers revealing that Hitler's "new order" had resulted in the death of 400,000 Jews. News filtered out of occupied Europe confirming that the Germans were murdering Jews throughout German occupied countries. Other newspapers had reported the Nazis had killed millions of Jews, but American journalists tended to be cautious about these claims. Such stories rarely appeared on the front pages. Adrian, having read these reports, prayed for Simon, hoping he was not caught up in the horrors of the Nazi regime.

In August, Adrian signed a contract with Three M Studio for an additional year from September 1, 1942, through August 31, 1943. In early September Adrian received another letter from Jonny. He read it to Suzanne while she was feeding Dominik in the kitchen. "Jonny says his unit was sent to Tunisia."

"Where is that?" Suzanne asked.

"North Africa."

"What are we doing in Tunisia?"

Adrian looked up from the letter. "We're there helping the French so the Germans and Italians can't reinforce their units there." He looked back down at the letter. "He says war is like being in a state of continuous fear. There's no release. He says he's instructed to be ready to react at a moment's notice. After a while, he says, "You begin to realize that everything you once thought to be unimaginable was now to be anticipated.""

Adrian ran a shaky hand through his hair and sat down. His other hand fell, still grasping the letter. Jonny's words were chilling. He couldn't imagine himself being in such a situation. He remembered Jonny coming to him after he received his Greetings letter, how he said he was uptight about it, and how he couldn't keep his feet still while they sat by the pool talking. He prayed Jonny could bear up under such stress.

"The poor boy," Suzanne said. "When you get a letter like that you realize how lucky you are to be safe at home." She stopped feeding her son for a moment and kissed Adrian's cheek. "I hope Dominik never has to face anything like that. I can imagine how Jonny's parents must feel getting such a letter. It sends shivers up my spine." Adrian thought how right she was. Jonny's letter stayed in his mind all evening. Behind the image of the young man in Tunisia, he saw the other young man in Poland. *What was Simon going through now?*

Three months later, on the evening of December 13, 1942, Adrian was at home listening to the radio. The broadcaster reported that the Nazis were gathering millions of people, mostly Jews, and callously killing them with brutal effectiveness. This news raised Adrian's worries further. The phrase "concentration camps" had now been turned into "extermination camps." There had been earlier news filtering out of occupied Europe that summer, following Poland's defeat, that the Germans were murdering Jews, but, as before, newspapers relegated such stories to the inside pages.

One morning Suzanne came into the kitchen while Adrian was

reading the newspaper while drinking his coffee. "Why do you look so glum?" she asked.

"More news is coming out of Europe that the Germans are murdering Jews in large numbers. I just hope my aunt and uncle have been able to hide Simon's background from them."

Suzanne came behind Adrian and patted his shoulder. "Don't you think he'll be able to protect Simon from any harm?"

Adrian reached for her hand and squeezed it. His posture hunched when he let go, and he whispered under his breath, *"I hope so. I hope so."*

In January 1943, Martin told Adrian the merger with Eagle's Nest Motion Picture Studio would be taking place on March 1. His contract would be honored through August. Eagle's Nest had a group of distinguished musicians well known to Adrian, all of whom he respected. He'd be added to that group when the merger became official. Martin explained that Three M Studio still would make its own pictures under the name of its production company. It would have greater access to actors, production staff, studio space, sets, costume designers, make-up artists, and all the other assets a studio needed. Most importantly, Eagle's Nest owned movie theaters around the country to which the Three M Studio would have access.

Adrian had reconciled himself with the upcoming merger and his place in it. He was pleased for the Marcus brothers and for himself. He'd helped them achieve their dream. They, in turn, had shown their appreciation by giving him a new contract through August 1943 that would give him the flexibility he wanted to become more independent and to be in direct contact at the studio with other well-known musicians.

"So, you're happy with this?" Suzanne asked at dinner in their kitchen.

"Very much so. I'm not only getting the opportunity to collaborate with other musicians I admire, but I'm also going to be around some of Hollywood's greatest stars. The best thing right now is I'm not going to have full responsibility for scoring a film. I'm very content to leave that up to someone else and to be free to take on the work I want. This will allow me time to finish the concerto

I've been working on for the past three years."

"It will be nice to see you under less stress and to have you home more. I'm happy for you." She patted his bottom.

In early February 1943, Adrian had the opportunity to play at the Los Angeles Odeum Center with their Philharmonic Orchestra. He performed the Mozart Violin Concerto No. 3 and realized how much he had missed the energy of live performances. Nothing could match being onstage, feeling the audience's anticipation and admiration, and feeling the music take over him as he became one with it. Then, when the music ended, there was nothing like the sound of applause that brought the world back to let him know what he had given it.

The response to his performance at the Los Angeles Odeum was so heartfelt that the management offered him a contract to perform Mendelssohn's *Violin Concerto in E Minor* in the spring. He accepted at once. Martin and his brothers had given him the freedom in the last months of his contract with them to perform at these concerts.

33

"HE DIDN'T SAY WHY."

In late February 1943, Adrian was at the piano in his living room when the phone rang. Suzanne was in the kitchen cleaning up a spill from Dominik's cup.

Adrian answered the phone. It was Mr. Richards, Jonny's father.

"I'd like to stop by tomorrow to see you, if that's OK," Mr. Richards said.

"Sure, is everything all right?"

"I'll be over at one," was all Mr. Richards said before hanging up.

A cold feeling settled over Adrian. He felt nauseous with foreboding. He walked into the kitchen.

"What's the matter? "You look like you've seen a ghost," Suzanne said.

"That was Jonny's father on the phone. He wants to see me here tomorrow. He wouldn't say why."

Suzanne sat down. "Oh God. Do you think Jonny's been hurt?" She reached for Adrian's hand. "Or worse?"

Adrian sat next to her. He reached for Dominik. He hugged the boy and pressed his face against his son's smooth cheek. His son's weight in his arms calmed him a little. After he handed Dominik back to Suzanne, he poured himself a glass of water and gulped it down.

Adrian didn't sleep that night. He tried not to think about what Mr. Richards wanted to tell him. He left the bed and went down to his basement office and took up his violin. The stormy waves of Sibelius' D minor concerto gave vent to the tumult inside him.

Saturday morning Adrian took an early swim in the pool. He showered and had only coffee for breakfast. He played ball with the girls on the lawn, but he had difficulty concentrating. Time passed slowly. He kept looking at his watch, waiting for one o'clock.

Finally, it came. Adrian was prepared for the worst. He felt shaky. He practiced saying hello to Mr. Richards to keep his voice controlled. His cheek and mouth muscles were tight. He paced back and forth in the living room waiting for Mr. Richards's car to arrive. When it did, he pulled his body tightly together and put on a smile.

Mr. Richards was a distinguished looking man, tall and trim, with graying hair and a mustache. He wore a dark suit, white shirt, and a dark tie. Adrian saw this as an ominous sign.

Adrian greeted Mr. Richards and invited him in. Mr. Richards declined Adrian's invitation to come into the living room, saying he could only stay a few minutes. Standing in the entranceway, Adrian surveyed Mr. Richards's body for clues to the news he was about to receive. The man stood straight with his arms hanging by his side, looking as if he were trying to keep his composure. There were deep circles under his red eyes, and his face looked drawn downward by sorrow. Adrian prayed Mr. Richards sad expression was because he had received news Jonny was only injured or, at worst, reported missing.

Mr. Richard's chin trembled. "I've got bad news," he said. "Jonny's dead. He was killed in a skirmish and buried in Tunisia." Mr. Richard's shoulders shrank, and he turned his head sideways to hide his emotions.

Adrian felt a tightness in his chest. He clenched his fists, trying to hold himself together, to not cry out, *no, not Jonny, not that vital, brilliant, ambitious young man.* It was what he had braced himself to hear but what he hoped with all his heart he wouldn't.

Somehow Adrian contained himself and thought more about the man standing in front of him. He wanted to touch Mr. Richards's shoulder to offer his genuine sympathy, but he held back, feeling this would break Mr. Richards's attempts to maintain his control.

"I'm so sorry," he said. "I was very fond of your son. I considered him a friend."

Mr. Richards bit his lip. His eyes looked downward. "Jonny was fond of you too. He spoke of you often." Mr. Richards looked back up and breathed in. "I came to tell you how much my wife and I appreciate all you did for our son. Not everyone gets the chance to help someone get his start to fulfill a dream. Before he left for basic training, Jonny gave me a letter to give to you in case…" Mr. Richards stopped, took out a handkerchief, and wiped his eyes.

Adrian stood quietly while Mr. Richards reached into his breast pocket and pulled out an envelope.

"I don't want to take any more of your time," he said. "I need to get back to my wife. She's taking this hard. She wanted to come, but she couldn't pull herself together."

From the living room window, Adrian watched Mr. Richards walk to his car. He saw Mr. Richards bang his fist on the hood of the Lincoln and fall against the door. He couldn't see Mr. Richards's face, but from the convulsions of his shoulders, Adrian knew he was crying. Adrian's heart felt like it was breaking for him.

Adrian sat in the living room reading the letter.

Dear Adrian,

I hope my father never has to deliver this letter, but I wanted to prepare for the worst. I didn't want to leave this world without telling you the influence you've had on my life. You've been a mentor and a friend. I felt I could always come to you and talk about things. You showed me what it was to be kind to others by sharing unselfishly. I'll never forget your generosity in giving me full credit for the lyrics to "Nickel and Gold." I promise to pass that on.

Not everyone gets to fill a dream at my age. Just think, I cowrote a title song for a popular movie, and that song became a hit. It was nominated for an Academy Award. Never mind it didn't win. Many people die without feeling they've achieved anything. If I die achieving nothing else, I have that, thanks to you.

Don't feel sad for me. Think of me as someone who came into your life and appreciated you, saw the good in you, someone you brought joy to and helped fulfil a dream. Smile when you think of me, like I smile when I think of you and what you've given me.

Your friend,

Jonny

Adrian held the letter close to his chest. For the past eighteen years Adrian had felt remorse for having abandoned his son. Despite whatever success he had achieved in his life, his guilt and shame over Simon were deep. He had been able to repress these feelings and hide them from others, but they arose persistently. Losing Jonny brought these feelings to the surface once again. Jonny gave him the opportunity to act toward a young man like he imagined he would have toward Simon. Now, he'd lost them both. His grief was as deep as it was when the contessa died.

Adrian found Suzanne in the twins' room helping them build blocks while Dominik knocked them down and they all laughed gleefully. Suzanne looked up. He could see she could tell something was terribly wrong.

He sat on the floor with her and the kids and tried to join in their play while Suzanne read Jonny's letter.

When she finished reading, Suzanne moved closer to him and laid her head on his shoulder. He heard the deep sadness in her voice.

"Oh, Adrian, I'm so sorry. I know how much he meant to you. He was so full of life and ambition. Why do things like this have to happen? I feel so bad for his parents."

Her words brought forth the flood of tears Adrian had been holding back. When the girls heard their father sobbing, they stopped playing. They went to their parents, fell into their bodies, and started to cry. Dominik crawled to Adrian and tugged at his trousers leg. Adrian reached for him and held him tightly as if he would never let go.

Later, when the children were napping, Adrian and Suzanne sat in the living room. Adrian described his meeting with Mr. Richards and how he'd held himself together until he reached his car.

"I feel so sad for Jonny's parents," Suzanne said. "When is the memorial service? We must go."

Adrian realized he didn't know. The next day he called Mr. Richards. During their conversation, Adrian learned the date of the service and agreed to play the violin to honor Jonny.

After consulting with the family, he chose "Ave Maria" and "The Larks Ascending."

At the memorial service, Adrian played the two pieces when the priest called for a period of silence and reflection. He stood to the side of the altar, out of sight of the worshipers. He wanted to be alone, unseen, while he played. He felt he wouldn't be able to control his emotions and would cry, but he played flawlessly as he thought about his first meeting with Jonny and the relationship they had forged after composing "Nickel and Gold." He could almost see the look in Jonny's eyes when he gave the young man full credit for the lyrics to the song, and he imagined hearing the roar of Jonny's motorcycle pulling into his driveway to seek his advice when he got his Greetings letter. All thoughts about Jonny came together as Adrian played, forcing back his tears.

After playing, Adrian joined Suzanne in the pew. He took her hand in his. She squeezed it and laid her head on his shoulder. He did his best to hold himself together.

"I'd like to do something special for Jonny," Adrian said to Suzanne after the service. "I'd like to establish a scholarship at The Walker School of Music in Jonny's name." It was the best way he could think of to carry out Jonny's pledge to pay forward his own success.

Suzanne thought that was a wonderful idea. After discussion with Jonny's parents, Adrian set up the scholarship guidelines with the Walker School. It helped them to know that each year a first-year piano student would have the support they needed to follow their dreams.

In March 1943 the studio announced the merger, as Martin had promised. Martin told Adrian Eagle's Nest needed him right away to replace a violinist who was drafted right in the middle of filming for a major motion picture. The film's composer, Igor Federov, had written the scores for previous films Adrian admired. He and Adrian developed a friendship and worked together whenever Adrian was available.

34

REDUCING RESPONSIBILITIES

After Jonny's death, Adrian found himself thinking more about his own future and what seemed most important. In June he spoke to Suzanne while they were in their bedroom preparing for bed. He sat on the edge of the bed watching her brushing her hair at her vanity.

He started straightforwardly. "I've decided I'm not going to ask for a renewal of my contract with the new studio, if offered," he said. "At least not if it's for any responsibility other than playing in the studio's orchestra under the music director."

Suzanne stopped her brushing and turned to look at Adrian. "Go on. You've got my attention."

"I want to reduce my responsibilities, so I have time to work on composing. I'd also like to accept some guest solo appearances to keep my name out there and maybe teach a few classes at The Walker School."

Suzanne smiled. "That sounds good to me. I'm sure the children will enjoy having you around more often. For that matter, so will I. Suzanne paused as if she were in thought, and said, "There are things we need to think about. Our lease runs out on this house in September. Emily told me the owner will be back then and won't extend the lease. We need to either rent another house or buy one." She ran her fingers through her hair. "If we decide to buy, that means furnishing it and a host of other things I won't be able to manage alone with three small children." She reached out to take his hands. "This weekend I'm asking Inga to sit with the children while we seriously talk about these things."

That Saturday, they sat at the kitchen table while Inga cared for the children, and they made several decisions. One was to keep the house in New York. If there were ever a possibility of their moving back to Manhattan, the house would be there for them. They decided, also, to continue to rent a house in Hollywood rather than buy one. Suzanne brought up a subject Adrian hadn't thought about. Her father was getting older and had only an older brother and Charlotte in New York. There was a likelihood, if they remained in California, Suzanne would want him to come live with them. Adrian agreed. He was fond of his father-in-law.

They discussed Adrian's career. He told her how he'd felt about performing at the Los Angeles Odeum and how much he missed the rush of live concerts. Suzanne agreed to his performing at concert halls in other states if he discussed them with her first before making commitments. He agreed.

35

CONSIDERABLE PROGRESS

In June 1943, two months before his contract with Three M Studio was to expire, Adrian met with Arthur Silverman following the success of his May performance of the Mendelssohn Concerto with the Los Angeles Odeum Philharmonic. He signed a two-year contract with the symphony for the upcoming season as associate concertmaster. During those two years, his contract allowed him to appear as a guest soloist with the Eleventh State Symphony as well as orchestras in Pennsylvania, Ohio, and New Jersey.

In September 1943 Adrian and Suzanne moved into their new rental three blocks from their previous one. They signed a two-year lease. The house had three bedrooms, and there was a small pool house for guests, which also served as Adrian's studio. He separated from the Three M Studio and Eagle's Nest, but he told the new studio's music director to call upon him when he needed a violinist to fill in.

Adrian felt secure in his decision to return to performing in concert halls. "I know the conductors of the orchestras where I'll be performing, Suzanne, either personally or by reputation. I'm proud to have the opportunity to perform with them. I'll never be away more than a weekend, I promise you." Suzanne accepted this. It was what his career required.

In November 1944, Suzanne's father had a minor stroke, coincidentally on the weekend Adrian was playing another solo engagement at Union Hall. He spent three days with his father-in-law and brought him back to California to live with them. Suzanne's

216

uncle and Charlotte took care of winding down her father's affairs in New York.

Before Mr. Reitman came to live with them, Adrian and Suzanne had visited a USO center once a week to talk with military personnel on leave and to provide entertainment. Adrian made it a point to let the attendees know he had a son stuck in Poland and how much he appreciated their service. He knew it was highly unlikely, if not impossible, any serviceman would have met Simon, but Adrian felt compelled to ask. During his free time, Adrian secluded himself in the pool house working on his concerto. By the midpoint of the 1944–45 concert season, he'd made considerable progress and felt he could finish it before the next season, during which he hoped to present it.

36

"WE MUST REMAIN HOPEFUL."

On April 11, 1945, Adrian was in the living room listening to Jonathan Rayburn, a local newscaster, whose broadcast covered California , Arizona, and Nevada. His guest had just come back from a delegation that had visited one of the liberated concentration camps in Germany. The guest's voice quavered as he gave a shocking description of the atrocities of the Germans. He described dead bodies piled high around the camp and prisoners left behind who were barely alive and so starved that their eyes were sunken and their bones showed prominently beneath their skin. The guest's words were so descriptive that Adrian visualized what it would have been like for Simon to be living in such a camp. He felt nauseated and felt the contents of his dinner rising from his stomach into his throat. He rushed to the bathroom to vomit. Suzanne heard Adrian's convulsive heaving and came to the bathroom to see what was wrong.

Adrian breathed heavily as he described to Suzanne what he'd heard. She helped him to their bedroom and insisted he lie down while she got him a glass of water. He grabbed her wrist to stop her and asked her to sit with him for a while. She sat holding his hand and rubbing it.

"What if Simon were living in a concentration camp like that man described?" Adrian said to Suzanne. "What if he were dead, or treated so badly he was near death? That would be my fault. If I had stayed in Poland with him or brought him to America, he'd be alive and well today. But I was too selfish, too immature. I may have killed him, Suzanne. Because of me, he may be a corpse lying in a ditch with countless other corpses." Adrian pulled away from Suzanne and rolled over, wallowing in self-loathing and guilt.

Suzanne tried to comfort him. "You don't know that," she said, her voice pleading. "For all you know, he's safe somewhere with your family and protected from harm. You can't punish yourself for things that may not be true just because you feel guilty. For the past six years we've lived with the hope of finding him. Think of it that we're much closer now that the Allies are liberating these camps."

Adrian rolled back over and fell into her arms. He hoped she was right, but right now, after the horrors described on the radio, he was beginning to lose hope. That night he slept restlessly. He had a dream Dominik had fallen and broken his arm.

"Where's Daddy? I want my daddy," Dominik cried from a hospital bed.

"What's your daddy's name?" the nurse asked him.

"Daddy. His name is Daddy."

When Adrian woke up the next morning, he had the uneasy feeling his dream was about Simon.

Adrian walked from the bedroom into the kitchen where Suzanne was on the phone. When she hung up, she told him she had arranged for Inga to sit with the children.

"You need to get your mind off last night. I'm taking you to the movies, and afterward, you're taking me to dinner."

"But—" he started, thinking he might sit by the radio to listen more about what the news was reporting about the concentration camps.

"No buts. You need to get your mind off last night, and I need a break from the kids. Dad and Inga will be happy to have the children to themselves for a while."

"What are we going to see?"

"There's a musical comedy starring Frank Sinatra and Gene Kelly that should distract us for a while."

"Who's the female lead?"

"Kathryn Grayson."

Adrian lifted his eyebrows in approval. Suzanne swatted him with a dish towel. *She's right*, he thought. *I need to get my mind off the news*.

While waiting for Suzanne, Adrian played with the twins and Dominik tossing a ball around on the lawn. Watching his healthy children reminded him of his young niece, Katrina, in Krakow. He remembered how Chana had told him how spirited the child was despite her disability. Adrian convinced himself that if the Germans had imprisoned Simon, he would possess the same spirit, having been raised by his aunt and uncle. He would have survived. He felt bad about how he had acted last night and the burden he had placed on Suzanne to hold on to hope.

On their way to the movie theater, Adrian told Suzanne his thoughts about Katrina and how his aunt and uncle would have instilled strength in Simon to survive any hardship. He apologized for his behavior the night before. She leaned over and kissed his cheek.

They arrived at the theater early before the movie was scheduled to begin and waited to see the previews of coming attractions. Instead, a newsreel came on showing General Eisenhower giving a tour of the newly liberated Ohrdruf concentration camp to a group of American reporters. The newsreel showed the General walking around a cluster of slain prisoners tossed into shallow graves and showed images of prisoners as described by in the broadcast Adrian had listened to the night before. Adrian felt Suzanne's hand grab his.

"Maybe this was a bad idea," she said. "I should have checked to see if there was a newsreel. I'm so sorry, Adrian. Maybe we'd better leave."

It was too late. The bile was rising in Adrian's throat. He made a leap from his seat over the feet and knees of others in his aisle in a frantic effort to reach the men's room in time. After he had pulled himself together and splashed water on his face, he found Suzanne waiting for him outside the restroom. The expression on her face showed regret for bringing him here. He took her hand, and they left the theater. They walked for a while saying nothing to one another as they breathed in the fresh air. They came to a small park and sat on a bench. She held his hand tightly. Finally, Suzanne said, "We can't give up. We must remain hopeful that Simon is alive, and we'll find him." It was his son for whom she was holding on to hope. She was his rock. Her words gave him the renewed encouragement he needed.

A month later, on May 7, 1945, Germany unconditionally surrendered to the Allies in Reims, France, ending World War II and the Third Reich. Adrian held on to Suzanne's earlier words and hoped that the end of the war would bring them that much closer to finding Simon and bring peace to their lives.

PART THREE
HOLLYWOOD

37

A BIZARRE QUESTION

On October 14, 1945, Adrian looked in his dressing room mirror at Union Hall and smoothed his hair with his palm. The crowd of well-wishers was gone. He felt exhilarated by his performance and the reception it received. He planned to head back to his hotel room, order a drink from room service, and call Suzanne to tell her his final East Coast performance of his new concerto had gone as well as the others.

He saw movement in the mirror. He turned around. Four people, their faces unfamiliar to him, stood awkwardly in the doorway.

"Hello," he said.

A man came forward and held out his hand. "Mr. Mazurek, I'm Richard Sherman. This is my wife, Cheryl, my daughter, Robin, and her fiancé, Dr. Stanton Kent."

Adrian shook the man's hand and smiled politely. "What can I do for you?"

"First, let me say what a treat it was to hear you. This is the first trip to New York for my wife and me. I've always wanted to come to Union Hall, and my daughter was able to get tickets for tonight."

Adrian tried not to appear annoyed by his being held back from getting to his hotel. "Thank you. That's very kind," he said.

"My daughter is a nurse in the army and is recently back from Germany. She had an experience there…" The man hesitated, looked at his daughter, and said, "I guess I should let you tell it, Robin."

The young woman cleared her throat and looked up at Adrian.

225

"I'm a little embarrassed," she said. "It didn't come to me until I reread the program during intermission. I may be…" she stopped and looked at her fiancé.

"Go ahead," the young man nudged her. "Tell him."

"Mr. Mazurek, do you have a son?"

What a bizarre question, Adrian thought. To be polite, he said, "Yes, I do. His name is Dominik. He's three years old. Suddenly his posture stiffened. "Why do you ask?" *She can't be asking about Dominik. Did she see something, someone in Germany that's caused her to ask me this? Could this have something to do with Simon?*

The young woman looked at her fiancé and then at her parents. "I'm sorry," she said. "I feel so embarrassed."

Adrian didn't dare hope too much. "What brings you back here to ask me that?" He pointed to a chair and invited the young woman to sit. He sat across from her, leaning against the arm of his chair.

Robin looked into Adrian's eyes. "I cared for many young Polish men the army liberated from a concentration camp. I didn't think anything about it at the time, but when I looked at your name in tonight's program, it came back to me."

Adrian moved to the edge of his chair. "What did? Please tell me." His foot started tapping uncontrollably on the floor.

"One of the men asked me if I knew a violinist named Adrian Mazurek. When I said I didn't and asked why, he said he was his father."

Adrian's chest tightened. *After all this time, could it really be? This can't be a coincidence. Maybe she got the name wrong.* "Are you sure he said Mazurek?"

He spoke with an accent," she said, "but I'm fairly sure. He asked when he noticed I was an American. I thought it strange for a moment, but things were so hectic, there was no time to concentrate on anything. Sometimes it comes back to me because the young man in the bed next to him died within seconds of the boy asking me, and we rushed to try to save him."

"What about the boy who asked about a violinist?" Adrian tried to control his voice. "Did he live? Did you catch his name?"

Her words stumbled. "No, I didn't, not right away. I'm sorry. Everything was moving so quickly. New prisoners arrived all the time, and they needed our help so much. I did see the boy walking around the camp a few weeks later. I stopped to ask how he was. He looked like he had put on a little weight. It was awful there, Mr. Mazurek. Their captors had starved the prisoners. Their digestive systems couldn't tolerate food. So many died."

Adrian's face turned white. He sat up straight.

"Oh, I'm sorry. That was cruel of me," the young woman said. "The younger men seemed stronger, had more of a will to live. I'm sure he was one of those."

Simon, Simon. Were you that strong? Could Adrian hope that much? "Please go on," he managed to say.

"A few weeks later, the boy told me he had a girlfriend the Germans had forced him to leave behind at Auschwitz. In the event the Allies freed them, he said, they'd made plans to reunite at his parents' home in Krakow. He said he needed to leave the camp as soon as he felt able."

Adrian thought quickly. Simon would be twenty now. He certainly might have a girlfriend. *Contain yourself*, Adrian thought. *This could be nothing but a coincidence. Thousands of Jews had lived in Krakow before the war and would go back there to find their families.* Regardless of his warnings to himself, Adrian wanted to believe this could be Simon. He sat listening to Robin speak. He looked down at his hands. He had clasped them in a praying position. His throat began to tighten. It was difficult for him to swallow.

"The last time I saw him," Robin said, "he had a change of clothes and a backpack of food. He jumped onto the back of a truck leaving camp." Robin lowered her head. "I hope I haven't made a mistake coming here to tell you this, Mr. Mazurek. I hope I didn't upset you. It's just, well, like I said, when I saw your name, it all came back to me."

Adrian swallowed hard and rubbed his hands across his thighs. He told Robin he did have a son in Poland around that age with whom he had lost contact during the war. He told her what she'd said gave him optimism that he might find him. He asked the family to join him for dinner and a drink at the restaurant in his hotel. He hoped Robin could tell him more.

They agreed. He hailed a cab, and they headed for his hotel.

Over dinner Adrian told them more specifically about Simon and how he'd lost contact with him and his aunt and uncle after the war broke out. "Ever since then I've tried unsuccessfully to find my family in Poland."

He pressed Robin to try and recall the young man's name. He asked pointedly if the name could have been Simon.

"I know it sounds foolish, Mr. Mazurek, that I would remember a foreign last name like yours but not a first name like Simon that easily could sound American."

Adrian placed his hand over hers. "Please don't be sorry. You've given me so much already. Can you tell which army division you were in? I may be able to get records from there."

"The Red Cross recruited me for the Army Nursing Corps after I graduated from nursing school. They sent me to a camp near the town of Schwerin, Germany, where the Germans freed prisoners from a concentration camp called Sachsenhausen. That's where Stanton and I met. He was an army doctor. The Red Cross should have records of those we rescued." She gave Adrian the army unit in which she served.

Adrian looked at Dr. Kent hopefully. "Did you see this young man?"

Dr. Kent shook his head. "If I did, I have no recollection. You can't imagine the conditions we worked under back then."

"Would you contact me if you think of anything else that might help me find my son?" Adrian said.

They agreed and exchanged information. Adrian paid for dinner and thanked them for their help. He couldn't wait to call Suzanne to tell her about his meeting with Robin.

Back in his room, he noted it was past midnight in New York but still early enough in California to not wake Suzanne. He called her immediately and told her about what he'd learned.

"If I sound over the top, it's because I am, Suzanne. Simon is alive. I'm convinced of it. See you at the airport tomorrow. I love you." He hung up and fell backward onto his bed and stared up at the ceiling with hope in his heart. He had a lead now. Simon was alive, and he'd find him.

38

WHOM MIGHT I KNOW?

U pon his return to Hollywood, after he and Suzanne had put the children to bed and Mr. Reitman had gone to his room to read, Adrian told Suzanne more about his conversation with Robin and about the boy she had met at the hospital. He was so excited he could barely sit still.

"Oh, Adrian, it's like a miracle. It sends shivers up my spine. I can imagine how you felt hearing her story. What are you going to do now?"

"I'm not sure, Suzanne. I need time to think this through."

"Why don't you come to bed and think about it in the morning when you're more refreshed? Dad and I can help you come up with some ideas."

"I'm sorry, Suzanne. I just can't get my mind off this. I'm going to sit by the pool and think."

"I understand. Don't stay up too late."

Adrian went out to the pool and sat in the dark.

Whom might I know? Who can help? It came to him: Eleanor Roosevelt. President Truman had appointed her a delegate to the United Nations after her husband's death. Adrian had read about the United Nations Relief and Rehabilitation Administration, but he didn't know much about it. He felt angry with himself. He'd gotten so involved in his concert schedule he'd lost sight of what was going on in Europe. Perhaps he could have contacted his son by now. Mrs. Roosevelt would be sympathetic and want to help. He'd write to her tomorrow.

The next morning over breakfast Adrian told Suzanne and his father-in-law about his idea. They agreed that would be a good start.

"It's funny how things work out," Mr. Reitman said. "If you hadn't scheduled your concert in New York that night, you might never have met that nurse. What are the odds Simon would have asked that nurse if she knew you, and what are the odds she'd have recalled your name if she hadn't been at that concert? I guess it's true what they say."

"What's that?" Adrian asked.

"God works in mysterious ways," Mr. Reitman said.

"Amen," Adrian said.

After breakfast, Adrian wrote to Mrs. Roosevelt telling her of his belief his son was still alive, citing his contact with Robin. He asked for whatever help she could provide through her position with the United Nations. He posted the letter that afternoon and waited for her response.

39

VERY SINCERELY YOURS

On November 20,1945 Adrian ripped open the envelope as soon as he saw the stamped return address from the United Nations Relief and Rehabilitation Administration.

My Dear Adrian,

I was happy to read your letter telling me of your fortuitous meeting with the nurse who treated Simon. I can only imagine the hope that gives you, and I shall do what I can to help you locate your son.

The United Nations will soon appoint a young man as the UNRRA director of the Föhrenwald Displaced Persons camp in Germany. I shall give him your letter. He will be able to determine whether Simon is at Föhrenwald or, through his contacts with directors of other camps, at another location.

I have followed your career since the passing of our dear friend, Rose. She would be proud you have returned to concert performing and have attained such prominence. I miss her dearly. I'm sure you do, too.

Please give my regards to Suzanne and those lovely children of yours.

Very sincerely yours,
Eleanor

Adrian went immediately to the kitchen to show Suzanne and Mr. Reitman the letter.

"How wonderful," Suzanne said. "

Mr. Reitman reached out his hand. "Let me see the letter." Adrian handed it to him. After reading it, he returned it to Adrian. "What a lovely letter," he said. "What a lovely woman."

Now all there was to do was wait and see where this might lead.

40

ONE MARKED VIA AIRMAIL

On Saturday, March 30, 1946, after breakfast, Adrian walked down the driveway to the mailbox. He sifted through the envelopes and saw one marked "Via Airmail" with German postage stamps. The return address read "Simon Baron, Föhrenwald Displaced Persons Camp, Föhrenwald, Germany." He dropped the other letters he was holding. With trembling hands, he ripped open the one he'd long awaited. He began reading it.

> *Dear Mr. Mazurek,*
>
> *I understand you are trying to contact me. I'm living at the Föhrenwald Displaced Persons Camp in Föhrenwald, Germany with my wife Rachel. Rachel is the daughter of Rabbi Rosenschtein, the Rabbi of the synagogue across the square from the bakery. The rabbi played an instrumental part in my survival. We're expecting our first child in November. I hope the news that you will become a grandfather pleases you.*
>
> *Rachel and I have been living here since last September. We have decided, when immigration laws allow, to move to the United States. If the U.S. accepts us, I would be happy to meet you. Perhaps we can write back and forth before then to get to know each other.*

Adrian didn't read any further. Right then, that was all he needed to know. He picked up the mail he'd dropped and ran up the driveway and into the house to show the letter to Suzanne and his father-in-law. While standing, he read the complete letter to them. When finished, he fell into a chair and rested the letter on his chest.

"You must write back immediately," Suzanne said.

In his exuberance, Adrian reached for Suzanne's hand. "I will," he said and pulled her into his lap. He wrapped his arms around her. "I couldn't have done this without you, Suzanne. You've been my rock." Then he looked at his father-in-law and added, "Nor without your support, Dad. Thank you."

"Don't forget to write to Mrs. Roosevelt to thank her for bringing you and Simon together," Mr. Reitman added.

Still clinging to Suzanne, Adrian said, "I will, but first I'll write to Simon,"

That afternoon Adrian sat in his studio and wrote a letter to his Simon.

> *Dear Simon,*
>
> *I was both happy and excited to hear from you. I want you to know how sorry I am for whatever suffering you and the Baron family experienced during the war. I know I cannot make up for it, but I shall try in whatever way possible if it takes me a lifetime to do so.*
>
> *I am happy to learn I have a daughter-in-law and a grandchild on the way. I cannot wait to welcome you all to the United States.*
>
> *You will be receiving a special package I've been preparing over the many years to give to you once we found one another. I hope it will show how much I have thought about you and how much our reuniting means to me.*
>
> *Sincerely,*
>
> *Adrian*

Adrian struggled with how he should sign the letter. He didn't want Simon to feel that after all these years he was presuming to take the place of the man he had called "Father" throughout his lifetime. He decided it would be best signing the letter "Adrian."

The next morning, Adrian went to the post office with the letter he'd written and the box of cards and notes he'd accumulated for Simon. He had them specially wrapped to send by air mail. Inside the box, on top, he'd placed a recently taken photograph of himself, Suzanne, the twins, Dominik, and his father-in-law. He marked their names and relationships to Simon on the back of the picture. He wanted Simon and Rachel to consider themselves a part of their family immediately.

41

AT A KOSHER DELI

When Adrian learned from Simon's letter announcing Ephriam's birth that he and Rachel were living a religious life very different from that of his own family, he wrote back saying their religious differences would not be an obstacle between them. He hoped they could form a family that accepted and respected each other's way of life. For a while he felt comfortable with this sentiment and fantasized what life would be like when Simon and his family finally arrived in the United States. He envisioned his new family living with him for a while until they settled into a home of their own. He pictured family dinners, he and the kids tossing a ball with Effy, the nickname given to his grandson, Ephriam, on the lawn, and introducing his new family to Hollywood, and their friends.

One evening after the children were settled in bed and Adrian and Suzanne were in the living room reading, Adrian said, "It will be nice to have a toddler in the house, if only for a month or so before Simon and Rachel find an apartment. I can't wait to meet Effy and spoil him and introduce Adrian and Rachel around."

Suzanne put her magazine down. "You know, Adrian, when they come to live in Los Angeles, it will require a lot of adjustments in our lives as well as theirs. I think we'd better start thinking realistically about what we need to plan for."

Adrian looked puzzled. "What do you mean?"

"Well, for example, shouldn't they have their own apartment upon their arrival where they can keep kosher and live within walking distance to a synagogue? Will we be able to participate in their holiday celebrations, and will they feel comfortable participating in ours?"

Suzanne's remarks unsettled him. "I'm sure they wouldn't mind staying with us for a short time. Wouldn't it be better for them to make their own choice about a home rather than choosing one for them? His tone was decisive.

"I know you want the best for them, dear, and so do I, but look at it from their point of view. It would be crowded here, and they might not feel comfortable at first."

Adrian was perturbed by Suzanne's remarks. They contradicted his image of what it would be like when his newfound family arrived. He felt some anger toward her. When she suggested they go to bed, he said, "You go along. I want to finish reading."

"You're upset by what I said, aren't you?"

"No, I'll be in soon." He picked up the book he was reading and fumbled through the pages without looking at her.

"Don't forget to turn off the light."

Adrian sat in the living room thinking.

I've waited so long to find Simon and want to give him a fine life to make up for what he's endured. I want to demonstrate this as soon as we meet eye to eye. I want it to show on my face, and in my deeds. Right now, we have nothing in common on which to build an immediate and sound relationship. I have to find something that will bind us together, even before Simon and his family arrive. He worried that with immigration laws being what they were, it might take quite a while before Simon and Rachel would be able to come to the United States. He felt he needed to get some perspective. *What can I do before my son's arrival and what after? How can I develop a relationship with Simon before then?*

After a few days of stewing over Suzanne's remarks, Adrian set up a meeting with Martin to discuss what was on his mind and to get some ideas from a Jewish perspective. He, Suzanne, Martin, and Joanne had remained friends after the Studio's merger.

They met at a kosher deli near the Odeum Center. Martin wiped mustard off his lips after taking the last bite of his corned beef sandwich. He smiled after listening to Adrian's worries. He pushed his empty plate to the side and sat back in his seat. "I remember the day you came to the Three M Studio, and we talked in my office. You were excited to participate in making movies that would encourage the American public want to enter the war? You told me you thought doing so might contribute to helping you find your son. Well, you have. You're luckier than most. Rejoice in your good fortune. My parents haven't found any of their European relatives. Their hearts still ache for them."

"Suzanne is right, Adrian. They should have their own place upon their arrival so they can live as they are accustomed to religiously."

Martin leaned forward and folded his arms on the table. "Joanne and I will help you learn our Jewish ways so you can feel more comfortable when you meet Simon and Rachel. You'll come to our home for our holiday dinners. We'll teach you as much as we can, and what we can't, we'll get you to the right people. Don't worry. Be happy you found your son. You're a grandfather now and a father-in law as well. Rejoice."

Martin leaned back and took a sip of water. "Keep in mind, my friend, with immigration laws as they are, it might take some time for Simon and his family to get visas to the United States. This will give you time to get to know him and your daughter-in-law better through your correspondence and to learn what they want."

He's confirming Suzanne's thoughts, Adrian realized.

Martin leaned forward. "Be assured, Adrian, Joanne and I are behind you. My father is a generous contributor to the Los Angeles Jewish Welfare Fund. He has lots of contacts. He and my mother are fond of you and haven't forgotten the role you played in making our movie venture successful. They, we all, will be happy to help you."

Martin had a sudden burst of enthusiasm. He sat up straight and threw his shoulders back. "I've got an idea. A couple of months ago Manus consulted with an Orthodox rabbi about a script he was writing. He found the rabbi friendly and willing to help. He might be someone who can help you sort out your concerns. I'll get his name and call you."

"Thanks, Martin. I appreciate that."

That evening, Martin called with the telephone number of Rabbi Isaac Abelman, the chief rabbi of Beth Shalom Synagogue in the predominantly Jewish neighborhood of Boyle Heights. The next day Adrian called the rabbi's office and set up an appointment.

The rabbi was congenial. He listened carefully to Adrian's story about his reunion with his son and how their coming together was complicated by their religious differences.

"Yours is an interesting situation. I see you're earnest in wanting to reunite with your son and are willing to accept the differences between the two of you to make your relationship work. I haven't experienced a situation quite like it, but members of our congregation have welcomed foreign relatives who, even though Orthodox Jews, have had cultural differences that have required adjustments."

The rabbi rolled his chair a few inches back from his desk and said, "I'd be pleased to welcome your son and his family to our congregation if they were to choose to join us. Our Sisterhood, I'm sure, would be more than happy to help Holocaust survivors resettle. From what you've told me about your daughter-in-law's background, our religious school director may find her very beneficial as a potential employee in our Hebrew and nursery schools."

They ended their meeting by shaking hands and the rabbi asking Adrian to keep him informed about Simon's progress with his immigration status. "If there is anything we can do to help you learn about our religion and our customs, please feel free to ask. I'd be happy to meet with both of you if your wife would like to join us. I'll have my secretary place you on our mailing list in case you'd be interested in attending any of our services, particularly during our holiday observances. That way you could become better acquainted with your son's way of celebrating. If you thought it would help, we could share our bulletins with him as well to see if this might be a synagogue he and his wife would be interested in joining when they arrive."

Adrian was pleased with this visit. He'd felt comfortable with the rabbi and what he thought to be a sincere interest to help him. Before heading home, Adrian drove around the neighborhood to get a feel for it and to see if there were apartment buildings that would be appropriate for Simon and his family. He saw many in a neighborhood that was well tended. There was public transportation two blocks away from the synagogue and a kosher food market, butcher shop, and bakery nearby on the bus route.

Despite his earlier rationalization that he and Simon would be able to form a close relationship despite their different religious practices, Adrian couldn't forget how Chana's separation from her devoutly Jewish family had affected their relationship and how unhappy she had become in an unfamiliar setting. Adrian didn't want their differences to prevent a barrier between him and Simon's family. He was determined not to let this happen here in the United States.

Adrian was overjoyed when he received a letter from Simon telling him he was playing the violin in a small chamber orchestra at Föhrenwald.

Dear Adrian,

I believe my violin may have once belonged to you. My parents discovered it in a chest drawer when they had it brought up from the basement when I was four years old. I began taking lessons at the age of six. I used a child's size instrument back then. As I grew older, I used the one we had found in the chest. When I became a student at The Krakow School of Music, my professors said I had exceptional talent, not only for playing , but also for composing.

After the Nazis invaded Krakow, I learned you were my biological father and a violinist. I suspected you may have left the violin in the chest of drawers for me. When I was forced into the Krakow ghetto I left the violin at home in a secret room behind my closet to keep it safe. I found it still there after I was liberated from Sachsenhausen. I've kept it with me since.

Apart for my love for Rachel and Ephriam, playing the violin has been and is my greatest pleasure. My skill with the violin may have saved my life. I was selected to play in the men's orchestra in the Birkenau-Auschwitz camp. The musicians received special privileges there.

I have never given up on my desire to become a professional violinist and a composer. I made the decision to immigrate to the United States to further my violin studies to accomplish these goals. Since arriving at Föhrenwald , I've been composing a concerto and have finished the first movement. My objective is to have the entire piece completed by the time U.S. laws allow us to immigrate. We Are looking forward to meeting you and your family.

Sincerely,

Simon

Adrian remembered the night he and his uncle had moved his chest of drawers to the basement to make room for his infant son and how he had left one of a pair of violins made by his father in a drawer of the chest. He had hoped Simon would later find it, and it would be what would bring them together. That day had come.

Adrian bought a small recorder and sent it with tapes to Simon, He asked him to record the first movement of the concerto he was composing and send it to him. Simon sent it back quickly. When Adrian listened to it, he realized whatever he had worried about that might stand between him and his son in their religious observances and otherwise, would be overcome by their connectedness through music.

He felt the piece to be beautiful. "It has a richness and a complexity, with a wide range of tonal colors that shows Simon's versatility," he said to Suzanne. He asked the conductor of the Odeum Symphony Orchestra to listen to it and give his opinion. The next day the conductor returned the tape and said, "You know,

Adrian, you may have spawned a genius. I'd like to meet your son when he comes to the United States."

With the knowledge he and Simon shared a love for the violin and for composing, Adrian's uncertainty about their having a common bond to bring them together evaporated. He couldn't wait for them to share this together. He had so much to offer to help Simon with his desire to become a concert violinist and composer.

While waiting for immigration laws to change, Adrian, Suzanne and the kids attended Passover Seders and other holiday celebrations at the home of Martin and Joanne as well as at the homes of Orthodox Jewish families from the Odeum Symphony Orchestra. They and the children attended Beth Shalom Congregation during Purim to enjoy the fun of the holiday. On Hannukah they wrapped presents to be given to families who couldn't afford gifts for their children. Suzanne brought home library books on Orthodox Judaism and holiday celebrations to learn more about Orthodox customs and traditions. Adrian wrote Simon he was scouting out apartments for him and his family in the same neighborhood as Beth Shalom Synagogue that would meet their lifestyle.

In June 1948 the Displaced Persons Act was passed by the United States Congress and became effective in June 25, 1948, This Act allowed 200,000 European displaced persons, who were able to secure the necessary visas, to immigrate to the United States. It wasn't until September Adrian received a letter from Simon saying that with the help of a Hebrew Immigrant Aid Society worker placed at Föhrenwald, he and his family had received the visas necessary to come to America. They'd be traveling from Föhrenwald to Bremerhaven on October 13-14 and boarding the USS General W.M. Black to New York on October 15. They would arrive in New York fifteen days later. He asked Adrian to arrange for them to fly to Los Angeles as soon as possible after their arrival.

Upon receiving Simon's letter, Adrian sent him funds to arrange for a first- or second-class cabin with a note.

Simon,
"First and second-class passengers receive speedier

quarantine inspections upon arrival in New York and bypassing Ellis Island. This will up the pace of our reunion in California."

Adrian

Adrian and Suzanne prepared for their arrival as soon as they had heard from Simon. Adrian signed a lease on a furnished two bedroom second floor apartment two blocks from Beth Shalom Synagogue, where Simon had written them he and Rachel would like to become affiliated. Women from the Beth Shalom Sisterhood helped Suzanne set up a kosher kitchen for the new arrivals, and they supplied new bed linens and a welcome basket of toiletries and items they would need immediately. Mr. Marcus had assured Adrian he'd have a job available for Simon until he found something more to his liking. Martin was trying to arrange a place for Simon in the Eagle's Nest Orchestra. No matter what, there would be a job waiting for him during his resettlement period.

42

CHOCOLATE AND RED ROSES

On October 31, 1948, two and one half years after Adrian had received his first letter from Simon, he, Suzanne, and their children stood behind the metal barrier watching the silver speck grow larger and glide gracefully from the sky toward them. Adrian held on tightly to Dominik's hand as the boy waved a small American flag with his free hand. The twins also waved miniature flags.

"Is that Simon's plane, Daddy?" five-and-a-half year-old Dominik asked.

Adrian tried to hold back the tears of joy welling in his eyes. "Yes. Your big brother, Simon, his wife, Rachel, and their little boy, Ephriam, have finally come home to us."

Adrian felt sad his father-in-law had passed away and wasn't there to share his joy. Mr. Reitman had been a support to him and had looked forward to this day almost as much as he had.

Adrian licked his lips. He felt his heart pounding as the plane landed and slowed to a halt.

He smoothed back his windblown hair. "How do I look?" he said to Suzanne.

With a smile, she gently patted his cheek. "You look fine. Stop worrying."

He looked at his watch. *What's taking them so long to put up the stairs and open the door?*

Finally, two men rolled out the ramp to the door of the plane.

The door swung open, and Adrian caught a glimpse of a man waiting to disembark. He was too old to be Simon. Several others came down the stairs.

Adrian held his breath and reached for Suzanne's hand. Then he saw a young man coming down the steps from the plane carrying a violin case in one hand. With the other hand, he helped a young woman holding a child.

Simon. Adrian was sure of it. He caught his breath. "That's him," he said to Suzanne, He let go of Suzanne's hand and waved as high and as heartily as he could toward the young couple. Then he took Suzanne by her hand again, and marshalled her, Dominik, and their seven-year-old twins to the gate.

His son, now standing in front of him, was a grown man. The years seemed to fade away. Looking at Simon, Adrian saw the baby he'd left so long ago and the girl he had loved and lost. A feeling of warmth radiated throughout his body. "You have your mother's eyes and her hair," he said.

Simon held up a photograph. "You look just like your picture." Adrian took it and stared at the photograph of him and Chana. He was surprised to see the picture. He felt touched Simon had carried it with him. He noticed the tear and its repair and felt what it represented. *He must* have *hated me. I'll make it up to him, I swear.* He showed it to Suzanne.

Adrian handed the picture back and let his eyes linger on Simon's a little longer. "Your mother was a loving woman. She'd be so proud of you," he said softly.

Then he turned to Rachel. He pulled himself together and smiled widely. "And you're my daughter-in-law, Rachel. I've waited so long to meet you." He looked at the little boy she was holding. "And that little tiger in your arms must be my grandson, Ephriam."

Rachel handed the boy to Adrian's outstretched arms. "Ephriam," she said, "meet your grandfather." Adrian nuzzled his nose into the child's thick, brown, curly hair. He deeply breathed in the child's freshness and kissed the boy's cheek. This was his chance for a new beginning with his long-lost son. Adrian then turned toward Suzanne and the children and said to Simon and Rachel,

"This is your family: my wife, Suzanne, our daughters, Gabriela and Elinore, and, this young man with the flag, is Dominik."

The girls presented Rachel with small bouquets of red roses. "They're lovely," Rachel said. Her eyes sparkled in the sunlight as she thanked them.

Simon put down his violin case and kissed Suzanne's hand. Then he kneeled to give his newly found sisters and little brother colorful wrapped pieces of chocolate. The children looked at their mother. "It's all right," she said. "This is a special occasion."

Suzanne pulled a small package from her purse. "For you," she said, handing it to Ephriam.

Ephriam, still in Adrian's arms, took hold of it, and with Rachel's help, unwrapped the paper. He held out a small wooden truck with rubber wheels for his mother to see.

Adrian handed his grandson back to Rachel and smiled. He pulled out one last gift from his jacket pocket for Simon. It was a Los Angeles Angels baseball cap. "If you're going to be an American," he said, "you must look like one."

Simon took the hat and put it on backward. They all laughed, Adrian the loudest.

Suzanne, catching Simon's sense of humor, smiled at Rachel, and said, "Like father, like son."

Adrian helped his son turn the hat around. Then he picked up Simon's violin case and took hold of his son's arm. He looked over to Rachel and Ephriam and jerked his head forward.

With Suzanne and his children right behind, he said, "Come, let us take you to your new home."

EPILOGUE

On Sunday, March 19, 1949, Norman French wrote in his "Backstage" column in the *Hollywood Tribune:*

Last night at the Los Angeles Odeum Center, four thousand people listened to performances by father and son violinists, Adrian Mazurek and Simon Baron. Mr. Baron is a survivor of both Auschwitz and Sachsenhausen concentration camps. This was his first American performance of the concerto he wrote during his and his wife's nearly two-and-a-half-year stay at the displaced persons camp in Föhrenwald, Germany. He and his father were reunited only three and a half months ago.

Following Mr. Baron's performance, father and son joined together to play *Bach's Double Violin Concerto in D minor.* Each played on coveted violins made by Dominik Mazurek, Mr. Mazurek's father, at his luthier school in northwest Poland. The school, unfortunately, no longer exists, a victim of the Nazis' takeover and destruction of many Polish villages and towns.

Mr. Mazurek and his son were separated twenty-three years ago when, after the death of Mazurek's wife, he left his son in the care of relatives to come to the United States to continue his violin studies at The Walter J.S. Sanfried Music School in New York. When the Germans invaded Poland and war broke out, he was unable to reunite with his son, who was being raised by his Catholic aunt and uncle. When the Germans discovered the young boy's Jewish heritage through his mother, the Germans forced him into the Krakow ghetto and later into Auschwitz. As the Allies advanced, Auschwitz sent him and others to Sachsenhausen.

Because of his musical training at The Krakow School of Music, the young man became part of the Auschwitz-Birkenau men's orchestra. At the end of the war, father and son, after nine years of searching, found each other with the help of our former First Lady, Eleanor Roosevelt, and the United Nations Relief and Rehabilitation Administration. It took more than two years for Mr. Baron and his family to get their visas to immigrate to the United States.

Mr. Mazurek, the former concertmaster of The Eleventh State Symphony Orchestra in New York, moved to Hollywood in 1940 to become the Music Director of the then newly formed Three M Studio, which, after a successful run of films, merged with Eagle Nest Studios. Afterward, Mr. Mazurek pursued a concert career as Assistant Concertmaster with The Los Angeles Odeum Symphony Orchestra, and as a composer and a soloist. He has played in most every major concert venue in the United States.

It has been announced that Mr. Mazurek will be assuming the position of Concertmaster of the Los Angeles Odeum Center Symphony Orchestra at the end of this season upon the retirement of Nathaniel Orfendorf, the concertmaster for the symphony since 1938.

The long separation between father and son appears to have had no effect on their relationship. On stage they expressed emotions that seemed to warm the hearts of the audience. Eagle Nest Pictures is planning a movie based on the lives of this father and son. Arthur Goldberg, the writer of the moving *The Andersons and the Steins* film series, as well as other films and plays since, is writing the screenplay. It is rumored Mr. Mazurek and Mr. Baron will be performing parts of the score.

Mr. Baron's concerto expresses his personal journey through the Holocaust, beginning on a peaceful day in 1939, when the sudden arrival of the German Army bursts the idyllic life of an ordinary, happy family. The young man becomes aware he is not who he believed himself to be when the Germans discover his birth to a Jewish woman. Despite his efforts to distance himself from his adopted family to protect them, they experience the cruelest of hardships, for which the young man blames himself. In the end, he is the lone survivor, but he finds love and eventually builds a family of his own. The music follows him on that journey from its horrific first day, to his liberation after the surrender of the Nazis, and his long awaited reunion with his birth father, Mr. Mazurek.

For those wanting to experience the full range of emotions of people caught up in the horrors of war, I recommend you reserve your tickets early when you find a venue playing this concerto. You will experience a beautiful piece of music played by a man with God-given talent and the sounds of a perfectly crafted instrument.

The End

Author's Note

One must write a novel about the Holocaust with the utmost sensitivity and respect for those who suffered and/or died through it. A person as far away from it as I am can only imagine and endeavor to convey what they experienced. The reality and emotion that I strived to put into writing this story will never compare with the testimonies of the survivors. I've tried to keep that perspective throughout this book and the first in the series, the companion book A PRODIGY IN AUSCHWITZ: SIMON, already released.

It is my hope these books will serve two purposes: [1] to educate those who are too young to remember WW 2 and the Holocaust and encourage them to want to learn more, and [2] to sensitize anyone of any age, race, ethnicity, religion, political ideology, sexual orientation and/or gender identity to the happenings in today's world as well as to what these happenings could lead to if we don't pay attention and learn from past events. Working together creatively as human beings, rather than destructively, is the more fruitful path.

Afterword

Writing can be a lonely art if it were not for interesting authors and, through their writings, the real and fictional compelling characters and places you meet along the way. I'd like to pay tribute to some of the authors and their subjects whom I've met in my research for my companion novels, *A PRODIGY IN AUSCHWITZ: BOOK I, SIMON* and *A VIRTUOSO IN AMERICA: BOOK 2, ADRIAN* and how their works helped in the development of some of the characters and their backstories in these novels. I hope what follows will enhance the knowledge of the reader not only about the Holocaust but of the role that music played at that time in history and inform music lovers, especially of the violin, about some of the important concertmasters of our great symphony orchestras. It is my goal as well to introduce other people, like Henry Cohen, who may not be widely known.

ANNE MISCHAKOFF HEILES

One of the first books I purchased for my personal collection to gain knowledge and understanding of the role of a concertmaster was *America's Concertmasters,* by Anne Mischakoff Heiles, published by Harmonie Park Press in 2007. The author was the daughter of Mischa Mischakoff, one of the outstanding concertmasters of the mid- twentieth century. This masterpiece of extensive research on over 180 concertmasters beginning with Ureli Corelli Hill in 1831 to Brian Reagin in 1997 provides invaluable insight into the professional standard's and decision making processes of the many concertmasters written about. One such example is the wisdom offered by one of the concertmasters interviewed by the author of the need for the concertmaster to have qualities of leadership and diplomacy that enable him to deal with differences between himself and members of the string section of the orchestra. This is displayed in *A VIRTUOSO IN AMERICA: BOOK 2, ADRIAN* when Adrian has to deal with the difference of opinion between him and his violinists regarding the bowing for one of the orchestra's upcoming concerts. I can only imagine and greatly admire the commitment the author gave to this project.

When I contacted the seller, she laughed when I gave her my name and information for mailing purposes. Her reaction to my name puzzled me until the book arrived, and I saw the handwritten inscription dated 4/7/18 on the opening page. It read "Dear Papa Fred, Wishing you a Happy and wonderful Birthday! With love, from ***" (name withheld for privacy purposes). It was almost as if fate intended this book for me, another Fred, to participate in carrying on the author's work through mine. I feel honored to be among those to give Anne Mischakoff Heiles the recognition she deserves for writing such a historical piece.

SZYMON LAKS

I first became familiar with Syzmon Laks when reading his autobiography, *Music of Another World*, translated from the Polish by Chester A. Kisiel and published by Northwestern University Press Jewish Lives in 2000 and the National Jewish Book Awards Winner, *Violins of Hope* by James A. Grymes, and published by Harper Perennial in 2014. He and others mentioned in these books inspired the fictional character known as Maestro in *A PRODIGY IN AUSCHWITZ: BOOK ONE, SIMON.*

Syzmon Laks was born to a family of assimilated Jews in 1901 in Warsaw, then the third biggest city of the Russian Empire. In 1921 he attended the Warsaw Conservatory to study musical composition and conducting before moving to Paris in 1926, where he developed as a conductor. In 1941 he was arrested by the Germans and deported. In 1942 he was sent to Auschwitz-Birkenau in Poland. There he became the conductor of the camp orchestra. In

1944 he was sent to the Dachau concentration camp in Germany, where he remained until the war ended.

Unlike Maestro, Laks survived the Holocaust. When liberated, he moved to Paris and became a French citizen. In the 1960s he resumed composing. Before his death in 1983, he'd compiled an impressive anthology of musical and literary works.

*This information was gathered through my reading the aforementioned books. Other sources of information about Syzmon Laks or any profiles of Polish artists is available through the Adam Mickiewicz Institute and The United States Holocaust Memorial Museum in Washington, DC.

ALMA ROSE

Alma Rosé was the leader of the Auschwitz-Birkenau Women's Camp Orchestra. Like it's equivalent, the men's camp orchestra, it played marching music for the women prisoners as they left and returned from their work details, and music for other administratively assigned functions. She, like her father, Arnold Rosé, was a prominent virtuoso violinist and is often cited as the niece of another revered family member, her uncle, Gustav Mahler, a leading conductor and composer of his time.

Ms. Rosé was a captive at Auschwitz for a brief time from 1943 to 1944. She is said to have died of a mysterious illness at the age of thirty-seven which has been speculated to be the result of food poisoning.

As their capo, Ms. Rosé is credited with helping to make the lives of her orchestra members better than the other women prisoners in the Birkenau Women's Camp. It is said she was responsible for convincing the camp administration to exclude the women from performing during inclement weather, of allowing them to have hot showers, and to be provided with more food than other camp captives.

Several books have been written about Alma Rosé. There is a

section about her in the aforementioned National Jewish Book awards winner, VIOLINS OF HOPE by James A. Grymes, *Alma Rosé: Vienna to Auschwitz* by Richard Newman with Karen Kirley, published by Amadeus Press on March 3, 20023, *The Violinist of Auschwitz* by Ellie Midwood and published by Bookouture, a British digital publishing company, on November 18, 2020. You may find ALMA ROSÉ, A FEATURE FILM by Francine Zuckerman, Director and Produced by Francine Zuckerman and Salley Blake on the digital website: ZFILMS.CA.

THE VILLAGE of KOLBUSZOWA

In preparation for writing my novels of the Holocaust, I read the true life reminiscences of Norman Salsitz in his book *A JEWISH BOYHOOD IN POLAND, REMEMBERING KOLBUSZOWA*. I'd been looking for a village in Poland to serve as the back story for Adrian and Chana. This paperback edition of the book by Norman Salsitz as told to Richard Skolnik, and published by the Syracuse University Press in 1999, presents a vivid descriptions of life before and after the invasion of the Nazis. Christians and Jews lived separately but in harmony among each other in this hamlet of about three thousand residents as long as the customs and norms of the time for each population weren't broken as they were by my characters, Adrian and Chana. The strength of the book lies in the colorful details of the captivating stories that display what life was like in this small village, especially for Jews, through the eyes of a young boy. The descriptions of the weekly marketplace provided a memorable and interesting setting for Adrian and Chana to have their secret meetings and are somewhat reminiscent of today's farmers markets and state fairs.

In an article on the internet to which Professor Benjamin Vogel was a contributor, I found that " the implementation of the domestic system into instrument making," including the violin, was probably used in the Polish village of Kolbuszowa. I thought the combining of Adrian and Chana of breaking the religious norms in my novel and of having a violin making school in Adrian's background would give more back story to Adrian as well as to the enhancement of the plot. I also felt this information might be of interest to those studying the history of violin making to anyone seeking a source of reference to explore this.

*This information came from "The project mounted by the Institute of Music and Dance in Warsaw in a year marking two major artistic events-the 13th International Henryk Wieniawski Violin Making Competition and the 15th International Violin Competition in Poznan, Poland. The online database showcases violins held in the Polish Ministry of Culture and National Heritage's Collection of violins administered by the Polish Union of Artist Violin Makers in Warsaw. Also featured are violins played by prominent Polish musicians and contestants of the Wieniawski competition, often at the onset of their careers, which today mostly belongs to private collections around the world. We are deeply grateful to the owners for allowing us their use,"

Norman Salsitz's memoir received high praise and reviews from Kirkus Reviews, the Polish Heritage, and the Library Journal.

DAVID MANNES

David Mannes came to my attention upon acquiring a copy of his autobiography, *MUSIC IS MY FAITH* published by W W NORTON & CO, INC IN 1938. I honestly don't remember why or how I acquired this book except for the fact that I was accumulating books on concertmasters that I felt would help me in my research in writing about Adrian. Although Adrian applied to and was accepted into the fictitious Sanfried School of Music in New York upon his arrival in that city, the Sanfried School was not based on the Mannes Music School David Mannes and his wife, Clara, founded in 1916. I became more interested in David Mannes upon reading Chapter FIFTY-SIX of his autobiography titled CREDO in which he discusses "his certain philosophy" and a "certain phantasy…without which no vision can be sustained."

The paragraphs quoted below reflect what I was wanting to convey in my Author's Notes in Books 1 and 2 of *CONCERTO*.

"Above all- at least to me-music is the only universal language. This is a platitude only because it happens, like other platitudes, to be based on incontrovertible truth. The only times when I have witnessed a state approaching the brotherhood of man have been moments of music, when hundreds of hearts beat to the same rhythm and lifted to the same phrase, and when all hate, all envy, all greed were washed away by the nobility of sound. Words are so often the agents of destruction; music-good music- can only build. And to learn the language of music- or at least to respond to it- one needs only an ear and a heart. It is only the deaf or the spiritually atrophied who do not somehow feel themselves exulted and purified in the presence of great music.

There are other ways besides music of trying to bind mankind in a common fight against the overwhelming forces of materialism and greed, of intolerance and rapacity, but they all have this in common with music: that they are based on creation and not on destruction. That is why I mistrust such drastic means of hanging the world and the spirit of man as revolution. Any gain through violence is bound to prove transitory. For revolution is admitted to be, in the main, based on initial destruction: on a clearing of the ground, a raising of all things that were built through the generations. And the loss of this precious human residue is seldom compensated by the new structure that replaces it.

The more I know of people the less fit I feel to judge them. And the more I know of myself the better I understand the doubts and fears that encompass them. It is only natural to dislike certain traits and qualities in people, but one should think twice before condemning them. It is usually people without imagination for the sufferings of others who sit in judgement upon them; people who have never known the cleansing agony of doubt. That doesn't mean that one should never be sure of oneself; rather that one should never be satisfied with oneself. When that happens, the spirit closes up and becomes sterile. There is no end to the development of the soul-and to the wonders of living."

Mannes was the concertmaster of the New York Symphany from 1903-1912. In 1912 he severed his relationship with the New York Symphony and in 1916, he and his wife, Clara Damrosch Mannes, a celebrated musician in her own right, established the Mannes Music School in New York City, the forerunner of the prestigious conservatory and degree granting college affiliated with the New School in Manhattan.

Despite the companionship one can derive from reading and becoming familiar with those whom one might never know or get to know otherwise, there is no substitute to being around real live people and learning about both writing skills and getting feedback on one's own writing. I suggest, where possible, new writers join a writing group, be it one focused on writing in general or devoted to a specific literary genre, whatever matches your goal. It was in one of these sponsored by my local library that a group of ten of us met weekly with a professional author and were trained in the elements of writing. At the end of each session, we were given a prompt from which to write a story in a defined number of words to discuss at the next meeting. Within our diverse group of people of different ages, backgrounds, and genders we would offer our opinions about what was good and what could be improved. Within such a group, not everyone agreed, but our teacher was able to provide us with comments that drew upon the basics of writing that would benefit us all.

I remember coming to some of these meetings feeling proud and assured of my presentations only to feel disheartened by some of the reactions of others. Other times I felt appreciative. I know there were times when my classmates felt the same. In the end, having a group of people with different opinions helped me define what I believed in and to develop my own style. With a combination of the skills I learned, and by either accepting or rejecting some of the comments offered me, I finished my novels. I thank Kris Faatz, our teacher and my fellow students, Cece, Christina, Gerald, Loni, Melissa, Rachel, Rebecca, and Toula for being so supportive in helping me complete a long -time goal. The staff of the Lutherville Public Library were extremely patient with me in coming to my aid as I was learning their computer system. I appreciate my friends, family and others who supported me through the process and who gave me the confidence to believe I was not being self-indulgent in deciding to publish. I thank everyone at Palmetto Publishing for their support in leading me through the process of producing the first editions of these companion novels and those at Historium Press who have made it possible to produce the second edition of my works.

Photo copyrighted by Rebecca Goldman Wyatt

About the Author

Fred Raymond Goldman was born and raised in Baltimore, Maryland. His fraternal grandparents immigrated to the United States from Poland, his maternal grandparents from Russia.

After obtaining a BA degree in Psychology in 1962 from what is now Mc Daniel College, he went on to obtain a Master of Social Work degree in 1964 from the University of Maryland.

Finding his true talent lay in administrative work, he held positions in Jewish communal service agencies of the Associated Jewish Charities of Baltimore, first as the Administrative Director of the Sinai Hospital Drug Abuse Program, which operated a methadone maintenance clinic that coordinated with other constituent agencies of the Associated to provide personal and employment counseling to aid in the rehabilitation of patients. He later was employed as the Assistant to the Director of The Jewish Family Services. He retired in 2005 after serving 23 years as Executive Director of the Har Sinai Congregation, a prominent Reform Jewish synagogue in Baltimore, now joined with Temple Oheb Shalom.

His desire to achieve a lifelong dream of writing a novel began after his retirement when he joined a writing group at his local library. There he began his four year journey of research and writing the novels you are about to read.

He remembers learning little about the Holocaust as a child other than six million Jews perished under the Nazi regime. No one in his family was directly affected or, if they were, they never spoke about it. It was a prompt given by the instructor of his writing group that led him to want to learn more about the Holocaust and to eventually write about its effect on those abroad as well as the effect of WW2 on citizens of the United States. It took four years of research and writing to complete and self-publish his two volumes. His work took on more meaning to him given the outbreaks of war in Ukraine and Israel and the political and social environment including anti-Semitism and other discriminatory behaviors against certain populations. Having ten grandchildren, he wanted them and others to understand, through his writing, that the effect of past events, if allowed to recur, could lead to such suffering today.

The author and his wife of fifty-two years, Abigail, live in Lutherville, a suburb of Baltimore. It is his hope that in each of his books you receive not only a worthy read but an informative one. Read the Author's Note for more of what he hopes to achieve by writing his two companion novels.

An Excerpt from
A Prodigy in Auschwitz

1

THE SQUARE

Morning of Saturday, September 2, 1939, Krakow, Poland

Simon was one of the first to notice the disturbance among the starlings roosting in the sycamore trees bordering the east and west sides of the square. He heard their pitched chorus and the flapping of their wings seconds before hundreds of them flocked to the sky, creating two formations before joining into one large configuration. They moved swiftly, twisting, turning, changing shapes, and creating an astonishing spectacle to those watching below.

As the progression of movements among the birds increased, Lena and the other young girls with whom she was playing ran to the benches where those caring for them were sitting. Lena pressed closely against Simon, her older brother. "What is it?" she whispered.

Simon put an arm around Lena's shoulder. "Don't be scared," he said. "I saw this in a movie. Watch, it will be spectacular. You'll have something special to tell the others at lunch."

She pulled closer to him when the birds formed a spiral-like circle that temporarily blocked out the sun and caused a brief darkening over the square. Two worshipers wearing prayer shawls came out of the front doors of Beth David Congregation, a square-shaped, flat-roofed building on the west side of the square. Its congregants were comprised of Jews who followed the rules and practices of *Halakhah*, the strict observances of Jewish laws. They looked up into the partially blackened sky, stared at each other, and shrugged before returning inside their house of worship.

"This is unusual," an observer sitting near Simon said. "Starlings take flight at dusk."

An elderly woman occupying the same bench shook her head. "It's a bad omen. Something terrible is going to happen."

A man sharing an adjacent bench seemed to have overheard their conversation. He stood, covered his brow with his hand, and stared up into the sky. He looked back at the two women and waved his hand dismissively. "Nonsense," he said. "Something has frightened them, probably a predator, most likely a peregrine falcon."

"I've heard birds can sense sounds and movements from ten miles away," another woman said. Her lower lip and chin trembled. "Do you think there may be an earthquake coming?"

"Don't listen to her," Simon said, attempting to reassure Lena. She was holding on to his arm tightly as she watched the dazzling configurations above. "Something must have scared them, like the man said. Soon they'll move on to find other trees to roost in. You'll remember this for years and hope to see one again." The starlings executed the shapes of a duck, a feather, and a giant bird before flying off into the distance and disappearing.

With energy befitting a four-year-old, Lena skipped off to rejoin her friends soon after the starlings' show ended. "I wasn't scared," Simon heard her boast.

Simon sat quietly, listening to more chatter while watching over Lena. They were on the square opposite the bakery their parents owned and operated. It was his responsibility to care for Lena every Saturday morning from nine until noon, when his parents would turn the bakery over to their staff and call him and Lena in for lunch as a family in their quarters upstairs. After lunch, Lena would play under the care of their older sister, Katrina. Simon would be free to prepare for the Poland Independence Day Concert on November 11. His school, the Krakow School of Music, presented this concert annually.

Simon was the youngest student ever selected to represent the violin department at this event. He'd be performing the solo violin portions of the first movement of Tchaikovsky's Violin Concerto in D Minor, which required great skill in executing both its fast running scales and its delicate main theme. None of his immediate family on his father's side had any musical talent. Simon wondered where his came from. His mother never spoke of her family. This puzzled him. When he asked her about them, she answered only that they were old and lived far away.

This year's concert was particularly important to Simon. The rector of the school had announced officials from the Alliance of Accredited Music Schools and Academies of Poland had accepted an invitation. This organization held a biennial competition and awarded prizes to experienced violinists and pianists seventeen or older. With the appearance of this delegation confirmed, Simon felt confident the coveted competition prize would be his in 1942, when he'd be eligible to apply.

Winning this competition would earn Simon the recognition and money to attract the most distinguished teachers, and this would lead to his objectives of becoming a renown composer and concert performer. Although his family earned a good living from the bakery, he knew it would cost them dearly to provide him with the continued education and training he'd need to attain his goals. He practiced the Tchaikovsky Violin Concerto every spare minute to reach perfection. Performing well and drawing the attention of the alliance attendees were foremost in Simon's thoughts.

Simon took his eyes off Lena long enough to see his fellow students, Bartek and Aleksander, walking briskly together on the walkway along the east side of the square. He waved to catch their attention. Bartek looked over at Simon and turned his head away. Aleksander gave him a weak nod. Simon rubbed his right hand. He remembered the soreness he felt when Bartek congratulated him by shaking his hand too long and too tightly. At the time, Simon wondered if he were trying to break his fingers so he could replace him in the concert. Alexander's smile was overly broad in his concession.

They're still angry Professor Kaminsky chose me over them.

Simon understood their being upset and their envy. He would have felt the same if Professor Kaminski hadn't selected him. Disappointed by their dismissal, Simon turned his attention back to conversations among people sitting nearby.

A woman pointed a shaking finger at the man who had seemed unconcerned. "I'm warning you. We're in for trouble. The Jews must know something," she said assuredly. "The synagogue is overflowing this morning."

"They have reason to be alarmed," the man responded with a scowl and said, "They have their own predators to fear. They're packing into their synagogues to ask for God's protection. It's no wonder after what we've all heard on the radio about what is happening in Warsaw and in other cities. They are afraid of more bombings and attacks and that Hitler will do to them what he's done to the Jews in Germany."

"God have mercy," another woman said. "We're all in for trouble. Germany wants our land. They'll take what they can get from us." She crossed herself. "We should pray for all Poles."

Simon's parents didn't talk about the Germans and what might be coming. They thought this would distract him from his studies. "Let him have his youth," he'd heard them say to his aunts and uncles. He realized now his parents were sheltering him from things going on in the world he should be prepared for.

I'm not a child anymore. I'm fourteen. They should trust me, he thought.

Oftentimes, however, when his parents didn't want him to hear something, they'd speak in his grandfather's native German. Simon learned to pick up the language to the extent he could understand what they were saying and, eventually, could speak it.

Simon looked at his watch. It was eleven forty-five. Soon he and the others on the square would hear the melodious sounds of the cantor chanting the closing prayer and the joyous voices of the congregants singing along. The rabbi, the cantor, and their families would be arriving at the entranceway to greet their fellow worshipers. Simon's parents would be handing over their aprons to their workers to manage the shop while they prepared to call him and Lena to lunch.

Simon felt a rumbling under his feet. He glanced around looking for what might have caused it. Lena and her friends were standing rigid, looking up the street. Simon's eyes followed theirs. He saw a parade of motorcycles followed by Nazi Germany swastika marked trucks moving toward the synagogue. The roar of their motors muffled the chanting and singing coming from the *shul*. Upon reaching Beth David Congregation, the motorcycles and trucks stopped. Simon felt a fluttering in his stomach.

German soldiers with rifles and pistols jumped from their vehicles and surrounded the synagogue. Elders on the square left their benches and scuttled away. Shopkeepers along the square and their customers came outside to see what had caused the commotion. Women clasped their hands over their mouths. Mothers with babies and children held on to them tightly. Soldiers grabbed the rabbi, cantor, and their congregants as they left the synagogue. They pointed rifles at them and pushed them toward where they had parked their trucks. Other soldiers pulled the congregants into the trucks.

Simon's heart raced as he watched the scene unfold. He clutched his arms across his chest trying to think what to do. He saw Lena run up and kick an offending soldier who was struggling with Rabbi Rosenschtein. The soldier grabbed at his leg, and the rabbi was set free, but another soldier grabbed the rabbi and led him to one of the trucks. Simon ran toward Lena, maneuvering through the crowd of worshipers and soldiers. Instinct had taken over. He was moving by pure adrenaline.

Simon reached Lena and clutched her hand. She was crying. He knew he had to get her to the safety of their parents quickly. The throng of soldiers and worshipers struggling with one another made it difficult to get through. The intruders herded Simon and Lena away from the square along with everyone else. A woman in front of them fell. Two soldiers hoisted her up. She screamed and struggled to get free. Simon used the diversion to grasp Lena's shoulders. His eyes looked down on hers.

"Run as fast as you can toward the bakery," he said. She stood frozen. Her eyes darted back and forth. "Run!" he shouted again and gave her a shove. He watched her little heels kicking up and down as she scampered away. Before he could see if Lena had reached safety, a German soldier gripped him by the back of the neck and propelled him toward the trucks. The screams of mothers and children crying out in search of each other pierced Simon's ears. He stumbled trying to keep his balance.

Simon heard glass shattering. The soldier dragging him stopped long enough for Simon to turn and see colored shards of glass falling from the second story of the synagogue. He looked up and saw two soldiers laughing. They had smashed the stained-glass Star of David. The soldier jerked Simon's head back and lugged him to one of the waiting trucks. Another soldier wrestled him inside.

Simon sat trembling in the shadows of the truck. He pressed his hands tightly between his knees and struggled to control his breathing. He prayed Lena had made it to safety. With the reality of his predicament setting in, Simon wondered where the assailants were taking him. *Did my parents see what had happened? Will Papa be able to rescue me? This is a crazy mistake. I need to tell the invaders I'm not Jewish, that, in fact, I'm part German, and my family is waiting for me.* Simon looked at his watch. It was twelve fifteen. He felt a pat on his knee. He looked over. Rabbi Rosenschtein was sitting next to him. He interpreted the rabbi's touch as a gesture of reassurance, but he felt none. The only assurance he wanted was to soon be sitting safely at home with his family. Although he was fourteen and felt ashamed to cry, he broke down. He couldn't stop the tears from rolling down his cheeks.